DEATH AFTER DEATH

DEATH AFTER DEATH

Edmund Glasby

Shadow Publishing

DEATH AFTER DEATH

ACKNOWLEDGMENTS:
'Hour of the Witch' originally appeared in
The Chaos of Chung-Fu (2013)
'Pale Lilac' originally appeared in
The Ash Murders (2013)
'Ghouls of the Undercity' originally appeared in
Ghouls of the Undercity (2014)
All other stories original to this collection

ISBN: 978-0-9572962-4-4
Shadow Publishing, 194 Station Road, Kings Heath,
Birmingham, B14 7TE, UK
david.sutton986@btinternet.com

ABOUT EDMUND GLASBY

As penance for past deeds, Edmund Glasby grew up in Morecambe and studied Egyptian Archaeology at University College London and Archaeology and Anthropology at Oxford— Morecambe, which has more than its share of the strange and unsavoury, provided him with a better education. After turning his back on academia, he now writes in the genres of dark fantasy and supernatural thriller, having been brought up on horror; his father was John S. Glasby the prolific supernatural fiction writer.

In 2010, his first novel was *Disciple of a Dark God*, a far-ranging dark fantasy epic. His first collection of all-new supernatural stories, *The Dyrysgol Horror and Others* was published by Borgo in 20013, and was followed by *The Ash Murders, The Chaos of Chung-Fu, Ghouls of the Undercity, Labyrinth of the Lost, Dark Shadows, Angels of Death* and a novel, *The Weird Shadow Over Morecambe.* For his UK publishers, Ulverscroft and Endeavour Press, he has also written four macabre detective thrillers, *A Murder Most Macabre, The Postbox Murders, The Doppelgänger Deaths, and Where Blood Runs Deep.*

When he is not writing he is the captain of a local archery club and he has won a trophy or two both at local and European level with the English longbow he made.

Contents

INTRODUCTION

Mario Guslandi

THESE ARE HARD times for fans of supernatural and horror stories. The few horror books you can find in actual bookstores or the ones mostly advertised by mass market online shops are novels, with the few exceptions of short story collections by the usual suspects, big names that I won't name.

If you're seeking either collections or anthologies of short horror fiction you have to actively look for them in the online catalogues and websites of the small, indie press devoted to the genre.

That means that, unless you're already familiar with certain small imprints, you may find it a little hard to locate those books and, to add insult to injury, when you do you often realize that said books are either sold out (the print run of the indie press books is always very limited) or overpriced or both. In addition, you end up missing excellent writers whose work is exclusively offered by the genre small press.

But now the good news. Here we have an excellent collection, written by a comparatively new author who has already established himself as a talented and confirmed short story teller in the dark fiction genre, and published at a reasonable price by the commendable British imprint Shadow Publishing.

Edmund Glasby's present collection assembles eleven supernatural tales (most of which are brand new), addressing the horror genre in all its various shades.

For instance, in 'The Last Night of October', a vivid tale of horror and witchcraft, the darkest secrets of a remote village are tragically revealed to an outsider during All Hallows' night.

'Hour of the Witch' is a clever melting pot, cooking some classical ingredients of horror fiction (the supernatural sleuth, the haunted house, exorcism etc) including some daring variations (a priest holding a séance!)

'Pale Lilac' is a vivid piece of graphic horror revisiting, in an effective and quite original way, the time honoured theme of the mad scientist.

Don't take me wrong, Glasby is not just an expert manipulator of classical horror clichés, but also a skilled creator of unusual plots and atmospheres. Outstanding examples are 'Where Dead Men Scream', an enticing, claustrophobic tale taking place in prison before the execution of an innocent inmate waiting for his own death, and the title story, 'Death after Death', a gruesome piece where a man is apparently haunted by his previous self.

Every now and then Glasby also tries his hand at something very different, as in 'Angels of Death', an offbeat mix of crime and pulp fiction, sparkling like a glass of champagne.

So, dear reader, take your seat in a comfortable armchair, relax, turn the lights down and enjoy this book.

Mario Guslandi
Milano, March 2016

THE BLACK SPIRIT OF THE STORM

On the wind it came, bringing madness and destruction.

THE STARK AND glacial wilderness of the Canadian North-west Territories surrounded the isolated geological research station. Here, close to the Yukon border, the glaring whiteness of snow covered the Mackenzie Mountain trails and swept down in a single stretch of eye-searing white to the pine tree-covered valley almost two thousand feet below.

Professor Alexander Moorcroft stared out into the far distance, his ruddy features displaying frustrated annoyance. This was supposed to be a flying visit and he had urgent business back in Toronto in a few days which he could not afford to miss. This was only the second time he had been here and the prospect of being stranded for the foreseeable future irked him considerably. 'You say there's absolutely no chance of getting down to the valley at all today? You're quite sure?'

'I'm saying it would be extremely difficult, if not impossible.' Chogan, the Native American engineer and expert on the local area, nodded his greying head emphatically and spread his hands out wide in a gesture of apology. 'It is far from usual to get such heavy snow cover at this time of year.'

'It appears that we're stuck here, professor,' said Doctor Ronald Chalmers, the team leader and the man responsible for the day-to-day running of the station. His face was furrowed into a tightly-controlled mask of impatience. 'News is that there has been a fresh fall of snow this side of the Wrigley Pass. Most of the trail leading to the valley has been completely snowed under and there are warnings of further falls.'

'I see.' Moorcroft walked away from the window and lowered himself into a nearby chair. 'And until it clears we're confined here.' He had arrived the night before and taken little more than a passing interest in the research team, intending to leave the next day with the samples he had come to collect. His gaze wandered swiftly from one to the other, taking in details with a practised eye in the realisation that he could well be cooped up with them for the foreseeable future. Firstly, there was Chogan, small and tough, thoroughly capable and completely at home in the mountains. A reliable man to have around in a crisis like that which faced them now. Thickset, with shoulders like an ox, and square, rugged features that might almost have been chiselled out of the very rock itself. This man knew the mountains like the back of his own hand and was well acquainted with their dangers and their hidden treachery.

By contrast, Chalmers was tall and fair-haired, bespectacled and in his early thirties. He had been based up here for the past three months along with his wife, Janice, who was herself a professional geologist. She was sat over to one side, busily going through some of the detailed paperwork. Two others, Sam Kuttner and Brian Munro, both research students, were elsewhere in the base.

'My guess is that it will be at least a couple of days before the way becomes passable. Perhaps more,' said Chogan, noting the frustration on the professor's features.

'Christ! If I'd known it was going to be like this I wouldn't have come here.' Moorcroft scowled. He hadn't prepared himself for this but perhaps he should have known better. He let out a resigned sigh. 'Ah well, I suppose I've got to make the best of an unfortunate situation. It's just one of those things, I guess.' Inwardly, now that the shock of impending isolation was beginning to wear off, he felt bored. There wasn't much for him to do, except sit this out and listen to the infrequent weather reports on the small radio. And they weren't very encouraging.

Chalmers threw a glance at his wife before heading over and sitting next to the clearly disgruntled professor. 'Would you care for a Scotch? I'll freely confess to you that it's how most of us get through the day. When you're based up here for weeks on end, as most of us have been, you take your comforts where you can.'

Moorcroft shook his head. 'Not for me, thanks.'

'Suit yourself.' Chalmers idly picked up a magazine. 'You know, one of us might manage to get down and assess things. Get a more localised view as opposed to what the regional forecast is. But I wouldn't advise anyone to be too hasty as there's another storm coming up. Mark my words, we'll be snowed under before nightfall.'

Moorcroft lay in his bed and listened to the wild fury of the wind as it howled and hammered outside. He could hear it as it shrieked around the base like a maddened beast, shaking the windows, piling the snow in great drifts against the walls. Desperately, he tried to shut out the awful, keening noise, and to make himself as comfortable as possible. There was something almost frightening about the insane violence of the storm outside.

He rolled over onto his side, closed his eyes and tried to get some sleep. But it was no use. The movement had brought him face-to-face with the window, looking out to the terrible blackness outside. In spite of the overall darkness of the berserk heavens, there was sufficient moonlight for him to make out some of the surface details. In the far distance, the gigantic sweep of the nearby peaks towered high above the base, sharp pinnacles of ice and snow that seemed to point accusing fingers towards the heavens.

Fear was cold along his spine as he stared outside. It seemed relatively harmless when looked at from the comparative comfort of his small room. But was it? Could anyone be sure for certain? Could it be that there *were* things as yet unknown to science and reason out there?

He was not by nature a superstitious man but even so he was afraid. It took all the mental discipline he possessed to face the madness of night that screamed outside with a bestial fury and still retain a tight hold of himself.

His thoughts stopped abruptly as he saw a bizarre shadow move past the small square window five feet away. Almost instinctively, he jerked upright, his eyes wide in his head. He tried to tell himself that it had just been the wind hurling the thick snow before it. But that wasn't the real explanation. He was sure of that.

And then he saw it again. There *was* something outside. Sudden, primitive fear came rushing, surging into his mind, lancing coldly into his brain. The age-old fear inherent in every man. The fear of the darkness—and the things that lurked therein.

Trembling, he looked about him. He moved his head very slowly, unwilling, yet unable not to look at that square of darkness; scared that at any moment he would see something terrible pressed up against the glass and that it would drive him insane.

Breathing deeply, he tried to tell himself that perhaps it was nothing more than an animal.

Above the wail of the wind he could hear the sound of movement outside and now he was convinced that there was something there. But what? In his mind, he began to hear faint tribal singing, the kind he was familiar with having been on several Native American reservations. Yet this possessed a nightmarish, soul-wrenching quality that played havoc with the mind, conjuring up ghastly images of the dead and the diseased and the foul, half-man, half-beast creatures that fed on them, of battlefields strewn with the rotting corpses of fallen braves at which the crows pecked and ancient, withered medicine men performing unholy rituals in the solitude of their tepees. Was it just his imagination or could he now hear an unholy drumming? Desperately, he fought against the whimpering horror that threatened to overwhelm him.

Curiosity battled with panic and the blind, howling terror in his mind. Forcing down the fear, he swung his legs to the cold floor and crossed over slowly towards the window.

The sound intensified, followed by a shrill caterwaul that sent tiny shivers of ice spilling up and down the muscles of his back. The hairs on his neck ruffled uncomfortably. Whatever had produced that dreadful screech certainly didn't sound like any animal he had ever heard before.

He reached the window and, mustering his courage, he put his face up to it, allowing him to make out the details beyond. Something unbelievably gaunt and tall—eight, perhaps nine feet in height—detached itself from the wall near the entrance to the base like an evil, threatening shadow gifted with movement. It moved, seemingly unimpeded, through the heavy blizzard before stopping at the main door to the base.

Moorcroft felt suddenly ill. A twin set of red, glowing eyes stared back at him. He caught a fragmentary glimpse of a hook-nosed face; grey-white and terribly wrinkled, framed by a long, ragged, black-feathered headdress, with slavering, pointed teeth in a caricature of a human mouth and rotting strips of beadwork and wampum-bedecked garments that clung grotesquely around an emaciated body. In one hand it held what looked like a tomahawk. He took a step away from the window, gasping for air, choking back the scream that rose unbidden to his lips. Then, unable to stop himself, he turned and ran shrieking out of his room.

A whirling chaos threatened to overwhelm him. That pair of lambent red eyes staring out of the ghastly corpse-face continued to burn in his mind. He fought desperately against the hideousness and the insanity that came crowding in, stumbling along the narrow passage, muttering incoherent profanities, trying to pull himself together, only vaguely aware of other doors being flung open, of light streaming brilliantly into the corridor so that it chased away the shadows. And then voices were shouting madly in his ears.

Someone seized his arm and held on tightly.

'Professor! For God's sake, pull yourself together!' Chalmers shouted. 'What is it? What happened?'

Moorcroft was shaking as he allowed the other to lead him to a nearby chair in the main lounge. Gratefully, he sank down into it. A drink was hastily prepared and placed into his shaking hand.

'What's going on?' inquired Munro, buttoning up his pyjama top. He was a small, bearded man who looked constantly nervous and almost as frightened as Moorcroft himself.

'I'm all right.' The professor took a sip from the whisky glass. 'Nothing to panic about. I'm all right now.'

'Something must have happened.' Chalmers came forward, his face a mask of concern. 'What was it? A nightmare?'

Moorcroft clasped his head in his hands and leaned his elbows forward on his knees. 'Maybe,' he said. 'I don't know. Perhaps I did dream it all. Though I could have sworn there was something in the snow outside the window of my room. Something that – God! It was horrible.' He shuddered.

'Well it couldn't have been one of us,' said Kuttner, the youngest of the team. He looked around, doing a quick headcount. 'We're all accounted for. Besides, it's thirty below out there and with this dammed wind it's probably more like minus fifty. Nothing human could survive out there for long.'

'Can you describe what you saw?' asked Chalmers.

'Only vaguely, I'm afraid. It was tall, with glowing red eyes and its face...' Moorcroft finished his drink in one gulp, wincing as the raw liquor burnt the back of his throat.

Chalmers looked doubtful. '*Red eyes?* Are you sure?'

'I don't know. Maybe I was dreaming. But it seemed so damn real.'

'Well if there is anything strange out there it had best stay outside.' Chalmers disappeared into his room and came back a moment later with his rifle. 'If it tries to get in, this will soon take care of it.'

'If it wasn't a dream he had then you're a fool if you think you'll be able to stop it with a gun,' broke in Chogan, stepping forward and turning to Chalmers.

Moorcroft looked up. There was a tight expression on his face. 'Just what do you mean by that remark?' he snapped.

Chogan began pacing the room, his face strained and hard. 'Who knows?' he muttered finally. 'Very few people have ever seen it face-to-face and lived to tell the tale. Yet, amongst my tribe, we have tales of the Wind-Walker.'

'Come on, Chogan, spare us the superstitious nonsense,' hissed Kuttner. 'I've heard your stories before. The professor just had a bad dream. That's all. Besides, if we're to be stranded here for several days, the last thing we want to hear is your ghost stories. That will do nothing for our peace of mind.'

'Well, I'm going to take a look around. Who wants to come with me?' Chalmers said, putting on his heavy fleece.

For a moment, no one replied.

It was Kuttner who eventually spoke up: 'I'll go with you. Just give me a minute to get my coat.'

'You're being fools, both of you,' said Janice. 'It's far too cold outside and you'll never find any tracks. That will have to wait until morning.'

Moorcroft had to agree. It was insane to go out there on a night such as this, to hunt around for evidence of something he may, or may not, have seen. 'Obviously it's up to you what you want to do, but I'm going to go back to my room.' He rose from his chair and, taking his drink with him, made his way slowly along the narrow corridor towards his room and stepped inside, closing the door gently behind him. For a long moment, he stood quite still, with his back hard against the cold, solid woodwork of the door, not daring to look at the black square that marked the position of the window. Then, finally, he managed to lift his gaze.

There was nothing there. He crossed over slowly, just to make sure. But the dark shadows outside were still. All was as it should be.

The events of the past quarter of an hour had made him feel light-headed. He turned his back on the window, went to his bed and closed his eyes, finally drifting off into a troubled sleep.

When Moorcroft awakened, it was from a ghastly nightmare in which he had been floundering desperately through knee-deep snow, pursued by ugly, screaming, whistling shapes, gruesome and distorted, that came rapidly nearer with every step.

He got up out of bed, walked across to the window and looked out.

It had stopped snowing sometime during the latter part of the night, but there were still a few dark clouds boiling threateningly above the high peaks of the surrounding mountains. He threw them an appraising glance, half-turned from the window, then stopped. He felt his stomach muscles quiver uncontrollably.

Outside, where he had thought that he had seen that creature last night, he could see Chalmers and Chogan, muffled in their heavy parka coats, scanning the ground. He could tell by the way they were looking around that they had discovered something. Fear suddenly blazed in him – stark, completely unreasoning horror that was like a mad thing in his brain.

So there had been something out there in the darkness. Something that had crept away into the shadows or had perhaps sought some other means of entering the base.

He had no time to mull these disturbing thoughts over in his mind. He lurched away from the window and hurriedly got dressed. All the time, his mind kept coming up with a multitude of burning questions that shrieked to be answered, but for which there were no answers.

Opening the bedroom door, he walked out into the corridor and entered the main room.

'Looks like you were right after all, professor,' muttered Kuttner. 'Chogan discovered tracks not an hour ago. Better have a look at them yourself.'

Moorcroft returned to his room and got his heavy coat. He was heading back, intent on going outside when, with a blast of freezing cold air, the main door opened and Chalmers and Chogan entered, hastily closing the door behind them. There was a look of confusion imprinted on their ruddy faces.

'Seems that there *was* something outside the base last night,' said Chalmers, taking off his coat.

'Any idea what it could have been?' Moorcroft asked.

'It's like nothing I've ever seen before in all my years in the mountains,' Chogan said, obviously picking his words with caution. 'We were hoping you might be able to help us. You claim to have seen this creature. Do you think you could describe it more accurately than you did last night?'

'Not really,' replied Moorcroft. He tried to think, but it was useless. Memory seemed to reach him through a thick fog. It was as if the thing he had seen the night before had been so horrible, so utterly alien, that his mind was baulking at the attempt to recall it. Dimly, he remembered something tall and grotesque, pale and cold, like the night from which it had come with a hideous, corpse-like face. And the glowing red eyes that had looked soullessly into his own. Briefly, he told them all that he could remember.

Chogan frowned. 'I see. As you said yourself, there wasn't much, but what little you've been able to tell us has convinced me that we're all in deadly danger as long as we remain here. I've heard many tales during my life in this land about the spirits — the manitous — that roam the mountain trails after dark. The worst of these is Ithaqua, the —'

'That's enough, Chogan,' interrupted Chalmers. 'I'll admit that those tracks out there belong to neither man nor any beast I know of in these parts but that isn't reason to suggest anything supernatural. Something had been prowling around the base last night, something that had no right to be here, but it's gone now.' He looked about the worried faces of those inside. 'You hear me? It's gone.'

'Surely we're safe inside anyway?' said Munro, nervously.

Chalmers turned towards him. 'Of course we are.'

'That remains to be seen.' Chogan had paced over to the large stone hearth where a welcoming fire blazed. 'Personally, I think one of us should try and make our way down the pass in order to see how badly blocked the road is. There's just a chance that the storm may have cleared away most of the fallen snow.'

'You're going to have trouble getting the snowcat down there. Besides, I've still got quite a bit of work to do repairing the treads,' said Kuttner.

'I wasn't planning on taking it. I'll go down on foot,' Chogan replied.

'You really don't want to stay here another night, do you?' asked Munro. Despite the fact that it was morning, he had already started on the whisky. 'What exactly is it you fear, Chogan?'

'Yes, what is it?' Moorcroft asked, not knowing whether he wanted to truly know the answer. It was clearly now a fact that something terrible in appearance and perhaps in nature had been outside the base.

Chogan looked briefly at Chalmers, contemplating whether or not to relate what he knew. A moment past before he began to speak: 'I am of the Mi'kmaq tribe, one of the Algonquian people.

There is a story we tell around our campfires when the sky is dark and the wind howls from the frozen North, concerning the evil spirit, the Wendigo. Of all the manitous it is the most depraved, glorying in acts of cannibalism and horror. It can change its shape, assume the forms of its totemic beasts, yet its true appearance is exactly as the professor described. It is said that it can possess the minds of men, drive them insane and turn them into raging, flesh-eating monsters.'

'Whilst I respect your customs, Chogan, it all sounds a load of scare-mongering rubbish,' said Kuttner. 'No doubt there was something out there but it sure as hell wasn't a ghost or anything of that sort.'

'If that's what you think, fine.' Chogan shrugged his shoulders. 'But I for one don't want to be here when the sun goes down.'

'So you think this thing will come back?' asked Moorcroft.

Chogan nodded. 'I'm sure it will. Last night it was just scouting, assessing our defences. That's why I think it is vital that I go and see if there's a way for us to get down to the valley.'

Half an hour later, Moorcroft stood at the wide windows and watched the short, thick-set figure of the Native American making his way down the snow-covered side of the mountain.

'With any luck, he'll make it all right,' said Chalmers. 'Once he gets to the pass everything will be plain sailing. He's a good man and I don't think he'll be foolish enough to take any unnecessary chances. If all goes well, he should be back well before sundown. And if he does find the way is passable then all of us could be out of here before it gets dark. I know my wife would much rather be heading for Wrigley than stay cooped up here any longer than is necessary.'

Moorcroft nodded. His mouth was set into a tight line across the middle of his face. Somehow, though, he didn't think things would be quite as easy as that. At the back of his mind, a little,

13

nagging thought kept skipping into the background of his brain, refusing to come out into the open, where he could recognise it for what it actually was – but whatever it was it was laden with dread. Shading his eyes against the wicked glare of the sun that was thrown up from the vast, white expanse of snow, he caught a final dark shadow as Chogan disappeared from view.

'I take it you're not buying any of this talk about evil spirits and the like, are you?' Chalmers asked, turning to the professor.

'Me? I don't know. I've been trying to wrack my brains for other possible explanations, and I can't come up with any. However, regardless of what I think, we should play this down for the sake of the others. The last thing we need is for panic to set in.' Moorcroft stepped back from the window.

'Chogan has been talking about a lot of weird things while he's been up here. This isn't the first time he's mentioned this *Wendigo*. He's told me quite a bit about it.'

'Given our circumstances, the less I hear about that, the better. Anyway, have you had any success in re-establishing radio contact?'

Chalmers shook his head. 'Not yet, although Munro's working on it. Mountain Rescue know that we're out here, however they don't know anything of our current plight. If we're stuck here for another couple of days and we've been unable to fix the radio then I'm sure they'll send out a helicopter or a patrol just to check on us.'

When Chogan failed to return seven hours later, Moorcroft, Chalmers and Kuttner went out to search for him. They had initially set out in the hastily repaired snowcat before being forced to abandon it after finding it unable to cope with the descent.

The raging wind swooped down from the mountain peaks at their backs.

Full darkness was still somewhere far away in the frozen

distance; a black, brooding thing that would come rushing up out of the sky as soon as the sun went down. And all around them, the snow, picked up by the heavy gusts, fell in blinding sheets across the face of the slope.

Despite the harsh conditions, Chalmers soon managed to pick up the guide's trail. 'We'll have to hurry,' he shouted as he led the way into the icy wilderness. 'At a guess, I'd say there's only perhaps a couple of hours of daylight left. Maybe less.' Violent gusts threatened to whip away his words.

Conversation became useless as they set off down the slope, the wind now screaming in their ears, slapping monstrously against their faces, freezing exposed flesh and chilling the blood.

Moorcroft kept his gaze straight ahead. His eyes, under the fur-lined hood of his heavy coat, were never still, watching intently for the slightest movement. But for a long while, there was nothing, only the two figures of his companions up ahead. Minutes ticked past, lengthening along with their shadows as all around them the high-pitched howling of the incessant wind blew loudly. A biting coldness ate into their bodies, numbing, stiffening their muscles. Surely they should have found Chogan by now, he thought as he glanced around, uneasily taking in the harsh terrain. Soon it would be impossible for them to go any further.

The wind picked up in strength, becoming a full-blown blizzard, a near whiteout. Within minutes, it had closed around them. A thick, virtually impenetrable wall of swirling snowflakes; a frozen maelstrom.

For the best part of an hour they ploughed on into the deepening snow.

In spite of the tight hold he had on himself, Moorcroft shivered and not just from the sub-zero temperature. His mind kept spewing up gruesome images of what might have happened to the Native American. He tried to stop it. But it continued, going around in circles, endlessly, and the result was just the same. Supposing, he thought, that the thing he had seen outside the base had ambushed Chogan. He shuddered. Even his usually calmly scientific mind had been seriously affected by what he had seen and by the anxiety of the past few hours. There was no denying it – this wasn't a land where men ought to be. Not out here, in the great, white spaces between the cruel mountain peaks, where the wolf-wind came howling down out of the Arctic North. A mad wind, that howled into the mind as well as eating at the body.

'*Chogan!*' Chalmers hollered. He shouted out the name twice more before turning round to the others. He briefly consulted his watch. 'There's nothing more we can do. Let's return to the base before it gets dark. It's possible that he's backtracked and we've missed him.'

For a time, Moorcroft had the dreadful, unnerving feeling that they were not going to make it to the base. A gloom had fallen and the uphill struggle, into the savage wind, tested each man's endurance to the utmost. Thus it was with a great sigh of relief that he saw the abandoned snowcat and then the welcoming lights of the research station glowing dimly through the dense blizzard that swirled all around them.

After ten more minutes, his leg muscles jolting with every step, and now that they were less than a hundred or so yards away, he crumpled to the snow with the utter exhaustion of it all. Sudden shock propelled him backwards. For there, lying face-up, half-buried before him, eyes staring sightlessly out of his face, was the body of Chogan. In one icy blue hand, grasped in a death-grip, was a strange bone amulet. The broken wooden shaft of his small ice-pick projected oddly from the frozen ground nearby.

'Christ! Wha... what—?' Kuttner choked on his words.

Moorcroft felt his legs weaken and quiver as he tried to stand up, his gaze glued to the sight before him. For one dreadful moment he was irreverently reminded of pictures he had seen of preserved mammoths exhumed from the Siberian tundra.

'We can't leave him out here,' muttered Chalmers as soon as he could speak and still keep his voice steady. He bent down and with a gloved hand gingerly touched the corpse. It was frozen solid.

'It looks as though he may have suffered a heart attack,' said Kuttner.

Chalmers nodded grimly. 'It's hard to say. We'll have to take him back.'

Despite the fact that they were so near, Moorcroft knew that it was going to be difficult getting the body back to the base. But unfortunately, it had to be done. Tired as he was, he helped as the other two began to clear away the snow and ice which had begun to encroach around the dead man. In the process, the fingers that grasped the amulet snapped off and, pocketing it, he continued more cautiously.

Carefully, Chalmers and Kuttner tugged and pried the body out of the compacted shallow grave, raising the frozen arms in order to drag it completely free. Once done, they hefted it between them and began picking their way through the banks of snow, their eyes always on the lookout for anything that might be lurking in the dense, yet becoming increasingly darker, whiteness, the bright yellow lights of the base leading them on.

Unburdened, Moorcroft led the way, frequently looking over his shoulder to reassure himself that his associates were still behind him. He would then turn swiftly, in order to peer out into the icy wasteland. But there was nothing but the driving snow.

Finally, the three of them reached the base.

Moorcroft banged heavily on the door.

A few seconds later, it opened and Munro peered out, a wood axe in his hand. He took an unsteady step forward as he caught sight of the rigid body on the ground nearby, half-hidden in shadow and a faint filming of snow. When he saw what it was, he hesitated, then took a sudden, fumbling step backwards even as the professor pushed past him.

Accompanied by a ferocious blast of cold air, Chalmers and Kuttner came inside, Chogan's grim remains supported between them.

Munro closed the door and turned to face them. 'What happened?' he asked faintly.

'We don't know,' Moorcroft answered. He turned to Chalmers. 'What are you going to do with him?'

'There's a small cold storage unit in the basement. I think it best that we put him in there.' Chalmers looked around. 'Where's Janice?'

'Don't worry, your wife's okay. She's in her room. You know what she's like. She's the only one who's been able to do any work of late,' Munro answered.

'Good. Come on, Kuttner, let's get Chogan downstairs before she sees any of this.' Heaving the dead weight of the stiff body off the ground, Chalmers, with Kuttner's help, made for the basement.

Moorcroft watched them vanish down the corridor, inwardly hoping that Janice would not appear at an unfortunate moment and witness the grim spectacle. No doubt she would be later informed by her husband. Not wishing to be subjected to Munro's questioning and thinking that he might be of some assistance, he set off after Chalmers and Kuttner.

Heading along the corridor, he passed his room, crossed the small canteen and went to the rear of the base. Beyond an open door was a flight of wooden steps that led down into the storage area. From beyond came the smell of faint diesel fumes and the constant rumbling of the generators which provided electricity to the entire station.

Gingerly, he started down. With each step the temperature plummeted so that by the time he reached the bottom his breath was visible as a frosty mist.

The small, densely cluttered room he entered was lit by a bright fluorescent strip light. All around him were shelves stacked with all of the items of hardware required for the running of the station. Oil drums and crates filled with geological drilling tools lay haphazardly in one corner. From beyond the door directly opposite him, he could hear the sounds of Chalmers and Kuttner bickering.

'Christ, Kuttner. Do you always keep this place in such a bad condition?'

'I've never seen it like this before. It wasn't like this when I checked yesterday morning.'

Not wanting to eavesdrop further on their conversation, Moorcroft opened the door and entered the room beyond, almost slipping on the thin sheet of ice which covered the floor.

Both men turned round.

'I'd watch your step in here, professor,' warned Chalmers, pointing to the white slickness that covered most of the ground. Icicles hung from the ceiling.

Supporting himself against an oil drum, Moorcroft could see that Chogan had been laid out on top of a work table in the centre of the room. 'Is it normally so cold down here?' he said, shivering.

'No,' Chalmers answered. 'Before we leave I'll be sure to put the heating up a notch or two.'

It was only eight o'clock but the weariness of the trek down and then back up the slope had fatigued Moorcroft considerably, so that he was now lying on his bed trying to get to sleep. His light was out and in the darkness he turned restlessly, listening to the continuous sound of the storm outside as it gusted relentlessly around the base. If anything it seemed to have become stronger, more savage, almost hurricane-like in strength.

Moorcroft lay in fear, unable to disentangle Chogan's

apparently natural death from that horrible thing he had seen the previous night; dreading the scrape of nails against the window or the chanting and the rhythmic beating of drums inside his brain.

Somehow, he managed to drift off.

Sometime later, he stirred out of deep slumber into a room bathed in cold moonlight. All was unusually silent, the wind no longer raging outside. For a time he was disorientated, unsure of his surroundings, unable to anchor himself to reality. And then, he heard it – the noise that had filled his nightmares, the scraping of nails – only this time it was closer, much closer.

It sounded as though it was directly beneath him – under his bed!

It felt as though he had been suddenly plunged into deep, freezing water. Brain-numbing, paralysing terror momentarily stopped his heart. He watched, stricken with fear as in the pale moonlight, a bone-white claw, attached to an almost skeletal arm over which the skin had been stretched taut, crawled over the side of his bed. There came a dreadful shuffling sound as whatever had lain hidden slid out, getting to its feet.

Shaking violently, unable to release the scream that threatened to burst his lungs asunder, he brought his knees up to his chest, cowering away from the grotesque living skeleton that reared before him. Red eyes stared out from a cadaverous, almost mum-mified face. Black dreadlocks into which beads had been fastened sprouted from its scalp and around its neck was a necklace of raven feathers and scrimshaw.

Fang-filled mouth opening, it reached forwards, raising its tomahawk, ready to scalp him...

With a violent start, he awoke from his nightmare. His heart was thudding away in his chest and his head was spinning. A cold sweat plastered his hair to his forehead.

Suddenly, there came a loud pounding on his bedroom door.

'Professor!'

Groggily, Moorcroft staggered to his feet and switched on the light, noticing from the wall clock that it had just gone ten. For one terrible moment he thought he was going to see that dreadful being stood, grinning, in the far corner, believing that he was still in his nightmare but thankfully there was nothing there.

'Professor!' The door was thumped again.

'Coming.' Moorcroft reached out and opened the door to find Kuttner standing before him. The man looked extremely agitated. 'What's going on?'

'Munro's missing!'

'What?' Moorcroft stepped out into the corridor. 'Where could he have gone?' He was about to ask something else when he saw Chalmers coming towards them from the canteen, his rifle in his hands.

'You're not going to believe this but Chogan's gone as well.' There was a look of utter bewilderment on Chalmer's face. 'His body's not where we left it. The back door's been unlocked so it looks like he's left the base and gone outside. Could be that he wasn't fully dead when we brought him in.'

Kuttner swore volubly. 'He was dead. There's no doubt about that.'

The realisation that he had gone from one nightmare into another struck Moorcroft forcibly. His mind reeled. None of this made any sense. 'Surely they can't have gone far in this weather?' he asked.

'I don't know what the hell's happening. Munro's coat and boots are still in his room but as he's nowhere to be found he must be outside somewhere.' Chalmers stomped into the lounge and started buttoning up his thick parka.

'I'll come with you,' said Moorcroft. 'Just give me a minute to get my stuff.' He ran back to his room and hastily got into his thermals. He took his heavy coat from where it hung and struggled into it, pulling the fur-lined hood around his face.

Chalmers was already outside by the time he arrived. 'Here, take this,' he said, handing over a powerful flashlight.

'I'll stay here in case they turn up,' said Kuttner.

Together, Chalmers and Moorcroft headed out across the frozen landscape. Swirls of snow fell around them as overhead the aurora borealis played a vibrant, scarlet-green atmospheric lightshow, providing an almost surreal backdrop.

It did not take long for them to locate a set of tracks; barefoot prints heading towards where they had left the snowcat.

Panning the flashlight beam straight at it, they were shocked to see shadowy movement inside the small compartment. There was someone – or something – inside.

Gulping back his fear, Moorcroft headed over, Chalmers to one side.

Suddenly the compartment door was thrown open. A blood-spattered thing that had once been Munro leapt down. He looked ghastly; his chalk-white face hollow and sunken, his mouth smeared with gore. In one hand he held a butcher's knife whilst in the other he gripped a severed hand at which he had been gnawing.

'Christ!' shouted Moorcroft. 'Shoot him!' he cried as the horror advanced towards them, snarling and drooling hungrily as it came.

'Get back!' Chalmers shouted, raising his rifle. 'Get back or I'll fire.' His warning fell on deaf ears. And now it was he and the professor who were backing away.

'Shoot him, for God's sake!' Moorcroft shouted.

Chalmers pulled the trigger. Having forgotten to remove the half-bolt safety catch, there came a dull click as the rifle failed to discharge.

And then the blood-covered man before them was changing, dropping to all fours. Bristling, dark grey hair sprouted from his face as his indoor clothes ripped and fell from him. His face elongated, becoming lupine as huge fangs grew from a mouth that was now a maw, a blood-coated muzzle.

Munro had become a wolf, a huge timber wolf, a malign, voracious intelligence in its eyes.

Moorcroft screamed as Chalmers began hastily fumbling with his rifle.

For a moment, the wolf bobbed its massive head from side to side, weighing up its opponents, gauging which of the two men posed the greater threat. Then, with a guttural howl, it expelled a freezing mass of ice and a vapour from its mouth. Glacial motes sparkled within the cloud of rimy breath, Chalmers its target.

Chalmers was quick to react. He leapt to his right, the frosty blast numbing his left-hand side instead of catching him full on. The cold was perishing, almost burning in its ferocity. With a scream of pain, he fell to his knees, dropping his rifle, his right hand gripping his frozen left arm.

The wolf then came at a leap.

Chalmers took its full weight. With a cry, he fell, the huge carnivore on top of him. Frantically, he battered at its snout with a gloved hand, his desperate blows having little effect.

In a savage frenzy, the wolf made to bite down, to tear the flesh from his face.

Chalmers managed to get his right hand in front of its snapping jaws. Three fingers were bitten off and greedily gobbled.

The sudden bang of the rifle going off startled the wolf, causing it to miss what would undoubtedly have been its killing bite. It looked around, its red eyes alive with a cold burning. It saw the other man, the man with the rifle and howled, the sound strangely human. Leaping off its savaged victim, it stalked threateningly towards him, hackles up, belly low to the ground, bluish wisps rising from its muzzle as it began to growl, indicating that it was about to exhale its cloud of freezing death once more.

With the flashlight resting on the snow throwing grotesque shadows, Moorcroft took aim and fired.

The wolf sprang into the air as the high impact bullet struck it in the throat.

Moorcroft shot it a second time and then a third as it limped away into the shadows.

Chalmers staggered over, blood streaming from his wounded hand, a thick coating of frost covering half his body. 'Did you kill it?'

'I don't think so but now's not the time to go after it. Wait here.' Moorcroft picked up the flashlight, headed over to the snowcat, climbed up and looked inside. Of all the things he had ever seen before this was undoubtedly the worst. Scattered inside were the barely recognisable, gory remains of the now thawed out Chogan. It took only the briefest of glimpses to fill the professor's mind with horror for it was clear that he had been partially devoured and that the thing that had been Munro had been feasting on him.

Bile rose in the professor's gullet. Stomach lurching, he jumped down and vomited.

'What is it?' asked Chalmers through gritted teeth.

Wiping spittle from his mouth, Moorcroft straightened. 'It's Chogan. That monster's been eating him. Come on. Let's get back to the base and get your hand seen to.'

Moorcroft sat by the fire, curiously examining the bone amulet that had belonged to the unfortunate Native American, wondering if it possessed any magic that could be of use against whatever it was that was outside in the dark. If it did, then clearly it hadn't provided its previous owner with any talismanic benefits. That is, unless Chogan *had* died from natural causes. For his corpse, prior to having been found mutilated in the snowcat, had borne no sign of external violence.

Alongside his wife, Chalmers sat shivering nearby, sullenly staring into his steaming coffee, his right hand heavily bandaged, the frost that had coated him having melted away, sloughing off like a snake's skin. He was in constant pain however and having changed into dry clothes, all had been shocked to see the blackened, almost frostbitten skin beneath.

Armed with the rifle, Kuttner was on patrol in addition to making desperate attempts to make radio contact.

The weather outside was atrocious. Cold, white death blasted at the base and despite Moorcroft's best efforts to regulate the inside heating it was steadily becoming colder.

Equally alarming was the way in which the lights constantly flickered, threatening to go out at any moment. The last thing they needed was for them to be plunged into icy darkness – a darkness, Moorcroft was certain, in which he would then see those malevolent red eyes. Consequently, he had the flashlight nearby.

'Chogan was right,' Chalmers muttered, deliriously. 'It is the Wendigo. And what's more it isn't going to let any of us leave here.'

Janice looked worriedly at her husband. She was the trained medic and although she had treated and cleaned his wound with alcohol and Betadine, it was still quite possible that it had become infected. She knew he seriously needed hospital attention.

Chalmers' eyes were wide and staring. 'I'm telling you, it's going to kill us all. And then it's going to eat us.'

Moorcroft had heard enough. Rising to his feet, he went in search of Kuttner, hoping against hope that he would find the other speaking into the radio, having made contact with the outside world. Instead he found him exiting the lavatories.

'How's Chalmers doing?' Kuttner asked.

'To be honest with you, I can't see him making it through the night,' Moorcroft answered truthfully. 'As things currently stand, I don't see any of us making it through the night,' he added.

'I still can't believe what you told us about Munro. Are you sure he turned into a wolf?'

Moorcroft nodded.

'And, are you sure you didn't kill him? I mean, if you say you shot him three times with this,' Kuttner held up the rifle, 'then I can't see how—' He was interrupted by a violent swirl of wind that rocked the entire base.

With a loud crash, the heavy rear exit door which had been securely bolted smashed open and an icy gale howled along the corridor, buffeting the two men as they turned in that direction, almost knocking them off their feet. Their eyes stung. A thin layer of frost instantly formed on their faces.

A tumultuous blizzard swept down the corridor with stunning force.

When it cleared, moments later, Moorcroft heard that dreadful mournful chanting accompanied by that frenzied drumming inside his head.

Stood in the wrecked doorway, illuminated by a swinging strip light which looked as though it was about to fall from its mooring at any moment, was that horribly tall, practically skeletal, fiend – that hideous aberration of a Native American shaman. Shadows danced weirdly around it.

Stooping slightly, brandishing its tomahawk, it stepped inside, red eyes glaring.

Kuttner screamed and brought his hands to his ears. 'Make it stop! For the love of God, make it stop!' Thick red blood began trickling between his fingers. He then began flailing at the air as though he were trying to shake off an attack from an invisible raven.

Moorcroft knew that for some reason – perhaps due to the powers of the amulet he had in his trouser pocket – the terrible noise wasn't affecting him anywhere near as badly. Scrambling for the rifle, he flicked off the safety, took aim and squeezed the trigger. He missed and the bullet ricocheted against the far wall. He was about to shoot a second time when, with a violent belch, the horror projected a thick stream of vaporous liquid from its mouth.

The super cold regurgitation blasted into Kuttner, striking him like liquid nitrogen. He crystallised almost instantly.

Then, to Moorcroft's revulsion, parts of the research student broke away.

Frozen chunks of solid man crashed to the floor of the passage. Little bloody ice floes separating from the main iceberg.

Something seemed to snap in Moorcroft's brain. A shrieking insanity tugged fiercely at his mind, rising up like a dark tide which threatened to engulf him, to bury him beneath its dark waters from which there was no escape.

There then came a loud crash directly behind him as the stretch of interconnecting passage which joined the canteen and the bedrooms with the main lounge caved in. Sudden, freezing wind and snow gusted in through the rent opening. Throughout the base, the lights flickered, dimmed and then went out.

Something had struck the professor on the head and in the darkness, he could feel what he assumed was blood trickling down his face. Taking the flashlight from his pocket, he flicked it on, dreading what he might see. He winced, noticing the shattered remains of Kuttner, not fully able to come to terms with the fact that this scattered pile of icy blue and red matter had once been a living being. It was a truly obscene way to die. Still, there was no sign of the monster – the Wendigo, as Chogan had called it.

He knew that he had to get proper shelter before he froze to death. Teeth chattering, well aware that he couldn't go back the way he had come, Moorcroft headed around the base to the front entrance, the beam from his flashlight throwing horrible shadows that seemed to shift of their own volition. The main door was wide open.

'Chalmers!' he shouted. His hands were shaking and his hair and eyebrows had become rimed with frost. He had lost all feeling in his toes.

There was no answer.

Shakily, Moorcroft entered, his flashlight in one hand, rifle in the other.

Bile rose to his gullet upon seeing the sight before him.

Crouched by the body of her husband, munching away at his bloody, torn open corpse, was Janice Chalmers – or rather the vile entity that now possessed her. She turned, hissing her displeasure at this intrusion, her snow-white face smeared with gore. Bloody hands which clenched the wrist at which she had been chewing, swung up to her red eyes in order to shield them from the beam of light.

Dropping the flashlight, Moorcroft raised the rifle and fired. The recoil jarred along his frozen limbs as the bullet blasted away a portion of the ghoul's head, knocking it back. He fired again, blowing a hole in the thing's chest.

With an unearthly screech, the thing began to shape-change.

The clothes it wore shredded and fell away as grey-brown fur erupted all over its body. Its face lengthened, becoming a fang-filled maw, a thick, shaggy mane around its neck. Hands became massive clawed paws.

Snarling, its metamorphosis now complete, the huge grizzly bear lumbered to its feet, its head brushing the ceiling.

Moorcroft sobbed with fear and horror, letting the useless rifle clatter to the ground. He knew he could not withstand an attack from this monster but raised his arms involuntarily, to block the terrible beast. A moment later the bear was on him, slashing with its claws, but they passed, ineffectually, straight through him. The creature bellowed with rage and frustration.

Galvanised by the bear's seeming inability to hurt him, Moorcroft scrambled backwards, away from it. He turned and ran, dashing headlong into the freezing night, floundering desperately through the thick snow, his mind and body temporarily oblivious to the cold such was his fear. The raging insanity of all he had seen obliterated his sanity and he was aware only of the adrenaline flooding him and the dreadful roars echoing through the night.

The day after the snow storm had ended, a small Mountain Rescue team had come from Wrigley to check on the geological station and see why none of their radio messages had been answered. The three men had got over the heavy snow by dog sled and were making their way up the slopes to the base. The snow had piled in drifts against trees and the going was slow and careful. One drift near the station was larger than the others and as a section of snow slipped down, they could see a flash of yellow underneath.

'That must be the snowcat,' their leader commented. 'Strange to find it over here. They normally keep it right by the station.' He used a long pole to brush more of the snow off, uncovering the windscreen.

All three men jumped as there came a shriek from inside the cabin of the vehicle.

'Jesus, there's someone in there! Quickly, get the snow off this thing.'

The shrieking continued as they worked, shovelling the snow away from the vehicle's door.

'Nearly there... done it!' The leader levered open the door and then recoiled in shock.

The interior of the cabin was spattered with gory remains – all that was left of Chogan. Huddled in one corner, stinking and dishevelled, was Moorcroft. His eyes were wide in terror and his clothes and face were smeared with blood.

'You can't eat me!' he giggled, brandishing a small bone amulet. The rescuers fell back in horror from the raving, wild eyed man as he continued to shriek, his voice tipping further into hysteria. 'You killed the others, but *you can't eat me!* YOU CAN'T EAT ME!'

The men looked at each other in dawning horror, taking in the lunatic before them and the just discernibly human remains he was squatting amongst and then, at a nod from their leader, the two youngest started off towards the geological station, dreading what they would find within.

THE VOICE-STEALERS

It would have been better if they had remained confined
to myth and legend.

DESPITE RETAINING MUCH of its historical and architectural opulence, the palace twenty miles north-west of Jaipur in the district of Rajasthan was far off the tourist trail. Built high atop a rugged hilltop overlooking vast stretches of dusty, barren land, it had been the dwelling place for countless nobles down the centuries until the time when the Rajput kings had concluded treaties in the early Nineteenth Century, accepting British sovereignty in return for local autonomy and protection from the expansionist ambitions of the Maratha empire. Its fine statues, tapestries and painted murals, although fading, portrayed many elaborate scenes from this time of its troubled history and provided a certain ambience for the banquet which was taking place in one of the grand state rooms.

Clive Mortimer Benford was one of those partaking of the sumptuous fare. He was a well-built, extremely wealthy American who had a passion for killing exotic wildlife in the name of sport. Hunting was in his blood and had been ever since his father had given him a longbow at the age of six and had taken him into the forested wilds, teaching him how to stalk deer and rabbits. On his eighth birthday, he had been presented with his own rifle and from that day on had gone in search of bigger and more dangerous game, namely mountain lions and bears. To him, animals were but things to stand alongside for photographs; poised over their bullet-riddled corpses or hung as trophies on the wall, or, in the case of the slices of dead camel on his plate, to eat. He began to cut up his steak. 'So just why were you kicked out of Oxford?' he asked conversationally yet well aware that his question was bound to offend his host. There was something about the young Indian prince, whom he had only recently met, that he didn't like—a certain cunning look in his eyes—and what was more, he was convinced the feeling was mutual.

'I wouldn't say I was 'kicked out',' Prince Deepak Singh, who sat at the head of the lavishly laid out table around which four others were seated, answered mellowly. 'Rather, we parted company. I guess Oxford wasn't yet ready for my ground-breaking discoveries. A pity, but at the end of the day, it's their loss, not mine.' There was nothing in his tone of voice to imply that he had been insulted by the nature of his guest's inquiry.

'You were studying for a doctorate in genetics if I'm not mistaken,' said Janice Carpenter in her shrill voice. She was a writer who had come out to India in the hope of finding material on mystical practices for a book she was planning. 'A fascinating subject I'm sure but one which I'm afraid is far too scientific for me.'

'Ever since childhood I've been interested in animal evolution and the manner in which some animals and plant forms survive and flourish whilst others become extinct due to their inability to adapt to their environment in addition to the damaging role that man has played on their survival, by which I mean habitat alteration, industrialisation and hunting.' Singh smiled and nodded at Benford whom he knew had come to India for the sole purpose of shooting game. 'For my dissertation, I collected material on a wide range of recently extinct fauna; the Javan rhinoceros, the Bali tiger, the quagga, the thylacine and of course, the much better known dodo. However, my particular interest lies in the field of cross-species hybridisation.' He raised a hand and clicked his fingers. 'More wine.'

His instructions given, two servants immediately came forward, filling glasses.

'*Hybridisation?* I assume that you're talking about the recent successes in breeding certain of the panthera strains?' Professor Hans Kugelbeck asked in his accented English as he dabbed at the corners of his mouth with a napkin. He was an archaeologist in his late sixties and had recently arrived from Munich with the intention of working on certain Harrapan sites on the Pakistan border.

Singh nodded. 'The genetic creation of the tigon and the liger are but two examples, but there are many more. One day —'

'Did you say tigon?' Benford interrupted. 'And what the hell's a liger? I've never heard of them and I've spent my entire life tracking down all manner of creatures.'

'Pardon me.' Singh gave Kugelbeck an apologetic smile before turning to face the brash American. 'The tigon is the offspring of a tiger and a lioness. The liger is in some ways its mirror-image, resulting from the mating of a lion and a tigress. I used to have a liger in my private menagerie. A truly incredible creature. The largest of the big cats. There is also the litigon which is the off-shoot of the lion and the female tigon but—'

'Are these things for real?' asked Benford. If so, he wanted to know where he could go out and hunt them – although that was a question which, given the current company, he didn't ask. Hopefully he'd have a chance to find out later.

'Very much so. As I told you, I used to own a liger. Unfortu-nately there was an inherent weakness in the genetic strain and she aged faster than was natural. In the end, there was nothing any of my highly-skilled veterinary staff could do.' Singh got to his feet. A small man, resplendent in his black formal suit and a silk, turquoise turban, he looked much younger than his thirty-three years. 'Now, there is still much for me to do, but as my guests feel free to wander the palace. In the morning, it is my wish that you all accompany me to see for yourselves some of the important work that I am currently overseeing. As some of you may know, my father ran a very successful stud farm, breeding some of the best horses in India, if not the world. Some were even sent to the polo grounds at Mumbai. I have gone much further, taking cross-species experimentation and selective breeding to levels hitherto unguessed at, advancing his work in ways that he would never have imagined.'

There was an unpleasant, queasy feeling in Benford's stomach as he sat staring out at the desolate landscape from inside the decrepit, wheezing bus. From the occasional groan from his fellow passengers he could tell that he wasn't the only one suffering. In all probability the meal last night hadn't fully agreed with them. To make matters worse, the conditions inside the bus were far from comfortable. Even with the windows down the heat was stifling and from where he sat he felt as though he was getting slowly cooked from the magnified rays of the sun.

Only Singh, who sat next to the driver, seemed unaffected.

The road the bus bumped and rattled along wound its way into the Rajasthan badlands. There were no villages or towns, only mile after mile of arid countryside, the sun-bleached uniformity broken only by an infrequent ruin.

There came a tap on Benford's shoulder. He turned in his seat.

'Excuse me my good man but am I correct in assuming that you came out here to hunt animals, yes?' asked a thin-faced, chinless man in an English upper class voice. He had introduced himself as Sir Reginald Ashmole when they had first got on the bus.

'Sure did,' Benford drawled. 'Why d'ya ask?'

Ashmole lowered his voice until it became an almost conspiratorial whisper. 'I may be able to assist you in your endeavour. You see, I know a man in Delhi who operates safaris with the more discerning customer in mind. For a suitable sum he's not averse to procuring certain of the more, shall we say, hard to find game.'

'Sounds interesting. Maybe—' Benford stopped as, with a sudden lurch, the bus came to a standstill.

Singh was on his feet. 'Apologies for the bone-shaking journey but I'm pleased to inform you that we've now arrived. Now, just a few short words about the facility before we disembark. There are basically two separate compounds. The first one we'll visit is what I refer to as the 'zoo'. It is here that most of the animals are housed and fed. In the second area are the laboratories where much of the actual genetic work is done. This facility is also home to the veterinary hospital.'

Janice raised a hand and then asked: 'Don't you think it's fundamentally against nature to be experimenting on these creatures in such a way?'

Singh smiled. '*Against nature?* Who's to say what precisely nature is? If man has the capability of creating a new strain of life through biological fusion then I see no ethical dilemma. Here in India we have a code of ethics when it comes to vivisection which is quite probably more stringent than that to be found in most Western countries. I can assure you that nothing is done here which breaches any laws. To me, the welfare of my animals is paramount. Well, if we're all ready, I see no reason not to start the tour.' He turned his back on the others and leapt down from the bus.

Privately, Benford doubted much of what the prince had said, nevertheless he followed, relieved to be no longer suffering the dreadful motion sickness which had plagued him for the past forty minutes. Shading his eyes against the terrible brightness, he could see a collection of single-storey buildings surrounded by a barbed wire fence. There was an overall drabness about the place and a thick, cloying stench, which reminded him of his uncle's pig farm back in Kansas, polluted the air. There was also a hellish screeching coming from over to his right and peering in that direction he could see, beyond the outer fence, a crude cage in which frenetic shapes, probably monkeys, leapt and scurried.

Once his four guests were off the bus, Singh began walking to a small sentry box which stood at the side of the main gate. Inside was a guard, a rifle slung over his shoulder.

Belching noisome exhaust fumes and throwing up a great cloud of dust, the bus pulled away.

Benford appraised the man with the rifle. Admittedly savage animals were kept here but it wasn't as though there was any threat to the public for the installation was miles from anywhere and he doubted whether it ever got any casual visitors. Even if several of the lions or tigers did manage to escape he doubted whether they'd get far in this sweltering heat and with no water for miles around. From past experience, he knew that creatures which had been bred in captivity became soft, unable to fully revert back to surviving in the wild where meals weren't delivered at set times and where competition was fierce. Some became docile, almost domestic, dependant on humans for their existence.

Singh conversed with the guard in his own dialect. Moments later, the gate was opened and ushering his guests forward, he led them towards a large wooden barn-like structure.

The horrendous stench became more overpowering.

'Please forgive the smell,' commented Singh. 'This building we're now approaching houses the various pens in which some of the animals are kept. In addition there are a few cages, mostly for the primates and the big cats, over on the far side of the complex, which we may have the opportunity of visiting later.' He gave a nonchalant wave of his hand to two men who came out of a large side door carrying buckets. 'We're in luck. It appears that we've arrived at feeding time. I must ask you all to be cautious around the animals. Both for your sake and for theirs.'

The five of them entered the building.

As Benford had suspected the area inside resembled huge stables, divided into numerous stalls and pens with a central walkway down the middle. The noise inside was a chaotic cacophony of screeches, barks, yelps and roars which seemed to tear at his brain as assuredly as the claws of the strange-looking badger-like creatures he was currently looking down at.

Kugelbeck leaned over the side and then quickly drew his hand away as one of the vicious animals sprang for him. 'What are these?' he asked, turning to Singh.

'These are Rajasthan desert badgers. They're unique to this vicinity and are native to the foothills south of here. They are very aggressive and unlike badgers found elsewhere in the world they are purely carnivorous. Let me show you.' Singh removed a thick chainmail gauntlet that hung on a hook nearby and put it on. There was a bucket filled with meat scraps at the door to the pen and he took out a large chunk which he then dangled over the side.

The effect was startling.

The closest three badgers ceased snuffling about and made frenzied leaps at the meat. Two latched on with their razor-sharp teeth and dragged it from Singh's hand. There followed a violent battle on the ground as all six of them then fought over the meat, tearing it to pieces and devouring it in a show of terrible, raptorial hunger.

It reminded Benford of something he had once read about a school of piranhas stripping an elephant to the bone in no time at all. 'Hell, they sure were hungry,' he said.

'They always are,' replied Singh. 'It is most unfortunate but if they're not fed regularly they are known to turn cannibalistic. Consequently, in the wild they tend to be solitary creatures. Here, part of my research is concerned with trying to breed this compulsive hunger from them; to make them more sociable and —'

'What the hell's this?' asked Benford. He had wandered over to a pen on the other side, away from the badgers. The long, lizard-like creature he was looking at had a hardened shell on its back like that of a tortoise but its profile, to say nothing of its angular, snouted jaws, were more in common with those of a crocodile. There didn't appear to be any movement from it in the slightest, leading him to the conclusion that it was either fast asleep or dead.

Singh sauntered over. 'That is a mutant. A freak which I obtained from a North African trader. Preliminary tests have shown that its genetic makeup is part freshwater crocodile and part turtle. I believe it to be a true quirk of nature. A real one off.'

'A most peculiar animal,' commented Ashmole.

Benford had already passed on to the next holding area. This one housed five piebald pygmy horses, no larger than medium-sized dogs and whilst unusual, they held no real interest for him. He quickly walked on. Here was a large tank filled with dark water in which, initially, he could see nothing. Then, just as he was about to call to Singh to ask if there was anything inside, the surface rippled and two serpent heads reared before him, their twin forked tongues flicking the air. Hastily, he pulled well back.

'Please be careful!' warned Singh, rushing over.

Now that the initial shock had worn off, Benford tried to compose himself. It was only a couple of snakes after all and he had killed hundreds over the years. Both heads sank into the murky water once more. 'I didn't recognise either of them from their markings. What were they?'

'*They*? That was one creature. A genuine amphisbaena.'

'A what?'

'It is a two-headed snake. The product of successful genetic engineering.' Singh guided Benford away from the tank. 'For centuries they were considered extinct; monsters of myth and legend. Through a specialised breeding program I have restored life to a species which nature had turned her back on. Further work is needed on establishing in which habitat these creatures will thrive but it is my ambition to be able to release all of them to the wild one day.' He was going to say more when a somewhat nervous-looking technician came walking briskly forward and muttered something in Indian into his ear.

Despite not knowing what was communicated it was obvious to Benford that something was wrong.

Some of the colour bleached from Singh's face. Gulping, he turned to his guests. 'I'm afraid there's been a slight problem. If I can just ask you all to follow me outside.' Hurriedly, using an exit at the other end of the building, he ushered everyone outside.

'What's wrong?' asked Benford.

'It's nothing to worry about,' said Singh. 'Just a slight prob-lem.' He spoke again with the technician. After a few moments, he then dispatched the other to the security guard at the gate. He turned to those assembled. 'If you'd all just remain here whilst I go and find out what's wrong. I assure you it's nothing to panic about.'

The guard with the rifle rushed over.

'Please, wait here.' Snatching the rifle from his hands, Singh and the other then dashed over to a squat, grey building built from breeze-blocks.

Benford took in the confused faces of his fellow visitors, noting the concerned looks.

'What do you think's the matter?' asked Janice. It was clear she was trying to conceal her fear.

'Hard to say,' answered Benford. 'Could be anything. Some-thing to do with the electrics or the water supply. Maybe they've had an infestation of roaches.'

'Or something's got out.'

All eyes turned to Ashmole.

The Englishman shrugged his narrow shoulders. 'Well, it's

possible, is it not? I had a friend who used to work at Windsor Safari and he once told me how a tiger had managed to escape from its cage. By the time they'd succeeded in getting it back it had mauled its—'

There came a loud gunshot that caused everyone but Benford to jump.

'Good God!' exclaimed Ashmole, looking in the direction from which the sound had come with wide, staring eyes.

'That was a gun, wasn't it?' asked Janice.

'Sure was.' Benford took a few steps forward. Apart from themselves there was no one else around. The door to the building which Singh had entered hung open and he expected the young prince to come out having now taken care of the 'problem'. It seemed that an animal had escaped after all.

A minute passed and no one emerged.

There was a tightness in Benford's stomach – a tensing of muscles. His eyes narrowed as he stared at the doorway some sixty yards away. Another minute passed and he could now feel a tingling sensation in his hands. If something had broken free of its cage then surely it had been shot and was now dead. So where the hell were Singh and the gate guard?

'Do you think they're all right?' asked Janice nervously.

'Perhaps one of us should go and see,' suggested Ashmole, looking pointedly at Benford. It was abundantly clear that he didn't feel up to the task.

'Yes, maybe that would be for the best,' seconded Kugelbeck. 'Just to make sure that nothing untoward has happened.'

'Be my guest,' said Benford. Had he a gun in his hand he would have been the first to go and investigate but unarmed he didn't relish coming face to face with whatever creatures may be inside. Given the bizarre nature of the animals he had seen so far it could be just about anything.

'Well, I...' Kugelbeck faltered. Mumbling darkly to himself, he mustered his courage. His face hardened. 'Very well.'

Benford felt a stab of guilt. He cursed his own cowardice. 'Hold up there! I'll come along with you,' he said.

Together the two of them headed for the door. A wind blew up, gusting dust into mini whirlwinds and causing the door to slam against the outer wall. The riotous screeching from the creatures in the stables behind them died down and a portentous silence fell over them, broken only by the banging of the door.

'I don't know what's going on but things aren't looking too good,' commented Benford. Tentatively, he edged towards the door, preparing himself to act without a moment's hesitation, his nerves coiled like a cobra about to strike. His nostrils twitched as an unpleasant odour wafted out from inside. It was very different from the animal stench he had come to associate with this place; more like vomit mixed with carrion which had been left to rot in the desert sun.

'Eugh!' mumbled Kugelbeck, pinching his nose. 'That's terrible. What is it?'

'Christ knows.' Switching seamlessly into stalking mode, Benford stealthily entered inside. The small room was drab, what furniture there was; basic and utilitarian. Directly opposite from where he stood there was another door, which was also wide open. Beyond, he could see a stretch of corridor lit by intermittently flickering fluorescent strip lights.

'Anything?' asked Kugelbeck.

'Nope.' Benford halted. He wasn't sure but he thought he could hear voices coming from the far end of the corridor where he could make out the entrance to a dark and shadow-filled room twenty or so yards away. The continual dark and light flashing of the lights was proving hard on the eyes. 'Say, is everything all right?' he called out.

With a sudden abruptness, the voices stopped.

'Singh!'

Silence.

'Singh!' Benford called out a second time, louder, his shout echoing down the passage. When there was no reply, he turned to Kugelbeck and shrugged his shoulders. The perplexity on the German archaeologist's face mirrored that on his own. 'I could have sworn I heard someone down there.'

'Maybe we should head back,' suggested Kugelbeck.

'I'll be damned if I will.' Ignoring the other's advice, Benford stepped out into the corridor. 'Singh! Quit fooling around, will you?'

For a long moment there was silence – an eerie silence.

Then came a sound, low and hushed. A mewling screech which came from nothing and warped into a man's voice. The words were in the Indian dialect but Benford was in no doubt that it was Singh speaking.

An abominable horror slinked from the shadows.

At first Benford thought it was some kind of horse or a large deer but as it came closer he saw that it had a shaggy mane like a lion and a head like one of those voracious badgers he had seen minutes ago. Its maw, however, was different. Gone was the snapping, razor-edged teeth. Instead, its mouth was more like a serrated, bony ridge; bladed and scissor-like – ideal for shearing away limbs. It was unlike anything he had seen before; a truly detestable composite chimera – an unholy mismatch of stag, lion and badger. There was an almost Pleistocene look to it.

'God help us!' cried Kugelbeck.

'What the hell is it?' asked Benford, not taking his eyes from the creature as it stalked forward, illuminated disturbingly in the flashing light. There was an unholiness about it; an almost palpable aura of evil which, accompanied by the horrendous stink, made his skin crawl.

'A leucrotta.'

Benford had never heard of such a beast. Unarmed as he was,

he knew he had no chance of tackling it. One snap from those jaws or one hefty kick from a hoof would spell disaster. Grabbing Kugelbeck by the arm, he dragged him back. Soon they were outside in the blazing heat and sunlight.

'Close the door and barricade it!' ordered the German.

'With what?' asked Benford. A pleading voice he was certain was Singh's echoed from inside.

'Come on! We must get away from this place. My God, what madness drove him to create such foul beings!?' Kugelbeck's eyes, wide and filled with terror, were focused on the doorway.

'What about Singh? We can't just—'

'He's already dead. According to legend the leucrotta's capable of stealing the voice of those it kills.'

'*What!?*' There was stark incredulity on Benford's face.

'Is anything the matter?' hollered Ashmole, coming towards them.

Benford turned to face the Englishman. He was about to reply when, in a dark flash, the monstrous quadruped sprang out, galloping swiftly toward them.

Rearing up on its hind legs it bore down on Kugelbeck, battering him to the dusty ground.

The attack on the German archaeologist was terrible as the thing he had called a leucrotta raised its hooves, bringing them down, savagely trampling its victim, pounding the now soggy remains, reducing the man to a bloody, flattened, leaking paste.

Benford had witnessed animal ferocity before, several times. Three years ago, his brother, a fellow hunting enthusiast, had been gored to death by a bull elephant whilst on safari in Kenya. He had seen a friend ambushed and savaged by a leopard in Tanzania and another torn apart by a grizzly bear in Canada but this was worse, far worse. The fury of the attack went beyond mere animal predation. There was a malign glint in the thing's eyes; almost as though this hellish fiend was taking delight in what it was doing. Whatever these biological throwbacks were it seemed that they were perfect killing machines and what was more they enjoyed killing.

'Oh my God!' mouthed Ashmole, his face aghast at the sickening violence.

Spattered in the German's blood, the evil ungulate made a sudden lunge and tore away Kugelbeck's throat, swallowing the vocal apparatus; the larynx, pharynx, trachea and tongue in one greedy gobble. It turned to face the shocked Englishman.

'Where the hell's Singh with his gun?' Ashmole screamed.

'He's already dead.' The words, spoken perfectly in Kugelbeck's voice, came from the dreadful bony-ridged, gore spattered muzzle of the hideous beast.

'*Jesus Christ!* It's true! It speaks!' Insanity came crashing down on Benford as his mind reeled. This was utter madness, a nightmare. Shaking, he staggered back.

There came a sudden high-pitched scream from Janice.

Benford spun round. To his absolute horror he saw a second leucrotta come trotting out from around the rear of the building. The creature tilted its head to one side, sniffing the air, picking up the scent of its prey. A babbling gibberish, spoken in Indian, poured from its mouth.

The beast that had killed Kugelbeck and presumably Singh, began to edge towards Ashmole.

As a hunter, Benford knew most of the strategies and the techniques by which animals in turn hunted their prey. He knew that lions would intentionally target the young and the infirm and that wolves would operate in packs to bring down larger creatures, possessing a high degree of social intelligence. However, in the eyes of these monsters he could see a depraved cunning that went far beyond this. Right now, he knew that of the three of them; himself, Ashmole and Janice, only one of them stood any chance of getting away. There were two leucrottas and if they were each to make a run for it in different directions...

As though they had read his mind, Ashmole and Janice turned and fled.

The leucrottas gave immediate chase.

Knowing that he had to seize the opportunity, Benford spun round and began to run. Heart pounding, he sprinted for a slightly more modern-looking building which he assumed was the laboratory Singh had mentioned. In his ears, he could hear the bloodcurdling screams from the other two but not once did he look back. This was a question of survival and he knew that to slow down or hesitate would assuredly mean death. He was nearing a door. Hands outstretched, he made a lunge for it, hoping that it wouldn't be locked. Mercifully, it flew open and he stumbled into a laboratory. Two long wooden benches, atop which were microscopes, centrifuges, incubators and a wide range of other pieces of scientific apparatus he didn't recognise, ran down either side of the room. Over to his right stood a fume cupboard near to which was another door.

A pungent, vinegary stink hung in the air, visible as a brownish-grey haze near the ceiling.

Risking a quick backward glance, he saw no signs of movement. Apart from Kugelbeck's mangled corpse there was nothing untoward. No trace of the leucrottas or the two who had fled from them. He could only hope that they had somehow reached safety.

He pulled the door to. What he needed right now was a weapon and some ammunition; preferably a high-powered rifle and a box filled with the kind of bullets that would blast those horrors to Hell and back. His spirits rose slightly at the thought of bagging one of them and displaying its head on the wall of his New York State hunting lodge.

However there were no guns here and as far as he knew the only one lay back somewhere in that other building, not that it had been of much use to Singh. He crossed to the other door and turned the handle. Beyond was a second laboratory. Two more doors, one to his left and one straight in front, permitted access to other areas.

Grabbing a chair, he wedged it tight against the door. He doubted whether it would stand up to a forceful kick from a leucrotta but it was better than nothing. Now that he was out of any immediate danger, he found it curious that there weren't any more staff around. So far he had only seen the gate guard, one technician and the two men who had delivered the meat and the slops. It seemed inconceivable that there was no one else. Unless of course they were now dead. He tried not to dwell on that thought for it gave rise to darker possibilities, such as the likelihood that there were more than two of those man-killers on the prowl.

Taking some deep breaths, Benford tried to calm his tortured nerves. He knew that he was once more in a life or death situation – something he thrived on when he was the one in charge; the one with the gun. Now, however, with the realisation that the hunter had become the hunted, he felt a surge of fear deep inside. He knew that those monsters were highly intelligent and that they could be anywhere, lurking in readiness to ambush him from the shadows. Gripping his hair, he tried to force himself to think rationally; coldly and logically, to try and detach himself emotionally from what was happening. He knew that was the only way to stave off madness and survive this experience. To succumb to the fear would almost certainly prove fatal.

Opening one of the doors, he found himself at the end of a short corridor. There was nothing visible save for a mop and bucket propped against the wall halfway along. The door at the far end was open and led outside. Benford was wrestling with the idea of taking his chances outside in order to see if he could make it to the main gate when, some distance behind him, he heard a door crashing open.

'Help me! For God's sake, help me!' came a yell.

It sounded exactly like Ashmole's plummy, aristocratic voice but Benford refused to believe that it was. Slowly, he began to edge along the corridor that led out.

A sudden, shrill scream made him jump. Half-expecting to see one of the devious leucrottas at the end of the corridor, his heart leapt when he saw Janice stood in the doorway.

She was looking, panic-stricken, over her shoulder.

'Quick. In here!' Benford hissed. When he saw her turn in his direction, he hastily beckoned her over. She came towards him in a mad rush.

Barely a second later the dark shape of a leucrotta sprang into the entrance. Framed in the doorway, the monster looked utterly wicked and unnatural – a freakish creation whose sole purpose it seemed was to kill. It barked, then uttered a demonic whinnying sound which echoed disturbingly down the corridor.

'Oh my God!' Janice cried, covering her ears.

'Come on!' Benford grabbed her by an arm and dragged her forcibly away from the approaching terror.

There were noises coming from the first laboratory he had entered—crashes as of some disruptive, destructive force taking the place apart. Above the wrecking could be heard sporadic out-bursts of a male Indian voice shouting madly intermingled with the mumblings of an English toff. It was a chaotic, mind-warping, glossolalic noise.

Benford looked for an escape. There was one more door he had yet to try. Rushing over, he threw it open.

Beyond was a flight of narrow stone steps descending into the darkness.

'It's the only way.' Benford didn't like the idea of having to go down there but staying where they were wasn't an option. Steadying Janice, he went down, using a hand to maintain his balance. Reaching the bottom, he was relieved to feel a light switch. He flicked it down.

Instant illumination lit the small basement.

The room was filled with all manner of things—spare parts for the machines upstairs for the main. There were also stacked animal cages, several large water containers, bits and pieces of furniture, a few old filing cabinets and a wide array of tools heaped in a corner. There were no firearms to be seen but there was a petrol-driven chainsaw, a wood axe and three six-feet long metal poles that had been sharpened at one end.

Benford's heart sank for, aside from the way they had entered, there was no exit. 'It looks like those bastard's have us,' he said, retrieving the wood axe. He peered around the corner of the wall, looking back up the stairs. Any moment now he expected one of the horrors to come into view. It was then that a small glimmer of hope sparked in his heart. The stairs were extremely narrow and almost precipitous in their ascent. Surely a horse-like creature wouldn't be able to negotiate them. He had barely managed it down, admittedly helping Janice, without tripping. Something on four legs would have no chance.

'There's no way out, is there?' mumbled Janice. It seemed her initial shock had faded and the reality of their imprisonment had registered. 'We're trapped!'

'We'll get out... somehow.' Benford tried to reassure her but his words lacked conviction. A shadow, which made his heart lurch, crept across the doorway above.

An elongated snout came into view—fresh blood dribbling from the saw-like ridge of the thing's mouth. A putrid stink filled the stairway as steaming, grey-black droppings fell from the leucrotta's rear end and splattered on the floor. The voice-stealing nightmare clip-clopped cautiously towards the first step.

Sickened, Benford watched, weighing up the possibility of goading the creature forward in the hope that it would stumble and come flying down the stairs, breaking its legs, or even better, its neck. He could tell that it was considering its options.

Warily, like someone testing the temperature of a bath, the beast extended a front leg and brought it down on the uppermost step. Unsteadily, it tried to put its weight on it, pitched forward and then managed to right itself. Pulling back, having now decided that such a risky manoeuvre was beyond it, the leucrotta retreated to the top of the stairs.

'Thank God! It looks like it can't get down the stairs.' Benford turned to Janice. 'I guess we're safe here.'

'But... for how long? We can't stay here forever.'

'I know.' Benford was thinking. 'Someone's bound to come out here to find out what's going on. Singh's sure to be missed. And I'd have thought that bus driver would be coming back for us. He'll get help.'

'So what do we do in the meantime?'

'I'd say there's little we can do but sit this out. There's a chance that now that those creatures know they can't get to us they'll go elsewhere. Also, if they're related to those Rajahstan desert badgers we first saw then when their food supply runs out they may turn on each other. If that's the case then no doubt one will devour the other. The survivor might be sufficiently weakened for us to either kill it or evade it.' Benford walked over and picked up one of the sharpened metal poles. Stabbing it in the air, he decided it would make a pretty effective spear.

'I wish I'd never agreed to meet Singh in the first place,' said Janice. 'I knew I should've turned down that palace invitation.'

Benford nodded. 'You got one too, did you?'

'Yes, as did the professor.' Janice perched herself atop one of the water barrels. 'He told me how pleasantly surprised he'd been. Like me, he couldn't understand why he'd been invited. Guess we'll never know now.'

Benford had thought little of it at the time. The hand-written letter, delivered by one of the prince's messengers, had been polite and courteous, inquiring as to whether he would care to attend one of His Excellence's banquets. How could he refuse? But now, the more he thought about it, a dark, paranoid notion began to blossom in his mind. Some of the colour drained from his face and he felt his stomach muscles tighten. Was it conceivable that there was a malign motive behind Singh's invitation? Had he brought them all here with the intention of offering them to these hellspawn? There was a pronounced variation in each of their voices; his rich American drawl, Kugelbeck's Germanic-slanted pronunciation, Ashmole's perfect, educated, well-spoken English and Janice's high-pitched tone. A uniqueness in their speech pattern and mannerism which would have been ideal for experimentation purposes in regard to the leucrottas. If that had been Singh's diabolical scheme it appeared that there had been a terrible mishap, with the monsters getting out shortly before they arrived. Try as he might to persuade himself otherwise, now that this theory had taken root, it was impossible to shake away.

'You look sick,' commented Janice.

Benford nodded. 'It's the smell,' he lied. The possibility that Singh had brought them out here with the intention of feeding them to the leucrottas made his blood boil. Although he hadn't seen Singh's remains, he was certain that the prince was dead – a victim of his own creations. He wouldn't have the satisfaction of killing the man himself.

There came a loud crash from directly overhead. This was followed by a maddened hammering that caused the ceiling to shake. It was like an earthquake. Plaster drizzled from the ceiling and the light flickered.

In his mind's eye, Benford could envisage one of the monsters stampeding around the room above, bucking like a wild stallion.

The noise lasted for several minutes.

A worrying silence descended, making Benford uneasy. While

that hellish din had lasted he knew where at least one of them was. Now, he had no idea. Had they both gone? Or were they waiting, trying to lure him and Janice into a false sense of security? The beasts were cunning, and he was only too aware that they possessed a level of intelligence far surpassing that of any normal animal. As a hunter himself, he knew the importance of being patient; to wait until an opportune moment presented itself. He knew that he could sit tight down here for as long as it took but he doubted whether Janice could. How much longer could she endure a diabolical game of cat and mouse?

'They're going to kill us, aren't they?' she whimpered. 'Just like the professor and Mr. Ashmole.'

'Don't talk like that!' snapped Benford. 'I've told you. We're going to get out of this. All we have to do is wait. Those monsters aren't going to stay up there forever. Maybe it would be for the best if you tried to get some sleep. Don't worry, I'll stay on watch.'

The gaping mouth stretched wider, like that of a crocodile about to chomp down on its prey. An utterly horrible exhalation blasted forth as the ridged jaws elongated further. A slimy, mottled tongue slobbered forth. The dark gullet grew in size, a black abyss from which came obscene gargling sounds. Then, a shape began to appear within the bottomless pit of the throat. It was a head. Kugelbeck's battered and bloody head. The dead German's mouth opened and —

With a jerk, Benford sprang awake. It was pitch dark and he was completely unaware of his surroundings. The vestiges of the terrible nightmare still lingered in his brain and the overwhelming sensation of disorientation caused his mind to spin. A cold sweat streaked his face and his shirt felt clammy on his back. Unable to check his wrist watch, he had no idea of how long he had been asleep—it could have been minutes. It could have been hours.

He could hear the rhythmic sound of someone lightly snoring.

A scream rose unbidden to his lips as realisation dawned. He had drifted off. Janice was sleeping nearby and to make matters a hundred times worse the lights must have fused whilst he had been out. Like a flash flood, a dark tide of uncontrollable fear flowed through him, freezing his blood, almost drowning him in its terror-filled embrace.

It was then that he heard the noises.

Ghastly sounds that came from somewhere in the darkness — evil whispers and unholy cries that played havoc with his mind; cruel taunts and pathetic pleas which drove an icy blade into his heart. There was a myriad of different voices that seemed to come from all around as though he were being tormented by a sadistic ventriloquist. It was an evil spell which conjured horrible images; peopling the frightening, impenetrable darkness with unspeakable demons. It was hard to tell whether the unearthly acoustics were real or whether they were mere figments of his overwrought imagination. On and on they went; an insane babble which gnawed at his mind, tearing at the very fabric of his sanity.

Yet the more he listened the more he became convinced that the sounds weren't the product of his sickened imagination. There were discernible patterns in the seemingly chaotic cacophony; a subtle continuous repetition which he was able to pick out. He became certain that the leucrotta weren't capable of independent human speech but rather they were but regurgitating phrases which they no doubt heard. Like monstrous parrots, their words and phrases were no more than an impressive display of mimicry. Such a realisation could prove useful.

Blindly, he reached to one side, his fingers tightening around the spear-like pole.

The voices stopped.

All was quiet for a very long time.

*

'Is anyone there? It's Dhiraj, the bus driver!'

Benford sprang up, fully alert. In the darkness it was hard to tell whether he had been sleeping or not. 'Janice! Wake up!' He stumbled over to where he knew she lay, still fast asleep. 'Get up!'

Janice stirred and began to mumble.

Benford began to shake her awake. 'The bulb must've fused. Someone's come to rescue us. We have to go.'

'It's Dhiraj, the bus driver!' came the shout again.

Benford made for the steps then stopped. Wait a minute, he thought. How could I be so stupid to be taken in by this ruse? This ploy was just the kind of thing those canny monsters used to such lethal effect. The real bus driver was in all probability nothing more than a hoof-imprinted puddle of rogan josh. However, there was one way of putting things to the test. 'What's your name and who do you work for?' he yelled, reasoning that if the answer that came back was nothing but a nonsensical regurgitation then he would have his answer regarding the other's true identity.

'Is that you, Mr. American man?' The voice was near and a moment later the door at the top of the stairs was opened. Outlined in the rectangle of electric light was a man.

'Thank Christ!' Gripping his metal pole, Benford headed up the stairs, half-dragging Janice behind him.

'I could find no one. I was about to head back to the palace. Have you seen His Excellency?' asked the bus driver.

It was clear that although riled, the man wasn't out of his wits with fear, leading Benford to the belief that he hadn't yet seen or learnt anything of the true horrors of this place. 'Singh's dead,' he said.

'*Dead?*' Dhiraj backed away.

'Yes, dead. There was a breakout by some of his animals. Didn't you see anything unusual outside?'

Dhiraj shook his head.

'Well, let's hope the coast's clear. Come on, if we want to get out of this place alive we've got to get going. There's no telling when they'll come back.' Taking Janice by the hand, Benford gestured for the bus driver to start moving 'Now, where's your bus parked?'

'At the main gate.'

'Good!'

The three of them left the laboratory building and slipped out into the cool Rajahstan evening. Twilight was still an hour away and the sky was a dismal shade of tangerine.

Benford was on constant lookout, dreading the sudden appearance of one or both of the leucrottas. At any moment, he expected one of them to come trotting around the side of a building or to hear the terrifying sound of galloping hooves behind him. His grip on the metal pole tightened. If one of them came for him he was determined not to go down without a fight.

Their shadows were long as they crossed the open compound.

Benford knew this was when they were at their most vulnerable. He did a full circle, ensuring that there was nothing sneaking up on them. Over to one side, he could make out a revolting patch on the ground—all that now remained of the flattened Kugelbeck. It wasn't that surprising that Dhiraj hadn't noticed it for the bulk of the professor's corpse had been dragged off elsewhere as evidenced by a bloody trail.

They were now nearing the animal pens. The noise from within was strangely subdued almost as though the creatures inside knew that there was something worse than them on the prowl.

Up ahead, beyond the entrance gate and the guard post, Benford could see the bus.

Janice made a sudden dash for it. Turning briefly in mid-sprint, she shouted: 'We've made it!' She reached the passenger door and

54

screamed.

From around the back of the bus stepped one of the four-legged horrors.

'Janice!' Benford cried, running forward.

The leucrotta heard his shout and turned to face him.

It was at that moment that the second beast, which had been hiding in wait behind a large boulder on the right, sprang from its concealment. It charged Benford, its downward bite blocked by the metal pole, its jaws clamped vice-like around it.

Locked in a savage tug of war which he knew he had no chance of winning, Benford was about to release the pole when to his shock and surprise the monster sheared it in half. Armed with two smaller poles, he fiercely brought both jagged-edged lengths of metal stabbing inwards, plunging one into the thing's left eye, the other into its throat. Dark crimson blood ran down his hands.

The beast went berserk. Rearing up on its hind legs, it kicked at the air.

Benford staggered clear. Through glazed eyes, he saw the other horror batter Janice to the ground, catching her with a kick to the side of the body, the force of which spun her round like a whirling marionette.

Then Dhiraj was screaming at the top of his voice, striking at it with his bare hands, pummelling its flank; his attack courageous but largely ineffectual.

It spun round. Snapping down, it caught the bus driver by the arm, severing it completely just above the elbow. Blood sprayed from his ragged stump as he reeled back before sinking to his knees.

'*Help!* For the love of God, help me!' That was Ashmole's voice coming from the wounded leucrotta. Next came a whining scream as the beast began to thrash around, dislodging the barb in its throat. Blood streamed from the one pinned to its eye.

Heart pounding, Benford made a run for it, heading back into the compound. The closest building was the stables. Once inside, he slammed the door shut behind him. There seemed to be no escape from this nightmare. The place stank and the noise bordered on the unbearable but right now he was past caring. He looked around for something to defend himself with but there was little of use here apart from— He stopped and stared at the six badgers. Suddenly the door behind him burst open.

Singh's voice cried out from the doorway. Then came Janice's high-pitched scream.

Fully aware that there was little else he could do, Benford pushed back the heavy bolt that locked the gate to the badger enclosure. He threw open the pen door and dashed for the exit on the other side.

The voracious badgers scurried out. A violent, frenzied attack on the leucrotta then ensued. It kicked and snapped at the much smaller beasts but what they lacked in size they made up for in numbers.

To add to the chaos and to make a greater distraction, Benford released the pygmy horses, knowing full well that they would fast become snacks for the untameable predators. He watched from the doorway, eager to be away yet captivated by the fierce spectacle. Two of the badgers lay still and lifeless, but the remaining four tore savagely at the leucrotta, its flanks now covered in blood and foam. And then it was on the ground, one badger snapped in half by its powerful jaws. They then targeted the soft underbelly, burrowing into the thing's abdomen, dislodging a heap of glistening entrails. Driven by an insatiable bloodlust, the badgers continued to bite and claw.

Benford had seen more than enough. He felt sick, yet he knew now was his best chance of escape. He dashed back to the bus, aware that the leucrotta he had wounded earlier was still out there somewhere.

It was getting dark.

Janice was dead. Dhiraj was dead. Everyone but himself who had come to this accursed place was dead.

Searching the bus driver's one-armed corpse, he soon found the keys to the bus. Wearily, he opened the door and clambered inside. He sat down in the driver's seat and started the engine. Throwing on the lights, he saw the wounded leucrotta lying sprawled in the road some thirty yards away. It wasn't dead but he was damned certain it soon would be. Forcing down the gear stick, he threw the bus into forward and stepped down hard on the accelerator pedal.

'*Help!* For the love of God, help me!' it cried.

Benford's hands tightened on the steering wheel as he aimed straight for it.

HOUR OF THE WITCH

It was a question of which of them, if any,
would still be there by daybreak.

JOHN MCQUEEN SAT at his desk, idly going through the mail that had gathered over the last few days. He had been away from work suffering from a heavy cold but now that he was back and feeling much better he thought it was high time that he started to make some money. For the past twelve years he had hired out his services as a private investigator and although he had never had any significant cases his profession had earned him a steady income.

Most of his mail was humdrum; enquiries regarding whether or not he was available to assist in locating missing dogs, discovering the whereabouts of stolen property and even one letter from a suspicious wife seeking help in tracking down an errant and undoubtedly unfaithful husband. He was just about to consult his logbook of old, unresolved cases when the office door opened and Mark Forsyth, his assistant, entered with a dark-haired woman; slim and pale with dark eyes and an oval-shaped face. She looked to be in her mid-forties.

'Mrs. Eleanor Campbell,' announced Forsyth, ushering the woman inside.

Somewhat surprised, McQueen got to his feet. 'Good morning. Please, take a seat.' He could see that the woman was nervous, her eyes never still, taking everything in.

'Mrs. Campbell has got quite an interesting proposition.' Forsyth drew up a chair, sat down and took a notebook and pen from his pocket.

'Well, Mrs. Campbell,' said McQueen, 'if you'll tell me what your problem is I'll see whether or not I can help.' Once she had sat down, he too took his seat.

'Just over a year ago my husband, Cameron, disappeared.' Mrs. Campbell removed a handkerchief from a pocket and dabbed at her eyes before returning it. 'He was an investigator like yourself, with the exception being that he delved into the supernatural. A paranormal investigator is what he liked to be known as.'

'*Professor Cameron Campbell?*' inquired McQueen, trying to re-member some of the details of the disappearance of the renowned parapsychologist that had made the headlines. 'I recall reading something about that in the newspapers. Didn't something happen to him on one of his investigations?'

'Not just Cameron, but his entire team of researchers from Glasgow University. Five of them in total.' Mrs. Campbell shook her head, clearly trying to come to terms with just whatever it was that had happened. 'They'd carried out investigations at alleged haunted sites all over Britain, hoping to discover evidence to prove the existence of the supernatural. Cameron had been the team leader, an expert in the field of parapsychology, the one who did all of the research in tracking down places of psychic interest. If only he hadn't found out about that awful house on Jura.'

More details of the case were slowly filtering back into McQueen's mind. 'Yes, I'm remembering more about it now,' he said. 'It was quite big news. All of them just disappeared, didn't they? The police carried out an intensive investigation both of the house and the surrounding area but no one was ever found. With-out doubt, a very mysterious case.' He gulped as a little shiver of uncertainty went through him. 'You've obviously come to me to ask whether or not I'd be willing to carry out my own investiga-tions regarding their disappearance, yes?'

She nodded. 'I was informed that you had some experience in such cases.'

'Not recently,' said McQueen. 'In fact, these days I'm something of a sceptic when it comes to the supernatural. I guess you could say I've seen too much but experienced too little. However, I must say I am rather intrigued by this and have been ever since reading about it. Clearly something happened out there at that godforsaken place, something that resulted in the disappearance of five people. Just what, well clearly there was something that the police were unable to discover.' He scratched at the day's growth of stubble on his chin.

'So you will help me? You'll take the case?'

McQueen took out a packet of cigarettes from a drawer, lit one and took a drag. 'What do you say, Forsyth?' he asked, looking at his assistant. 'Sounds interesting, doesn't it?'

'Certainly does,' replied Forsyth. 'Although I don't really see what new light we'll be able to shed on this. I guess the first thing we should do is head out to this house and see if there's any evidence to be found, anything which the initial investigation may have overlooked. If we turn up nothing, then perhaps we might get some valuable insights into the minds of those who vanished by tracking down any friends and relatives.'

'Maybe a look at the initial police report might help as well,' added McQueen.

'Yes,' agreed Forsyth. 'Although you know as well as I that ever since that new Chief Inspector took over getting our hands on such documentation has proved increasingly difficult.'

McQueen nodded in agreement. 'Yes, that may prove tricky.' He stubbed out the remains of his cigarette in an ashtray. 'But first, I'd like to ask you a few questions about your husband, if I may, Mrs. Campbell. I guess the most important question is; do you yourself have any notion regarding just what may have happened to him and his team?'

'I'm afraid not. I'm as baffled as everyone else. There was absolutely no reason for Cameron to go missing. And as for the others, well I've been in correspondence with some of the relatives and they're just as confused as I am. The last year has been sheer torture for me not knowing what's happened. Sometimes I can cope with it, but—' She broke down into a sobbing fit, reaching for her handkerchief once more. After a few moments, she looked up, her eyes tearful. 'Please, I need your help in this. I've come to expect the worst but it's the not knowing—that's what's really painful.'

McQueen and Forsyth exchanged concerned, yet uncertain glances. Was it something they could handle? McQueen seemed to think so, although he doubted whether their investigations would reveal anything of merit.

'I'm imploring you,' pleaded Mrs. Campbell. 'Please help me find my husband. I don't know who else to turn to. The police are no longer interested. I'll pay you whether you find anything or not. I'm certain there will be something that the police have overlooked. Some small clue which may reveal what happened to them out there.'

'Very well, Mrs. Campbell,' said McQueen. 'I will take this case on although I can't make any promises regarding the outcome. I'll also add that it is a little outside my usual field of experience, however I will give it my full, undivided attention. Now, how soon do you want me to start?'

'As soon as possible. The sooner the better.' A bright intensity shone in Mrs. Campbell's pale face now that she had told her tale and had secured the private investigator's service. It was almost as if she was a different woman from the one who had entered the office a few minutes earlier. 'I plan to travel to Jura myself within the week. I trust that's not too much short notice for you?'

It was certainly short notice but McQueen had the suspicion that this case could well be a significant one. If he were to discover the true explanation behind the disappearance of Cameron Campbell then he would be made for life. An opportunity like this did not come knocking every day, that was for certain. 'Very well, I'll see to it,' he said, reaching for another cigarette. He lit up and inhaled the smoke, drawing it deep into his lungs. 'In the meantime, I'll see what I can find out about this house. What was the name of it again?'

'It has no name. Only a reputation. You see I've done my own research, and from what I can gather it's not really even a house. More of a ruin. A crofter's cottage, which has now been reduced to little more than four walls and a shattered roof.' Mrs. Campbell reached into a coat pocket and removed a small photograph that she handed over. 'As you can see, there's not much of it still standing. It was once the property of a Mr. Tam McSweeney and his wife, Aggie. My husband's reasoning for it being haunted was based on some research he'd done which had suggested that the previous owner, an old crofter, had been killed by his wife sometime during the last century. She was reputed to have been a practitioner of the Black Arts, a witch.'

Looking at the photograph, nothing immediately suggested itself to McQueen. It was, after all, little more than a tumbledown farmhouse. The white walls were barely standing and the roof was sagging; just a jumble of criss-crossing timbers in places. Two small square windows and a dark doorway completed the unimposing structure. And yet, the more he looked at it, the more a strange sense of unease filtered into his mind. For a long time, he sat there, unable to think clearly, unable to wrench his eyes away. Whether due to some strange quirk of the lighting, shadows seemed to crouch around the deserted building where shadows ought not to be and he felt mild nausea arising from the pit of his stomach as he continued to stare at the image. This he immediately put down to an association of facts; nothing more than an acknowledgement that something inexplicable had happened to five people there. It was this alone, he reasoned, that caused his unease.

'Not much to look at, is it?' said Mrs. Campbell.

'No, I guess not.' McQueen handed the photograph to Forsyth, who looked at it with measured interest. 'So, Mrs. Campbell, I've told you that I am willing to take on this case. It will necessitate quite some organisation but I'm pretty confident about being able to join you at the weekend. Just to let you know, I always work with my assistant, in fact some would say he's the brains of the outfit.'

'And you're the brawn?'

McQueen smiled. 'Hardly. So don't go expecting any gumshoe -like behaviour from me. I don't drink cheap whisky, and as you can see I don't operate from a sleazy backstreet office, nor do I carry a gun. Unfortunately the law in this country forbids me from using one, not that I foresee the need for one for if I see anything ghost-like I'll be first out of the door.'

Four days later on the ferry crossing from the mainland to Port Askaig on Islay, McQueen stood next to Forsyth looking out across the churning grey water as the Paps of Jura, the name given for the three island mountains, loomed before them. It was cold, slightly foggy and very damp. And for those who had lived all of their lives as city-dwellers it was an imposing, foreboding and not particularly welcoming sight. It was no longer hard to imagine that something utterly inexplicable could have happened out here. It seemed as though they were going back in time; back to a remote past long-shrouded in myth and legend.

Having talked with the few passengers on board, most of whom were inhabitants of Islay, the closest island, they discovered that there were probably fewer than fifty islanders on Jura and that they would have to cross on the Feolin Ferry to reach their destination where it was planned they would rendezvous with Mrs. Campbell.

'Quite an impressive sight, wouldn't you agree?' commented McQueen. 'Though just why anyone in their right mind would want to live out here beats me.'

'I daresay you get used to it after a while. The solitude, the cold, the rain. In summer, one of the men downstairs was telling me, the midges here are diabolical. They're like mosquitoes. The sooner we're away from here the better. I don't like it one bit.'

'Well, although we didn't manage to get a look at the police report, if we can find something of significance regarding the disappearance of Cameron Campbell and his team we'll be famous. Think of that while you're having to put up with the hardships. Besides, I think our investigations will only take a day or two at most. We've got sufficient camping gear to stay in that place in reasonable comfort and then we'll be back in Glasgow. And like Mrs. Campbell said, we get paid whether or not we find anything. So it's a win-win situation for us.'

'I don't suppose you've ever considered the possibility that there just may be something behind all of this? You know, something *weird*.'

McQueen lit a cigarette, cupping it in his hand to shield it from the strong wind that was blowing. He eyed the other strangely. 'You mean, do I believe that Cameron and his associates fell foul of something supernatural?' He shook his head fiercely and took a drag from his cigarette. 'No, of course not. I don't buy that as an explanation. Something undoubtedly did happen, but I'm certain it didn't have anything to do with ghosts or demons. Five people cooped up together in a deserted building in the middle of nowhere—all it takes is for one of them to go mad. Kills everyone in their sleep, one by one, disposes the bodies somewhere they'll never be found and then makes good their escape. Or maybe, two of them working together. That'd be easier. Now clearly, I don't know just why they would do something as despicable as that but people being people it's not out of the scope of possibility as an explanation. To me, it sounds far more feasible than bringing in the supernatural.'

The ferry was now fast approaching the small harbour where they would be disembarking. Several small cottages dotted the coastline and seagulls cried and circled overhead. After ensuring that they had their rucksacks with them they headed downstairs and waited for the announcement from the captain to instruct them that it was all clear to get off the ferry. When it came, they were the first in the queue to walk down the metal gangplank where they were somewhat surprised to find Mrs. Campbell waiting for them. She was accompanied by two men; a stocky, middle-aged man with a short white beard who from his attire was clearly a priest and a younger man who bore some resemblance to her.

'Welcome to Islay,' greeted Mrs. Campbell. She gestured to her companions. 'May I introduce my brother-in-law, Father Archie Campbell and my son, James.'

For a moment McQueen was lost for words. He had not expected there to be others involved in this investigation although he saw no reason why their presence should complicate things. Indeed it could make things easier, providing they knew what they were letting themselves in for. After making his greetings, he and Forsyth followed them to their car.

'So just what are our plans now?' asked McQueen, unslinging his rucksack and handing it over to James Campbell who had opened the car-boot.

'From here, in about half an hour's time, we'll catch the Feolin Ferry over to Jura. Then it's just a relatively short drive along the only road until we get to the point where we have to head off across country. If the weather stays reasonable it should take us about three hours to get to the house,' answered Eleanor

Campbell.

McQueen shivered and turned up the collar of his coat as he stood beside the parked car and gazed out at the desolate moorland before him, the dark grey masses of the three mountains barely visible in the low cloud which threatened to descend and engulf everything. He shivered at something more than just the coldness of the early afternoon air. It was as though an invisible, clinging mist had risen up out of the ground beneath his feet, bathing him in an aura of impending horror. With an effort, he told himself fiercely that he had to forget that, to keep his mind on the job that lay ahead, and that somewhere out there on the other side of the island there was a ruined house that kept its own mysteries.

A chill light drizzle began to fall.

'*God!* What a place.' Forsyth tightened his bootlaces and then hoisted his rucksack onto his shoulders.

'It's fairly inhospitable, I agree,' commented James. Like the others, he was outfitted in a large raincoat and both he and Archie carried rucksacks as well. 'How my father persuaded the others to come out to this godforsaken place I don't know.'

Tightening a strap on his rucksack, McQueen strode over to join him. 'Did he really believe that the most haunted place in Britain was out here? I'd have thought somewhere like Edinburgh Castle or Highgate Cemetery would've been more his kind of thing.'

'Cameron did indeed think that the place we're going to was the most haunted,' answered Eleanor, before her son could answer.

McQueen glanced upwards, noting that the drizzle had now turned to a cold rain. 'Might be best if we waited in the car until this rain's stopped.'

'Depending on how long the rain's going to last we might not make the house before nightfall, and the path's hard enough to find in daylight,' reasoned Archie in his thick, gruff accent. 'No. I think we'd better head off now, rain or no rain.'

With no further talk, they set off across the bleak, uncompromising landscape, their boots squelching through the thick, peaty sludge of the barely discernible path. After about a mile the path degenerated into nothing more than a trail and in the gathering mist it became increasingly difficult for them to stick to it. The atmosphere had now become oppressive, cold and damp and it did not take long for the imagination to run riot.

Half-formed, tenebrous images seemed to lurk just on the periphery of McQueen's vision, leading him to think that there were things out there, unfriendly things which even now were observing their progress with a malign intent. The mist had become thicker, almost suffocating, the only sounds that of the occasional curse and splash from one of the others. As they progressed through the murk and the gloom, the notion that perhaps this was not one of his better ideas came to his mind and that, despite what he had said to Forsyth about enduring the hardships for the sake of fame, perhaps it would be best to turn back whilst that still remained an option.

With some measure of inner resolve, he took a hold of himself and trudged on, the ghost-like form of James, who he was following, just visible up ahead.

After the first hour or so the conditions deteriorated further so that, at least as far as McQueen was concerned, it seemed as though the very elements themselves were conspiring in an attempt to drive them back. A strong wind had now picked up, ice-cold fingers clawing at exposed skin and stabbing sadistically through their waterproofs. With it came an almost horizontal rain that drove at them with a vengeance that seemed born of an elemental fury.

The sky darkened with each passing minute and ill-looking

black clouds now replaced the ubiquitous greyness.

A cold sweat trickled down McQueen's spine; an iciness somewhat colder than the rain. On several occasions he was convinced that he heard hideous wails on the wind as though nature itself had become corrupted and had now found some fell voice with which to shriek at them, to warn them perhaps of an impending doom. The ground become soggier, the going more treacherous as deep pools of standing surface water now lay all around and one wrong step would result in an immediate drenching from which hypothermia could easily develop.

The others cursed and struggled on, each absorbed in their own thoughts and nightmares regarding where they were going.

They stopped briefly for a cheerless break, sipping from their flasks and devouring their packed lunches before setting off once more, hoping against hope that they were still heading in the right direction. In the thick fog it was now nigh on impossible to be certain and McQueen dreaded to think what would happen to them if they were to become hopelessly lost out here, for he did not think that there were any adequate search and rescue teams based on the island. Similarly, at least as far as he and Forsyth were concerned, neither of them possessed any appropriate survival knowledge nor, more importantly, had they informed anyone else of where they were going. The latter was an unsettling thought that, unwillingly, plagued his brain for the remainder of the trek.

Thus it was with some relief that, just as darkness was encroaching, James let out a jubilant cry that he could see the house up ahead.

At first McQueen could see nothing through the veil of water that curtained off his immediate surroundings. Then, spectrally, the ruined cottage just seemed to materialise out of the fog before him.

*

By torchlight, they began sifting through the detritus and rubble, stooping occasionally to take a look under many of the heaps of contorted woodwork and jumbled heaps of bricks. What remaining furniture there was lay mostly wrecked and decaying; a bookcase devoid of books against one wall and a few splintered chairs. It was clear that someone had been here, certainly within the last few years for there were small piles of cigarette butts of a brand McQueen knew to have been only released relatively recently. When he had questioned Mrs. Campbell, she told him that her husband had been a non-smoker, however they could have belonged to members of his team or indeed to the police who had searched the place after the disappearance.

After an hour or so of fruitless ransacking, they decided to camp up — McQueen, Forsyth and Father Archie Campbell setting up base in the ruined main room, whilst Eleanor and her son retired to one of the small side rooms, one which had clearly served as a bedroom of some description.

Outside, the wind and the rain battered without mercy at the derelict building as though trying to outdo each other in terms of ferocity. Despite their hasty, patchwork attempts to provide shelter and make the place somewhat habitable the interior was cold, the atmosphere, lugubrious.

'So what do you think happened here, Father?' McQueen asked as he unrolled his sleeping bag and looked for somewhere comfortable to lay it down.

'The Devil's work,' came the gruff reply. 'What else could it be?'

'Would you care to be more specific?'

'I always told Cameron that no good would come of his meddling with things which are best left alone. But would he listen? No! All the time he said he needed to have the proof to substantiate his beliefs. I repeatedly told him that faith should be enough — but alas, it was clearly not enough for him and for those other misguided fools who followed him out here.'

'So I take it you think something unnatural happened here?' asked Forsyth from where he sat, shining the torch all around, making the grotesque shadows dance like wraiths.

'Without doubt. It's one of the main reasons why I agreed to accompany Eleanor. There's evil here. I can sense it. It lives in the very bricks and timbers of this old house. When it shows itself I have all the means necessary to combat it and make it pay for whatever it did to my brother and the others.'

'Are we talking about an exorcism here?' asked McQueen.

'Exactly.' The priest grinned. 'For whereas Cameron sought only to prove the existence of such foul things, I believe it is my duty to permanently destroy such Satanic entities. As I said, I have come prepared. Crucifix. Holy water. Bible. Communion wafers.'

'What are you—some kind of vampire hunter?'

'No. Simply a humble servant of God. One on a crusade to stamp out the Dark and restore the Light to its true brilliance.'

'And what if nothing happens?' said McQueen. 'What if we just end up spending a couple of miserable, cold and wet nights in this deserted shell of a cottage—what then?'

'Ah, but that won't happen. You see it's my aim to draw out whatever evil resides here. Tonight, at the stroke of midnight, I'll conduct a séance to try and do just that.'

'Wait a minute!' protested McQueen. 'Who mentioned anything about holding a séance? That's completely out of the question and I want no part of it. What a ludicrous idea.' He lit a cigarette, his strong features visible for a moment in the flaring match-light.

'Scared of something?' taunted the priest.

'*Scared?* Of such a stupid thing as a séance? No, I'm not scared, but—'

'But what?'

'Well, it's just that I don't have any belief in anything like that. I don't see the point.'

'Surely we've got nothing to lose and potentially something to gain,' ventured Forsyth. 'Besides, it'll pass the time,' he added flippantly.

'Yes,' said the priest. 'And perhaps as another incentive, think on this: We may gain an insight into just what happened here on that dismal night over a year ago. If I do manage to contact the spirit world perhaps I can find out what really happened to Cameron.'

McQueen had not factored anything like this into his plan of operations. But he might as well humour the man and besides he thought it highly likely that Eleanor, who was paying for his services, would want him to participate. So disagreeing would be counter-productive. Later on, after the séance had failed, he might be able to work the conversation round to his theory that one or more members of Cameron's ill-fated team had gone berserk and murdered the others. In the shadowy light, he could see from his watch that it had just gone nine o'clock so that left nearly three hours in which to get some rest in readiness for midnight and whatever insanity that might bring.

The exhaustion from the three-hour trudge across the island struck McQueen with a fierce suddenness, dragging him off into a dark slumber as soon as he climbed into his sleeping bag. Almost instantly he was struck by a terrible plethora of dark mental images, each nightmare worse than the one before. Horrible, grinning skull-like faces swam into view before melting away into a swirling mass of blighted wickedness. Surreal, unnatural beings, neither man-like or animal-like, danced crazily through his silently screaming mind, insane shapes which seemed to fold and unfold before him.

And then, it seemed no sooner had he drifted off into a

troubled sleep that he was awakened by James.

'It's getting close to midnight. My mother was hoping that you'd join her and my uncle.'

'What?' asked McQueen groggily, temporarily unsure of his surroundings.

'They're planning on holding a séance in the next room. I can't say that I'm all in favour of the idea but there we are. I don't approve and I don't think it'll help in finding my father.'

Everything rushed back, colliding inside McQueen's brain like a dark tide battering at a sea wall. 'Yes. I must have drifted off for an hour or so.'

'More like three hours,' commented Forsyth, entering the abandoned room. The light from his torch made everything seem frightening and insubstantial, shadow-shapes seemed to slink away from the beam of light as though possessed of some sentient quality. 'I guess that hike across the island must've really taken its toll on you.'

McQueen got out of his sleeping bag and followed the others into the adjacent room. A small wooden table has been set up, around which five chairs had been placed. Eleanor and Archie Campbell were already seated, clearly awaiting their arrival.

'When you're ready,' said the priest, gesturing to the others to sit down in the vacant chairs. Once they had taken their seats he continued: 'Let us all link hands whilst I try and reach out to the spirit world.'

They linked hands as instructed. In his left, McQueen held Eleanor's delicate, long-fingered hand and in his right he grasped Forsyth's. Inwardly, he could not help but think that he was being a gullible fool for even considering participating in this occult nonsense. He had come out here in order to conduct a rigorous and methodical search for any evidence pertaining to the disappearance of Cameron Campbell and his team and now, here he was, gathered around a table joining in with their mumbo-jumbo!

He would have to see about asking for extra pay as compensation for this insult to his common sense.

'Is there anyone out there?' intoned the priest. 'Does anyone care to tell us what happened here?' He asked his questions with a quiet deliberation.

McQueen grimaced, his face a portrait in sceptical annoyance. Of course there were people there—themselves.

'Cameron. Are you there, brother?'

'Look, this is getting—' complained McQueen, getting ready to rise from his chair.

'Wait.' Eleanor threw him a sharp glance.

The room was suddenly very still. All sound ceased abruptly, as if someone had drawn a thick, impenetrable curtain across everything. Utter silence. A finger of ice traced strange patterns along the muscles of McQueen's back. His skin itched and crawled as though a thousand ants were creeping across it.

'Cameron, can you hear me?' In the dim torchlight the priest's face was half-bathed in shadow, giving it a sinister and slightly demonic look.

McQueen felt Eleanor's grasp on his hand tighten, her nails threatening to dig into the flesh of his palm. An eerie atmosphere crowded around them and the temperature dropped noticeably so that he was shocked to see that his breath was now steaming. A long moment passed. There was a low ringing in his ears now and somewhere, at the very edge of his vision, he detected a growing brightness coming from the corner of the room. He clenched his mouth shut to keep his teeth from shaking.

Within the darkness, in the corner of the room, a greenish, dense fog began to gather. The fog began to assume human form; condensing and then solidifying into a tangible being—perhaps not a true flesh and blood one, but a being nonetheless. The ghostly face was lined with pain and torment. Its eyes were tinged crimson and sunken, its face etched with deep lines and its hair was wild and unkempt.

It was the tortured spirit of Cameron Campbell!

'Cameron!' cried Eleanor.

'*You must all flee!*' wailed the spectre. 'There is a dark spirit here. It will destroy you all as it destroyed me. Your only hope resides in the fireplace. *Save my soul and your own lives...*' Its last cry was a bloodcurdling, fading scream from the netherworld, a truly terrifying caterwaul that shook all of them to the marrow, temporarily paralysing them with fear. Then, his warning given, Cameron's spirit was drawn back into whichever dark beyond it had temporarily been summoned from. It was compressed to a single glowing point, before blinking out of existence.

'What the hell was that!?' cried Forsyth, his eyes wild, his hands trembling visibly. Most of the colour had drained from his face.

A gripping terror clutched at McQueen, forcing him to swallow a lump in his throat. He could feel his heart begin to hammer inside his chest like a caged animal and a cold, damp sweat now leaked from his forehead. He could offer no explanation for what had just transpired; no reasoning enabled him to come to terms with what he had just witnessed with his own two eyes. He had known, instinctively, that what he had seen had been real. It was no trickster's hoax or phantasm generated by a troubled mind, for all of the others had seen it too. It had been something that had defied his logical ordering of the world and all within it, something that his practical, pragmatic outlook on life could not accept and yet it had happened. *He had seen it!*

Father Archie Campbell was the first to regain some semblance of composure. 'It was the doomed soul of my brother. May his spirit rest in peace.' He broke his hold on those seated next to him and, shakily, made the sign of the cross.

'The fireplace—I wonder what he meant by that?' voiced McQueen, turning his gaze to the ancient, half-collapsed hearth.

Charred fragments of wood and an overturned coalscuttle rested close to it but apart from that it looked completely ordinary.

'And what about this dark spirit?' asked Forsyth nervously.

James got up from his seat and strode over to the fireplace. 'There must be something here,' he said, kneeling down in order to examine the ash-strewn contents of the hearth. A moment or two later, the priest and Forsyth got up to assist him.

They searched around the wide hearth, removing the cast-iron grate and checking for any loose bricks that might conceal any hidden cavities or such like.

'Doesn't seem to be—' Forsyth stopped mid-sentence as there came a loud crash from the main room. It sounded as though someone had dashed the rotting bookcase to the ground.

All eyes turned in the direction of the doorway.

'What was that?' asked Eleanor.

'Damned if I know,' replied McQueen. He found himself being held by thoughts that he had never believed existed in his mind; an almost tangible fear, that was making him now believe in things that he had long consigned to the realm of superstition. Savagely, he tried to throw his gaze into the darkness of the doorway, to try and see whatever may be lurking beyond the shadowy opening. He stood rigid, his heart thudding within his chest.

'We'd better check,' said James, his voice tinged with uncertainty. Hesitantly, he advanced towards the doorway, directing his torch beam in front of him, holding it as though it were a talisman capable of keeping the things of the Dark at bay.

'I'm with you, lad.' Gripping his crucifix, the priest went first, venturing through the shadow-filled doorway. The rest followed.

The room beyond was much as they had left it only minutes before with one noticeable and horrible exception. An exception that shocked and stunned them all so that for the best part of a minute there was utter silence as they stood gawping, shaking, unable to react as fear paralysed them, gripped them and froze them to the spot.

In the torchlight, written on the nearby wall in what looked like dripping blood was:

I'M GOING TO GET YOU!

It was McQueen who was the first to break free from the hypnotic hold the grim lettering had on them. 'Right. I've seen enough. That writing wasn't there a few moments ago and none of us could have done it. This place *is* haunted. Let's get our stuff together and get the hell out of here.'

'Too right,' agreed Forsyth, staring around him, his eyes wide. 'That's enough for me. We should never have tried that stupid séance.' He moved towards his sleeping bag. 'I'm not staying here a moment longer. This place gives me the heebie-jeebies.'

'This *is* blood,' said James, after testing the viscous red liquid with his fingertips.

'That does it! Get the equipment packed up as quick as you can. Then we're getting out of this house of horrors.' McQueen turned to Eleanor. 'Sorry about all this but I hope you understand this goes far beyond what I'd bargained for. If you'd all take my advice you'd leave too.'

'What makes you think you can leave?' asked the priest.

'What?'

'I said, what makes you think you can leave?' The priest fixed the private investigator and his assistant with steely eyes. 'Maybe this 'dark spirit' that Cameron warned us about won't let us.'

'That's rubbish.' Hastily, Forsyth crammed his camping gear into his rucksack. He hoisted it onto his shoulders and stomped over towards the front door. All eyes watched him as he turned the handle and opened it.

A strong, cold gust of wind and rain blasted forth but nothing untoward occurred.

'See,' said Forsyth. He closed the door and turned to McQueen. 'Come on let's get out of here. I'd much rather traipse across ten miles of wilderness than stay a moment longer in this hellish place.'

Once McQueen had all of his gear packed the two of them stood by the door, ready to go and face the elements.

'Are you sure about his?' asked Eleanor, concernedly. She herself was in two minds about leaving but whilst there remained the slim chance of discovering something about her missing husband she felt compelled to remain. She was scared, more so than she had ever been but she felt some level of reassurance knowing that Father Archie and her son were with her.

'Damn sure,' said McQueen. He gestured to Forsyth. 'Come on, let's go. If we can get back to the road then—' He was interrupted by a door slamming shut somewhere along the small corridor that led to the partially destroyed kitchen.

'That's it. I'm out of here.' Forsyth opened the front door and stepped out into the pitch-blackness, his torch illuminating little but dense shadow. No sooner had he done so than the door slammed shut behind him as though blown by a terrible squall.

'What the hell?' yelled McQueen. He reached for the handle and tried to open it. It was held tight as though some fiendish strength on the outside was keeping it shut.

Then came the screams; awful, bloodcurdling cries that hinted at some evil beyond mortal comprehension. And still, despite McQueen's desperate attempts, the door would not yield.

Now they were one down and trapped.

For the past ten minutes McQueen had sat on his rucksack, slumped and shivering by the far wall, unable to fully take in the fact that they were now at the mercy of powers beyond his wildest nightmares. Despite repeated attempts to open the front door it now seemed that escape was impossible—not that any of them had the desire to venture outside after hearing the soul-wrenching screams of Forsyth. The windows could have been broken down and in some places escape could have been gained via clambering through the wrecked spaces in the roof but none had even considered them.

'Perhaps we should search the fireplace again,' suggested Eleanor, her words cutting through the dark melancholy that had now fallen about them.

Checking his watch, McQueen was surprised to find that it was only twenty-five minutes past midnight. It had seemed as though time had become distorted, detached almost from the bizarre reality in which he now found himself. Shaking his head from side-to-side he tried in vain to accept that something truly hideous and undoubtedly gruesome had befallen Forsyth. Just what, well that was something he tried not to think about.

All around them the dilapidated house creaked and groaned, the sound of the storm outside adding to the sense of overall horror and isolation.

'Let's go back into the other room,' said the priest. 'It's clear that there's no more we can do for our friend who went outside. Perhaps if we can find whatever it is that Cameron told us about we may find a means of defeating this evil.'

With no further words, they retreated into the other room whereupon James started a more intense search of the fireplace. After a few minutes during which both he and the priest had dismantled the surrounding structure it became abundantly clear that nothing was going to be found around the exterior.

'There's nothing here,' said the priest. 'Nothing at all.'

'I'll see if there's anything inside.' With that, James stooped low and, torch in hand, squeezed into the narrow flue so that he was now invisible to those outside from the knees up.

McQueen could hear the sounds of scrabbling coming from inside and he watched as a heap of soot and dust fell from within and piled around the young man's feet. He heard a cough and, after a few seconds, a dislodged brick tumbled into the hearth along with the shattered remains of a small, brown earthenware pot and some other small bits and pieces. 'What's that?' he cried.

Then, before any of them could react there came a horrendous scream from somewhere close by. And then, suddenly, James was hauled off the floor.

'Oh my God!' Eleanor screamed.

The priest made a desperate grab at his nephew's feet, to try and pull him back. He caught hold of one boot and it came off in his hand. And then, screaming, legs kicking frantically, James was wrenched out of sight, dragged up the narrow chimney! His second boot fell into the hearth, landing alongside the pot shards.

'No!' Eleanor staggered forward, her eyes staring, disbelievingly. She fell into the priest's arms even as McQueen stood staring, unable to help, unable to think clearly.

This was not happening, he tried to tell himself. It was a nightmare, a long and involved nightmare from which he would soon awaken. It was the only explanation his fracturing mind could offer in order to explain all that he had seen since setting foot in this accursed place. He felt as though his scattered wits had been thrown to the dogs; remorselessly shredded and devoured. Something completely outside all of his previous experiences now assaulted him. Whatever this foul thing was that they were now facing, he knew it was an evil thing, spawned out of Hell itself. Fear pulled and tugged at his mind.

Crouching low, McQueen steeled himself to peer inside the hearth but apart from the soot, crumbled brickwork, one boot, bits of pottery and a few spiders there was nothing. No trace of James. 'The fragments of that small pottery jug and those other things. It may be what Cameron was on about.' He stooped to snatch them up before hastily pulling back.

The priest loosed his hold on his sister-in-law who was now bordering on the inconsolable, tears streaming from her eyes in great wet sobs. James' boot was still in his hand and he stared at it, stupefied. His nephew was gone and this was all that now remained of him.

McQueen examined the contents in his hand with mild revulsion. For, amidst the shards of broken pottery was a small wool-like ball of what appeared to be human hair, a few human teeth and some nail clippings. Then realisation dawned. He held in his hand the shattered remnants of a witch-bottle, a vessel used to imprison evil. No doubt Cameron and his team had found it and perhaps unwittingly someone had broken it, unknowingly releasing the evil power that now dwelt here. And as long as the pot was broken the evil could not be contained.

As though that power had now become aware of his under-standing it launched a fresh assault at the house. The doors and the window frames shook with a sudden ferocity. Plaster fell from the ceiling and a mass of bloodied brickwork fell into the hearth.

'In the name of God, I cast you out foul spirit!' shouted Father Archie, his crucifix held aloft. 'Begone! Leave this place and never return.' His holy declaration resounded around the rubble-filled room. He began to sprinkle holy water around the place. 'By the power invested in me as a servant of God, I cast you out!'

A high-pitched keening scream reverberated around the small room. It was a truly hideous noise; a wild ululation, a banshee's wail that conjured up horrible images and made the three remain-ing shrink back towards the dark opening of the doorway. The dreadful howl echoed all around, piercing their ears and stabbing into their minds, instilling within them a terrible, brain-numbing sense of dread and despair.

Gritting his teeth, Father Archie fought back against the dark power, chanting the opening words of the Lord's Prayer. Fiercely, he gripped his crucifix, sweat now running in tiny rivulets down his face. Tiny electric pulses were dancing erratically down his arms as he strived to keep the holy symbol aloft, to push back and repulse the demonic entity that now threatened to consume them all.

It was a titanic struggle, and for one dreadful moment McQueen thought that the Dark was going to prevail. But then, with a savage grunt from the priest, the unearthly, cacodemonical scream stopped and, temporarily at least, some level of normality returned.

McQueen shook his head in order to clear the insane sound that had assaulted it. For a moment he felt he had been psychically wracked, mentally tortured to the verge of madness. Shaking, he checked his watch, realising that it was now almost ten minutes to one. The witching hour was almost over. Whether that would bring an end to the supernatural malignity directed against them he knew not but it was a small hope he had to believe in. He doubted whether any of them could survive a night filled with this eldritch insanity.

A deep hush fell over them all.

'Do you... do you think it's over?' asked Eleanor, tremulously.

'I don't know,' answered the priest.

'I think you did it,' said McQueen. 'By God, I think you —'

The evil power resumed its attack on them.

Accompanied by a mad cackling laugh, a barrage of bricks was launched malevolently at them. McQueen ducked, but Eleanor did not react quickly enough to avoid getting struck by them. One struck her raised left arm whilst another cracked against her left knee instantly drawing blood as well as a cry of pain.

A nearby window imploded, showering the priest with flying glass.

'Oh my God!' McQueen rushed forward and grabbed Eleanor, shoving her out of harm's way as a further bout of poltergeist activity brought a large roof beam crashing down, smashing into the floor where she had been only a moment before. Had it struck her she would certainly have been killed.

The three of them withdrew out of the small room. McQueen

slammed the door shut. Hastily, they made their way down the small interconnecting passage towards the rear of the cottage.

The sound of cruel, insane cackling pursued them. The walls splintered and cracked. Great ragged zigzags appeared in the coarse stonework.

A hurled brick smacked painfully off McQueen's left shoulder blade. 'Do something,' he screamed hysterically at the priest.

'Quick! In here.' The priest grabbed him and together they stumbled into the small bedroom in which Eleanor and her unfortunate son had set up camp. Archie slammed the door shut. 'I'll try and secure this room,' he said, sprinkling holy water over the door.

Eleanor sat, huddled in an almost catatonic state, her arms wrapped around her knees by her son's rucksack. Her eyes were blank and it was clear, yet not entirely surprising, that something within her mind had finally snapped.

A loud thump smacked against the door.

'Can we defeat this thing?' asked McQueen. 'I've got the pieces from the witch-bottle but I don't see what good—'

'That's it,' said the priest. 'If we can contain the personal items belonging to this fiend, this witch, then we may be able to trap its spirit. We'd be able to force it into a physical form. Only then would we be capable of truly destroying it.'

'Is there anything we can—' McQueen's searching eyes were drawn to the small thermos flask lying by the rucksack. 'That flask! We'll use that.' He rushed over and snatched it up, emptied out the dregs of tepid coffee and, after a reassuring nod from the priest, delicately dropped the hair, the teeth and the nail clippings inside.

'Just to make doubly sure.' Archie decanted a splash of holy water into the flask making the contents within hiss and steam.

The screams and curses in the corridor grew in intensity. The door shook and rattled like an aggressive lunatic in chains. It was thumped repeatedly. The handle turned repeatedly but thankfully the door would not open.

McQueen screwed on the lid and the priest made a small blessing over it.

The screaming stopped abruptly.

For a long moment there was an unearthly silence, the only sounds that of their laboured breathing and the incessant thumping of their hearts. It seemed as though even the storm that had raged outside all night had finally abated.

'Is it over?' McQueen stared at the door as though half-expecting it to crash open in a violent explosion and for some horror born of nightmare to appear. He looked down at the flask in his hand. Was it just his imagination or did he feel something shift inside? For a moment he thought about magic lamps and trapped djinns. Was there a similarity? He checked his watch. The witching hour was over and with it, he hoped, the terror that had plagued them.

'I think it is.' The priest listened at the door. Nothing. Slowly, he turned the handle. The door opened a few inches then met with resistance as though something on the floor was blocking it. He pushed harder and—

In the light cast from his torch, there, lying on the hard stone at his feet, were the grisly, ragged remains of some withered being. It was partially desiccated, the limbs and much of the skull-like face decayed and worm-eaten. Filthy, tangled greying hair, crawling with ticks sprouted from the head. A crude burial gown was draped around it. One skeletal hand was on the door handle. *It was the corpse of Aggie McSweeney, dead for over a hundred years!*

GHOULS OF THE UNDERCITY

Things other than flesh crawled in the darkness.

DAVID RICHARDSON SAT in front of the small mirror applying the final touches to his skull-faced make-up; the chalk-white powder and the dark eye-shadow. He grinned, appraising his teeth which he had already blackened, wondering whether or not to enhance his ghoulish appearance with a little fake blood. After a moment's indecision he chose not to, after all he had gone out in his blood-sucking vampire costume the night before and it was just possible that there would be some who had attended that tour there tonight. It wouldn't do to make his little business—providing 'ghost tours' around the city—look cheap for there were now other tour operators working out there and competition was relatively fierce. It really was a question of showmanship and originality and to that end he wouldn't settle for second best; aspiring to give his customers the most insightful and frightful experience that he could.

In this endeavour Richardson had two main advantages over his competitors. First—he possessed a theatrical background, both in acting and in make-up and costume-design, having worked for over twenty years on some of the, admittedly low-scale, productions that several playhouses in the city had put on. Secondly—he knew much of the ghostly lore pertaining to the city, including the knowledge of the dark, eerie and atmospheric places to visit. When he had started the business, in 1980, he had spent hours trawling the records in the library for the gems that added lustre to the facts that the other guides re-hashed time and time again.

85

On occasion he had, surreptitiously, joined some of the other, inferior—in his view at least—tours, making mental notes and learning one or two things; little tricks of the trade, so to speak. To his satisfaction, there wasn't much that he didn't already know, and plenty of mistakes. The only drawback he faced was the fact that he was a sole operator, a one-man show and, consequently, unlike some of the other tours he had been on he had no paid stooges ready to jump out of the shadows at opportune moments. However this was something he was rather pleased about, preferring a much classier approach.

Richardson had three different tours which he alternated throughout the week, each of approximately one and a half hours duration. By far his favourite and the one he would be leading this evening was a trip around the Old City, visiting several of the locations where over the years, apparitions had, allegedly, been seen. He would then lead his group into the tunnels and the catacombs beneath street level—into the so-called Undercity; a labyrinthine warren of vaulted, coarse-brick, underground chambers that dated back hundreds of years. In this dismal, unlit, subterranean environment unknown numbers of the poor had lived a squalid, cramped and disease-ridden existence, shut off from the world above. There were countless tales of bloodcurdling horror attached to this place; ones which he would relate and embellish with his own sense of macabre flair.

Consulting his wristwatch, Richardson realised he would soon have to set off for the rendezvous point just outside the cathedral—an interesting building in its own right and one into which he used to take tourists until the bishop had learnt about it and brought such activities to a halt. All of his tours began at eight o'clock, regardless of the weather and if the past few nights were anything to go by there would hopefully be a substantial number waiting. It had never ceased to amaze him how much people enjoyed hearing about such horrible facts and ghoulish happenings;

eager to learn more about the darker side of the city's history. For evil had happened here. This was undeniable—the evidence and the truth lay buried under the streets, in the cemeteries, in the dark cobbled alleyways and boarded-up houses.

Yet, in spite of all that he knew, Richardson himself was an ardent sceptic. Certainly, many terrible things had happened here; murder, grave-robbing, devil worship and the like but he didn't believe in ghosts. After all, if anyone should have seen one then surely it would have been him after two years intentionally visiting the places they were rumoured to haunt. But the truth of the matter was he had seen and experienced nothing that couldn't be explained in a logical manner.

That said, there had been numerous occasions when some on his tour—individuals claiming to be psychic or some such nonsense—had reported seeing things or having experienced something unsettling. Such 'experiences' included the sighting of an apparition of a young boy down in the Undercity crying in torment, the image of a shadowy Jack the Ripper figure close to where some of the most sadistic and gruesome murders had occurred and the sensation of icy, spectral hands closing around someone's throat. His tours were advertised as being not for the faint of heart and, to date, there had been over a dozen instances when individuals had steadfastly refused to go any further, nine cases of the hysterics, three faintings and one heart attack victim who, thankfully, had been resuscitated by an off-duty doctor who had also been on the tour at the time in question.

Satisfied with his cadaverous visage, Richardson rose from his chair and moved to where a range of mannequin heads sporting various fright wigs rested on a shelf. Tonight he opted for a straggly, grey, shoulder-length hair-piece which he believed would augment his ghastly facial cosmetics. He put it on and ran his hands through it, raking it with his fingers into even wilder tangles. To complete his look he went to his wardrobe and took out a black cloak with red lining which he fastened around his neck and then grabbed his top hat, his silver wolf-headed cane and his black valise. Inside the case he had a powerful torch, some spare batteries, a wad of information flyers that he would distribute after the tour, a thick bunch of keys enabling him to enter the Undercity, the cemetery and several of the abandoned houses that were of interest and a small, basic first-aid kit in case of minor accidents, mostly as a result of people tripping or banging their heads in the shadowy tunnels into which they would be going.

After checking that everything was in order, Richardson switched off the lights in his changing room and left his small office, exiting onto the street. It was dark and cold and there was a light drizzle in the air. Whistling jauntily, he made for the cathedral.

'Dare you venture inside the dark and terror-filled Undercity, where hundreds lived in squalor and poverty? Join me on a journey into a shadow-filled world of horror and crime, where cannibalism was rife and Satan Himself is said to have been summoned. Discover, at first-hand, the dark alleyways where Charles Butterworth, 'The Laughing Ghoul', stalked and murdered his victims in such a grisly and depraved fashion and learn just why the house at 333 East Street has such a sinister reputation, remaining closed all these years.' Richardson spoke eloquently, trying to tout for business among the passers-by for he had been sorely disappointed when, upon arriving at the cathedral, there had been only a middle-aged couple waiting, who had enthusiastically introduced themselves as Lester and Mary Cunningham, American tourists from Boston. A poor showing by any standard. Still, there remained a few more minutes to try and whip up some interest and, as this was a weekend night, there were a lot of people about. 'I alone have the key which will enable us to enter.' He spotted a tall, elderly, bespectacled man regarding him with measured interest. 'You sir, you have the look of someone who is unafraid of the darker side of life and who would be willing to venture into the hellish depths in order to come face-to-face with the living dead, to hear of the stories of mayhem and murder which have left their gruesome stain on this fair—or should I say *foul*—city.'

'Well, I think you may have just piqued my interest.' The man stepped closer. 'Yes, why not. I'll give it a go.' Noticing the advertising placard next to Richardson, he dug into his pocket and handed over the admission fee.

'Thank you.' Richardson put the money into his wallet. 'I can guarantee your enjoyment. Now if you'll just wait a few minutes over here—'

'Hurry up, Stanley. Oh, thank God we haven't missed it.' A large, forceful woman pushed her way through the passing crowd, practically hauling a small, bald-headed, bearded man. 'We heard about if from some guests staying at our hotel the other evening who told us how much they enjoyed it. This is our last night in the city and we didn't want to miss out, now did we, Stanley?' She threw a disparaging look at her husband. 'Well hurry it up, Stanley. Pay the man.'

With something of a pathetic, long-suffering look at Richardson, Stanley counted out the required money and paid up.

It was now only two minutes to eight o'clock and Richardson was preparing to start when a group of young men, four in total, turned up. At first, he was concerned, having dealt with brash and offensive types before, who either deliberately sought to ridicule his tours or else proved downright difficult with their disruptive antics. However this group of lads seemed to be relatively well-behaved. Besides, it was slim pickings this evening and he didn't want to turn away four paying customers. News like that would soon get around and the last thing he needed was negative advertising.

'Well, if we're all ready, let us begin. Please, follow me. I'm a fast walker and we've got much to see so do try to keep up.' With those words, Richardson set out, his group of nine close on his heels.

Striding purposefully to the side-street at the rear of the cathedral, Richardson led his party away from the main thoroughfares of the city which were now beginning to throng with crowds of weekend evening revellers. Their shouts and laughs faded altogether after a few minutes, the only sounds now audible that of the clatter of shoes on the pavement and the occasional snippet of hushed conversation. Even the group of young men were surprisingly quiet.

They were now entering an area devoid of street lighting and the crumbling houses that loomed high on either side were dark and foreboding, partially decaying structures that no doubt housed countless undesirables. The street before them narrowed further and now Richardson had to use his torch to light the way, informing everyone to stay close and to mind their step. About halfway along, he stopped and shone his torch down a downward sloping passageway that branched off from the street they were on. It was terribly dark along that cobbled lane and, even he had to admit, it was spooky.

'We now stand at the turning to Hobbs Alley—one of the oldest, and some would say, most haunted parts of the Old City. For those of you who don't know, the city you see today has been occupied for well over a thousand years. Now obviously there are only a few small traces of occupation going back as far as that, however much of the present-day buildings are in fact built atop much older structures, some dating back two, three and even four hundred years. The oldest building in the city that still stands is probably the Three Goats Heads public house which dates back to the early Twelfth Century.'

'Can we go there and visit the spirits behind the bar?' quipped one of the young men, his comment winning a few laughs from his mates.

Richardson took it all in his stride. 'Not on this tour, although that is one of the tours I run and there are some very interesting and unnerving tales to be told about that place. Its name, for instance, comes from a certain Black Magic rite which utilised said goats' heads, but I digress. Hobbs Alley is infamous for many things but perhaps its greatest notoriety derives from the fact that it was down there, on the twenty-seventh of February 1886 that the mutilated body of a young serving girl, Jayne Wheatley, was discovered. Three days later, a second victim, Rosie Travis, was also found. Then a third, Margaret Brent, again three days later, was found; brutally murdered, torn almost to pieces in an act of unspeakable violence.'

'Was that like Jack the Ripper?' asked Mary.

'Hell, Mary, that was in London. Remember we went on that tour last year,' replied Lester.

'Although there was some resemblance to the Ripper murders, this was the handiwork of a despicable being some would consider far worse, despite the fact that not so many have heard of him. I'm talking about Charles Butterworth — *The Laughing Ghoul*. I see by the looks on your faces that none of you are familiar with the name — a name that history has, to a large extent, chosen to forget, so wicked were his crimes.'

'Either that or you've just made him up,' remarked Stanley's wife.

'Why, not at all.' Richardson enjoyed it when others challenged his knowledge of the details. 'At the end of our little expedition I have certain pamphlets which I will distribute that provide all the information regarding this evening's tour. You'll be able to do some research of your own if you doubt any of what I say.'

'Why was Butterworth called The Laughing Ghoul?' asked the elderly gentleman.

Richardson turned. 'A good question but the answer will have to wait until later when all will be made clear. Well, if we are ready, we'll head down to where young Jayne Wheatley met her terrible, tragic end. Follow me and —'

'We're not going down there, are we?' asked Mary nervously.

'But of course. I assure you I'll keep the torch on at all times, however the ground is uneven so please take care.'

As a tightly-huddled group they went down, the alley narrowing the further they went. There was a cloying, unpleasant smell in the air and it was deathly quiet, claustrophobic, the atmosphere and the knowledge of what may have happened here playing on the nerves of all bar Richardson. After all for him this was familiar territory. He came down this alley with groups twice, sometimes three times a week.

Shadows shrank and crept back again as the guide swung his torch around the walls before directing the beam to the ground at his feet. 'It was here, in this godforsaken place that the body of Jayne Wheatley was found — well what was left of her at any rate. You see, when they found her she had been partially consumed. The flesh from her legs, torso and arms had been —'

'Hey, steady on. That's quite enough of that.' Lester shook his head with distaste. 'I thought we'd come to hear about some good old-fashioned British ghosts not this kind of stuff.'

'Well I'm sorry if I've offended you, but I normally only tone down my commentary if there are any children present. Although, that said, more often than not it is they who want to hear all of the gory details. Bloodthirsty little tykes that they are. However, I'll take on board what you say.'

A couple of the young men moaned at this, believing it a needless acquiescence on their guide's part. They weren't squeamish and wanted to hear it — guts and all.

'As I was saying, it was here that Charles Butterworth claimed his first victim. The other two were found close by. Butterworth's involvement was only discovered later and indeed only by pure chance, when human remains were found in his house—333 East Street. And it is there that we're going next. Now before we go I normally just ask everyone to stand still and try to mentally picture the scene as it would have been almost a century ago on that dark, terrible night.' Richardson deliberately covered the torch with his hand, dimming the light and making the alley even more horrifying.

Shadows seemed to seep and press in towards them as though possessed of their own malign intent. A preternatural, unnerving silence fell, descending upon them like a funeral shroud. It was bordering on the unbearable for some – the two women and Stanley in particular. It was a horrible atmosphere, whether one believed in the bloody murders or not. Varying levels of fear crept into the hearts of all but Richardson as the imagination conjured up ghastly images.

Two agonising minutes passed before Richardson raised his torch. 'Well... did anyone experience anything? On previous tours I've had people tell me that they've felt suddenly cold or even heard hideous laughter. On one or two occasions I've had people who claimed to have seen the ghost of Jayne Wheatley or even the phantom of Butterworth himself dressed very much in the same manner as I am.'

'I did feel a chill,' spoke up Stanley's wife. 'A creepy kind of shiver. It was most unpleasant.'

'It's an eerie place, I'll say that for it,' said the elderly man. 'Do people still live in these houses?'

'I don't know,' Richardson answered. 'I've never seen any lights on behind any of the windows but I assume they do.'

'Can we be going now?' inquired Stanley's wife. 'I don't like it here.'

'I think it's giving her the willies,' commented Lester cheekily. His comment received a dark glower from the woman in question but got a few chuckles from the young men.

'Indeed. Follow me.' His torch illuminating the way, Richardson took them further into the warren of dingy backstreets.

They went down narrow, uneven flights of stairs and up sloping inclines. At one point they exited onto a relatively major road and the sight of cars and lampposts provided some with a well-needed respite in what was proving to be a most unsettling experience. But then the modern street was behind them and they were once more back in the twisting, cobbled streets and alleys of the Old City.

A malodorous, fetid stench struck at their nostrils.

'Say, what's that God awful stink? Don't you people have working drains?' Lester's nose wrinkled in disgust.

'That, my friend, is the accumulated waste of several centuries,' answered Richardson. 'You see there were no latrines or sewers back in the days these houses were built and sanitation was virtually non-existent. Much of the effluent was merely tipped from windows where it would fester for weeks. Liquid waste would run down the street, leaching into the very brickwork—hence the better property, if one could say that given the conditions, was always at the top of the hill. The council have not yet tackled this area of the city as it is virtually uninhabited. Indeed, if they finally get round to modernising it I fear we will be losing a piece of history.'

The buildings around them were even more dilapidated than those they had already seen with smashed windows and broken doorways. Some bore the scars of past fires and a sense of wickedness seemed to hang over them as though, over the years, they had borne silent witness to acts of great inhumanity. Over to their right, away from some boarded-up houses which leaned like dying men against one another for support, was a burnt-out church-like building. Once a gathering point for the denizens of this area, now it lay desolate and heavily vandalised, its remaining walls and rafters broken and blackened. This area seemed almost detached from all that was sane and modern and it was doubtful that even daylight would improve the look of the place. At night, with a chill drizzle falling from the dark heavens and a gloomy, spectral mist now beginning to fall and with a character like Richardson, dressed as he was, it bordered on the nightmarish.

'And here we are, East Street. The house we have arrived at is number 333.' Richardson shone his torch at a dark, padlocked wooden door set in a stretch of very old wall, the stonework coarse and crumbling. 'It is here, within this very house of horrors that Charles Butterworth, the evil perpetrator of those heinous murders, lived; murders that went beyond madness and evil. Behind this door is the house of a truly depraved individual. What terrible sights the police must have witnessed when they entered we can only imagine but if the records are anything to go by then we can but speculate on the gut-wrenching horrors within.' Removing his set of keys from his case, he quickly found the one he needed, inserted it into the lock, turned it and opened the door.

By the light from the torch the gathered group could see that the space beyond was a small, bare room.

'Please be careful once inside as there are numerous loose beams and, as you can see, it is rather low-ceilinged, so please mind your head.' With that warning, Richardson entered. He waited until everyone was inside before closing the door.

A faint charnel smell hung in the air.

'Charles Butterworth was more than a killer. When the police came here on a tip-off they found far more than they had bargained for. The ground floor was fairly normal—obviously there is no furniture remaining from that time—but it is what they discovered upstairs...' Once everyone was inside, he led them along a shadow-filled corridor, showing them around several fairly nondescript ground floor rooms. They gathered in what had once been the kitchen.

'It sure is a creepy place this,' commented Mary.

Lester put his arm around his wife. 'I don't know; some nice wallpaper, fitted lights and some pot plants... I reckon —'

There came a loud creak from upstairs as though someone had stepped on a loose board. It came again and was then followed by the sound of a door closing.

'What the hell was that?' cried out several voices at once.

All was quiet.

Richardson swiftly panned the torch around. It was possible that there was someone else in the house with them although that seemed highly unlikely considering the fact that he had had to unlock the property in order to gain access. A vagrant, possibly? On a few occasions he had encountered drunks and homeless individuals down in the Undercity—those unfortunates who had nowhere else to go.

As a group they remained silent for a further thirty seconds.

'Maybe it's the ghost of Charles Butterworth,' said Richardson. 'Shall we go and see?' There was a slight apprehension in his tone. Realising this, he forced calmness back into his voice. After all, this was but an old, dark house—admittedly it had been the house of a psychopathic, cannibalistic murderer—but a house, nonetheless. To the others, however, the place was genuinely creepy. In the torchlight the imagination was free to run rampant and unchecked and for some – those perhaps more susceptible to the multitude of fears that came crowding in, ringing them around, notably the two women and Stanley—the pressure was becoming unendurable. It was as though some powerful, malevolent presence now lurked here; an evil that was just waiting, readying itself for the best moment at which to reveal itself.

In single file, with the guide in the lead, they started up the stairs. There was a small landing half-way up and there was no banister, making it relatively hard going, more so in the cramped conditions and dim light. There was some disgruntled muttering in addition to a few curses from the young men as they tripped, their ascent almost in complete darkness for they were at the rear of the group. Even with the background kerfuffle, Richardson strained his senses; attempting to hear anything out of the ordinary. He thought he detected a further groan from the floorboards in the room at the end of the corridor indicative of someone—or something—moving around in there but he wasn't certain. They had all heard a sound when they had been downstairs in the kitchen but he knew from past experience of being in these old buildings how sounds could be deceptive. A gust of wind down an old chimney, the scampering of rats or even the very settling of the building itself due to hundreds of years of age and decay could create a myriad of noises. Noises that those who had been 'conditioned', as it were, to believe in ghosts, would instantly attribute to the paranormal to the detriment of the mundane.

Gently, Richardson pushed open the door on his right. It was an unfurnished bedroom—rather that is what it had once been. Similarly with the room on his left. He shone the torch inside both permitting the others a brief look. For some reason and despite his rational thinking he was beginning to feel tiny trickles of cold sweat crawling down his back. He had felt like this on one or two previous occasions—more so when there had only been two or three in his group and that 'safety in numbers' feeling of security had seemed virtually non-existent. For perhaps only the second time on one of his 'ghost tours' he longed for a light switch he could just reach out for and click, instantly bathing his surroundings in bright, welcome illumination.

'Just what is it that's beyond this other door?' asked Lester. 'Are we going to see a ghost or what?'

Richardson turned, one hand on the door handle. 'I make no promises that we'll see any ghosts. Indeed, I, myself, don't believe in them. However, if they do exist then surely it would be in a place such as this. Over the years there have been several investigations by specialists in the field—ghost-hunters or parapsychologists—experts, who, allegedly, have witnessed and experienced dreadful and inexplicable things in the room beyond this door.'

'What kind of things?' asked Stanley's wife, her fleshy face shrouded in shadow.

'I believe they took several photographs,' answered Richardson. 'In some there were—unexplained shapes—things that weren't there at the time the photos were taken; blurred outlines of a man dressed similarly to the reported sightings of Butterworth. There were other things too. Things I'll explain once we're all inside. I should warn you that on previous tours I've had people feel suddenly sick and disorientated upon seeing what lies beyond.' When this precautionary statement got no immediate response, he pushed open the door and raised his torch beam.

A grotesque, corpse-like face grinned back at him!

It was almost as though the torchlight had struck a mirror, reflecting back his own hideous, made-up image. However this was a wall painting, daubed onto the coarse brick in garish reds and yellows. The painting was both surreal and unnerving and was clearly the product of an insane mind. The mouth hung wide and stretched; the eyes huge and staring. And as the group moved in they saw that there were many such murals – some mere caricature-like sketches others full-blown works of devilish artistry. All depicted that grinning, triumphant, ugly visage. No matter which stretch of wall one looked at there was a face, the eyes glaring out with a malevolent intensity. Within the confines of the room it gave the viewer the impression that they were caged; and that it was *they* who were the subject of diabolical scrutiny.

Thankfully, at least as far as Richardson was concerned, the room was empty. There was no vagrant lying huddled in newspapers and with a bottle of cheap rotgut close at hand. Such an encounter could have proven awkward and extremely embarrassing. Tourists eager to learn of the city's dangerous and squalid past were seldom as keen to confront these elements of its squalid present.

'Good God!' exclaimed Lester. 'Those faces! I take it that's Butterworth?'

'None other. Hence 'The Laughing Ghoul'. It was in this room that he was said to have practised his unholy ceremonies. One rumour has it that it was within this very room that he summoned forth the Devil and that it was this experience which drove him completely insane, making him paint all of these warped self-portraits. Another rumour says that when he called forth Satan, the Devil forced him into painting one face for each person he had murdered. Ah, but I notice your confusion – Butterworth only killed three times, you say. Alas no, you see when the police conducted a search of the house they discovered more bodies—or rather parts thereof. Where? I hear you ask.' Richardson pointed the torch beam to the floor. 'Why under the very floorboards upon which you now stand. Over twenty-five individuals, or so it is claimed, lay underneath.' He grinned upon noticing the shock and revulsion that flickered over some of the other's faces. In a perverse way he loved this little revelation. It never ceased to get a reaction.

Some looked down as though half-expecting putrefying, clawed hands to burst through the floor or to see withered, rotten faces gazing up through gaps in the boards.

'You're kidding, right?' asked Lester, his arm around his wife's shoulder, providing comfort for it was clear that she was feeling uneasy.

Richardson shook his head. 'I'm afraid not. It was here, in this diabolical shrine that many unspeakable atrocities were carried out. It is now well-accepted that Butterworth was a leading

Satanist and I'm sure he was not working alone. A cabal of devil-worshippers operated from this house, preying on the poor and the vulnerable, obtaining many of their recruits and their sacrificial victims from the surrounding slums and the Undercity, where we shall be going next. There used to be—' he was interrupted by the unsavoury sound of the American woman vomiting.

'Are you okay, honey? I think it's time we got out and got some fresh air,' said Lester.

'I agree.' With hasty strides, Richardson led them back along the corridor, down the stairs and outside. Here they all gathered, the two women looking pale and sickly in the poor light, their respective spouses trying to comfort them.

'Hey, Mister tour leader.'

Richardson turned to face one of the young men, an acne-faced youth in his late teens. 'Yes?'

'Well I've just noticed that the old geezer, you know, the guy with the glasses... well, he's missing.'

A quarter of an hour later, after having re-entered Charles Butterworth's house and conducted a thorough search within, Richardson found himself perplexed and at a loss for answers regarding the man's disappearance. The appropriate thing to do was to call the tour off and inform the police but when he had raised that as a course of action, both Americans and Stanley's wife had volubly stated that they wanted it to continue; a decision given some strength when one of the young men revealed that he had overheard the old man mentioning that he had seen enough. It could be, therefore, that he had just decided to make off without announcing his intent, in which case, assuming that he could find his way back in the dark safely there was no cause for alarm. Such things had happened on the other tours – indeed, now he came to think about it, it was rare that he finished a tour with the same number he had started out with.

'Well, are we going to see this Undercity or whatever it's called?' ventured Lester. 'Or are we going to get a full refund?'

'Yes, I, or rather we, came along specifically to see the Undercity, didn't we Stanley?' Stanley's wife pulled her expensive coat tight over her pendulous bulk. 'We've heard it's a must see. A once in a lifetime experience.'

Richardson was still mentally debating what he should do. It went without saying that the Undercity was the highlight of the tour and it would reflect badly on him if he were to cancel things now. He reached a decision, hoping that he was right about the old man having just opted to abandon the tour and make his own way back. 'Very well,' he said. 'On with the tour. We shall leave the maleficent Charles Butterworth behind and set out for the Undercity—a vast, sprawling underground labyrinth of tunnels and vaults wherein whole generations lived and died.' He felt somewhat better now that he had reached a firm decision, assured that he had at least gone back into the house, where the old man had last been seen, in an attempt to locate him. Case and cane in one hand, torch in the other, he marched off, confident in the knowledge that the others would follow.

They soon entered a further maze of narrow, deserted streets. The age-old houses crammed in around them oppressively and with each step that horrendous stench grew.

'In times past, this part of the Old City was often referred to as the 'Necropolis', which if we have any Classical scholars amongst us will know means 'city of the dead'. Although this area was never used as an actual burial site, at least not to my knowledge, there's little doubt that hundreds, maybe thousands, died in these dismal hovels. Many perished due to malnutrition and disease. Others fell victim to the likes of Butterworth and his cronies. There were also many fires in this area, although none as severe as the blaze of 1826 when almost a third of the Old City was affected. Many of the buildings we can see around us bear traces of that terrible conflagration. However, it was in the Undercity itself where one of the most calamitous fires erupted, killing scores of unfortunates. It must've been a truly terrifying experience; trapped underground, the flames and the smoke, the screams as entire families were burnt to death, unable to escape.'

Far away could be heard the faint sound of a police car siren – an incongruous sound considering their surroundings and a small, yet welcome reminder that they hadn't completely stepped outside the modern world. It was difficult to perceive the fact that they were in a city within a city; a frightening, ghastly enclave which lurked within the boundaries of an otherwise relatively sane conurbation filled with schools, hospitals and libraries.

Down a twisting street Richardson led them. On their right loomed a wall some thirty feet in height, its surface cracked and covered in obscene scrawls of graffiti suggesting that local street gangs had at one time frequented this area. Amidst the doodles and the gibberish, one slogan proclaimed *'Charles Butterworth will rise again!'*; the message painted onto the wall in thick, red, sloppy brushstrokes.

'There are a few entrances to the Undercity,' announced Richardson, opening his case and removing his set of keys. It was only now that the others realised that there was a cunningly concealed door in front of him. 'With several more being found each year. Most are but tunnels, little more than sewer entrances. This one, however, was perhaps the most commonly used by those who either chose or were forced to dwell therein.' He unlocked the door and pushed it open.

The stench that assaulted their nostrils was foul; an age-old smell mixed with the hint of sewage, as though a long-closed manhole lid had just been raised. Beyond the door was a stretch of tunnel at the end of which, just visible in the torchlight, could be seen another door.

Once everyone was inside, Richardson closed the door behind

them. He then went to the front of the group and led them down the passageway. It was dank and low-ceilinged, the walls curved slightly as though it was a sewer tunnel. The door he was approaching was far older in appearance, with a square metal grille set at head height. With a different key, he unlocked it, the torchlight revealing a flight of stone steps descending into a murky darkness. Water could be heard dripping from some-where, the steady sounds echoing off the walls.

'Please be careful on the steps.' Deeper and deeper Richardson led them down the sloping passages, through tunnels that rang with the muffling echoes of their feet and oozed a thick, viscid moisture from the walls until none but he was sure of the way back. Eventually they left the sewer system and exited, via an-other downward sloping passage, into a rat-run of interconnected vaulted chambers. Some were sealed off with portcullis-type gates and all were ancient.

There was an air of menace about these subterranean spaces; an aura of evil and cruelty that was almost tangible. In this place of darkness and death only the shadows seemed alive.

'All sorts of ghostly things have been seen down here. Not sur-prising, I guess, when one considers the grisly history which has literally seeped into the very walls.' Richardson continued with his spiel: 'In 1779 the crown ordered a violent, merciless assault on the inhabitants in an attempt to clamp down on the rampant lawlessness that, like a contagion, spread from here. Hundreds were butchered in their sleep or rounded up and dragged to the surface where they were either imprisoned or executed. Six years later it was the turn of the church. By order of the bishop the known entrances were sealed off, resulting in mass starvation.'

'I didn't think it would be so big,' commented Lester, eyes wide as he stared all around.

'This is but one part of the Undercity. Exactly how far it stretches no one actually knows however there are points of access in Grey Chapel Cemetery, Kirkwall Street, St. Cuthbert's Causeway and West Tower Road in addition to the one we entered by. It is said that there may also be entrances near the castle as well as one in the vaults of the cathedral where we started. At the height of its inhabitation it has been suggested that up to six thousand people may have lived down here. It must have been a very basic existence; food and fresh water being scarce and having to be scavenged from above. Sadly, it is a documented fact that cannibalism was rife and there are reports of folk being snatched from above and dragged down here for such a purpose.'

'I did a history lesson about Sawney Bean, the Scottish cannibal who lived on the Ayrshire coast,' spoke up one of the young men. 'He lived in a cave and ate people.'

'Ayrshire is a little outside my beat but I can't say that I've heard of him,' replied Richardson. 'Anyway, if anyone has any questions I'll be pleased to answer them.'

Lester ran a hand down the wall, feeling the dampness on the rough surface. 'You said earlier that these tunnels were several hundred years old. Well, I've been to Egypt and I've been inside some of the ancient tombs in the Valley of the Kings and I've got to say this place looks a damn sight older even though those tombs were thousands of years old.'

'The main part of the Undercity is three hundred, maybe four hundred years old. It could be that there are older parts as yet undiscovered but I doubt it,' Richardson replied, casting a casual glance at his watch. It was a quarter past nine; time to be winding things up. 'If you're all ready we'll start heading out. I'll be leading you out a different—' He stopped as everything went several shades gloomier and then suddenly dark, the light from his powerful torch dying before going out.

There were a few startled cries.

'Please be calm,' Richardson called out. 'The batteries on my torch must've died. Just a moment. I've got spares in my—'

'What the hell was that?' Lester called out.

'Something just moved past me,' cried one of the young men.

'Oh my God! Oh my God!' screamed Stanley's wife hysterically.

What followed was pure pandemonium. It seemed that everyone was screaming now as panic broke out. In the utter darkness people were floundering and tripping, colliding with others and stumbling, blindly, into the walls as the darkness become peopled by nightmares.

Richardson was fumbling desperately for his spare batteries. He slid one into place and then someone staggered into him, knocking the second battery from his trembling fingers. With a curse, he dropped to his knees and began feeling around hoping that it had not rolled far or down a crack in the floor. It would be pure hell trying to get these frightened people out in pitch darkness.

'Jesus Christ! Something's got a hold of my —' Lester's words were cut short as there came a scratching, ripping sound followed by an obscene, terrible gargling.

Yells and cries reverberated off the Undercity walls, chasing themselves in fading echoes down the age-old tunnels. In the terror-filled darkness it was clear that some had tried to flee from the ensuing madness for their screams now sounded further away. Someone nearby was whimpering, their pathetic mumbled words half-prayer, half-nonsense.

Like a blind man feeling his way forward, Richardson's fingers clamped around the missing battery. He slid it into place and... what he saw as the torchlight illuminated his surroundings once more caused his heart to leap and his stomach to lurch.

Crouched over the bloody, savaged corpse of Lester was a small, naked, thoroughly grotesque being, its skin pale, almost bone-white. The emaciated thing's face was wrinkled and sallow, its eyes huge and black, doll-like. Fresh blood dribbled out of its crooked, tooth-filled maw from where it had been feasting on its victim's torn throat.

Mercifully, Richardson only saw it for a second or two for it recoiled instantly from the bright light, hissing its wrath and shielding its eyes before scampering rapidly away. It vanished almost as quickly as it had appeared, its movements loping and almost spider-like as it clambered up one of the tunnel walls and disappeared into a crack in the ceiling. A blurred motion to his left made him spin round, catching at the corner of his eye a second white blur as another one of the things dashed out of view. He raised a hand to his mouth, grimacing and fighting to keep down his supper upon seeing the mutilated bodies of Stanley's wife and one of the young men, their ravaged, bloody corpses showing signs of bite marks.

Insanity threatened to tear Richardson's mind apart. The harrowing horror, the bloody carnage and the madness battered and yammered at his brain, sending it spiralling in a hundred different directions, each one darker and more chaotic than the last.

'Are they gone?' asked one of the young men, shambling back into the light. His face was ashen and he was trembling. Blood ran from a claw mark on his arm.

'What in Hell's name were they?' questioned another. Unlike his friend he appeared uninjured but there was shock and confusion imprinted all over his face.

'I don't know—but we have to get out of here,' answered Richardson. 'It could be that the torchlight kept them away. We've got to get moving.'

'I'm going nowhere without my husband. You've got to help him,' pleaded Mary. She stood gazing down at her very dead husband, clearly not accepting the fact that he was beyond help, after all there was nothing in Richardson's first-aid kit that could perform miracles. 'We have to get the police and an ambulance.'

'Come on, let's get going before those things come back.' One of the young men was practically pleading with Richardson to leave—to abandon the American woman if need be—after all he was the only one with a light source and this was now a survival situation. Tears would have to wait until they were out.

As Richardson hesitated, contemplating whether or not to drag the woman with him, there came the echoing clang of one of the portcullis-like gates closing. Several seconds later the sound came again, more muffled this time, further away and from a different direction.

'What was that?' asked Stanley. He had sat, huddled in a corner, his arms wrapped around his knees, his eyes wide and staring throughout the madness. Only now did he haul himself to his feet.

'I think they're trying to trap us; to block off our escape routes.' Richardson swung his torch around, shining it over the three shadowy exits from the chamber they were in. It had sounded as though the way they had come was sealed off as well as one of the forward tunnels. 'Those who want to see daylight again had better follow me.' He waited, giving Mary the chance to join him if she so desired and was pleased to see her nod her head and shuffle forward, tears running down her face, smearing her make-up.

There were now only five of them, one of the young men still unaccounted for having fled into the darkness, presumably dead. They had set out as a group of ten – now they were half that number. All of them looked shell-shocked, weary, frightened and some were blood-spattered. There were glazed, disbelieving looks in their eyes, indicative of those who could not come to terms with what they had just experienced.

'Everyone stay close, keep moving and keep your eyes open.' There was a determination in Richardson's stride as he set off down one of the passages—one which he hoped had not been blocked. His mind was a seething cauldron of writhing, chaotic thoughts but despite this he tried to mentally regain control, knowing that panic would not do him or any of the others any good. To succumb to the insanity would only compound the situation and would no doubt lead to them all getting killed. He forced himself to get a grip on his faculties; to think clearly and logically. He reckoned it would take them about ten minutes to reach an exit, providing it had not been blocked and that he could remain focused and remember the route.

They had been going for close on five minutes, the gnawing fear at what existed in the darkness and was no doubt in stealthy pursuit bordering on the unbearable.

Yet a little hope began to blossom in Richardson's chest as he firmly believed that he was heading in the right direction. The way had not been barred and the exit lay just ahead. When he got out he would head straight to the nearest police station and inform them of all that had happened. There were witnesses who would testify that he was telling the truth – no matter how incredible it might sound—that there were flesh-eating monsters, devils born of nightmare, haunting the Undercity.

'Keep moving. We're nearly out. Only another hundred yards or so.'

It was then, when safety and salvation seemed to be tantalisingly within their grasp, that disaster struck as Richardson's torch went out again.

Scurrying forth from the impenetrable midnight blackness, the savage, child-sized mutant degenerates that had laired down in the deepest parts of the Undercity and the old sewage tunnels fell, ravenously, upon them. With teeth and claws they bore down on their screaming, vulnerable prey, tearing bloody gobbets of flesh from their still-living victims.

Richardson stumbled in the dark, one hand outstretched, reaching for a wall, supporting himself and managing to stay upright. There was nothing he could do for the others now. Only his own survival mattered. Swinging his silver-headed cane in fierce swipes, he edged away, each backward step bring him closer to the exit—or so he hoped.

The gurgling, chomping, slavering sounds that echoed all around were terrible. In his mind he envisaged those poor, hapless victims being torn apart and greedily devoured. He was thankful that he could not witness such gory proceedings.

Step-by-step, he kept retreating.

The sound of scrabbling and the patter of bare feet filled his ears and he was sure the horrors were approaching, no doubt readying themselves for an attack.

'Get back! Get back I warn you!'

'*Sssh... sssh... feeeeed usss,*' cried out an unholy chorus of sibilant, unearthly voices. '*Weeee... huuunger. Sssh... more... brrriing more.*'

Richardson's mind darkened.

'*More...*' came a pitiful wail; an ululation of the dammed.

A terrifying phantasmagoria of hideously laughing, wide-mouthed faces swam at him from out of the darkness, faces he recognised and had seen many times before. The painted faces of Charles Butterworth. And then a hellish realisation hit him and he knew why these ghouls of the Undercity had not attacked him; *had dared not attack him.* For his soul belonged to Butterworth, had done so for over two years when he had first set foot in that accursed room in 333 East Street. It had been that Satanist who had formed a pact with these creatures over a century before. He had been their feeder, providing them with morsels from above, until his execution. They still hungered and Butterworth's spectre had found a way to honour his pact, using Richardson to deliver unknowing victims to them, after all they preferred their meat fresh and as the majority of those he brought were visitors to the city, taking the tour on a whim, their disappearances had never led the police to Richardson. As a further measure, and to ensure no suspicion on the part of Richardson, Butterworth only took full possession after the creatures had claimed their victims, only entering the forefront of his host's soul and mind when the devilish deed was done.

With Butterworth now in full possession, Richardson found he could see in the dark. He could see that the ghouls were after more but they would have to wait for another night or two and even then it was rare that it was deemed safe enough for them to take an entire group as they had done on this occasion. They must have been starving, poor things. Whistling jauntily, he straightened his hat and made for the exit. In many ways, he was the greatest ghoul of the Undercity.

WHERE DEAD MEN SCREAM

In a man's last few hours he will see many things.

NIGHT HAD FALLEN at the John Royce Penitentiary — one of the most notorious criminal holding units in Western Texas. The few inmates who had managed to fall asleep twisted and turned in nightmarish fever while those awake, cried out through thinned lips. Others banged on doors, rattled the bars of their cells or hollered loudly, so that their unnerving yells echoed and re-echoed along the empty corridors, down from one floor to another.

This was the way it always happened. An evil, restless night; made immeasurably worse by the intolerable heat of summer, without a breath of air stirring through the whole of the grey, gaunt building.

On the ground floor, away from the cells and the worst of the noise, Brett Chesterfield sat uneasily in his chair and looked across at the tall, square-shouldered figure of the Governor, Mantley Harris. The husband of one of his more distant cousins, he was a huge, thickly jowled man, with the kind of stubble that would no doubt serve to light a struck match. He *seemed* unmoved by what was going on, treating it as a normal, everyday affair but, underneath, Chesterfield guessed, he was as nervous as everyone else. Near the door, one of the guards sat tensely on the edge of his chair, sweat streaking his rugged, tanned face. He looked the kind of man who wasn't averse to breaking the odd limb whenever the need arose.

The Governor looked up after a pause and drawled genially: 'I know you've been here before, Brett, but I understand this is your first assignment on an execution.'

'Yes. To be honest I had no idea it would be like this,' Chesterfield answered hoarsely. 'Tell me, does it always affect the other prisoners in this way?'

Harris shrugged. 'More or less,' he replied. 'They seem to know when it's going to happen, even if we take the most stringent precautions to keep it a secret. I swear that no one leaks the date fixed for an execution, yet somehow they know all the same.'

'Listen to them now.' Chesterfield sat tautly upright in his chair. The hellish screams and yells, muffled a little by distance, still continued to reach them, reverberating along the corridors which were empty except for the occasional patrolling guard. It was akin to wild animals; wolves or coyotes, baying mournfully at the moon.

'Mark my words, it'll get a lot worse before dawn,' said Harris. He lit a cigar with a lighter and took a deep draw. 'You get used to it. If you'd been through it as often as I have. At first, it gets you down.'

'Can't you stop them?'

The other spread his hands helplessly. 'What can we do? Most of the time, they're muttering and screaming in their sleep. We can't stop that. Some of the others do it deliberately, I know, trying to draw attention to themselves. We can usually shut them up to a certain extent, but it's the atmosphere that's more to blame than anything else. That, and this damned heat. For a time we tried to drown them out with music but all that did was add to the noise. There was talk of getting soundproof windows installed but then the finances ran dry and nothing was done.'

The guard near the door glanced up at that and laughed loudly. The sound was harsh and grating, unpleasant on the ear.

Chesterfield looked at him in sudden surprise. 'Is it possible that there's something here that these men can *feel* – or rather, sense?'

The guard shook his head ponderously. 'There's nothing here that can't be put down to imagination,' he declared. 'I've seen almost as many executions as the Governor here and I maintain that the men themselves are at the bottom of it all. They know through the prison grapevine when a man's going to the chair. Don't ask me where they get the information, but I know for certain that they were aware about Tommy Vincento almost a week ago. I heard a couple of them talking about it in the yard during exercise.'

'What does that prove?' asked Chesterfield curiously.

'Simply this. That it only takes one or two of them to stir up the rest. Those bastards who start all the trouble get up at two or three in the morning and make all of this god-damned row just to disturb the other prisoners, to get them going. You know how a thing like this will spread once it's started.'

'That's possible, of course,' agreed the Governor. He puffed on his cigar, blowing out a cloud of acrid smoke before straightening the articles on his desk with a slow, careful motion. He seemed a little more ill at ease than Chesterfield had noticed a few minutes earlier.

'Would I be correct in guessing that you think there's something more to it than that, Governor?' said Chesterfield.

'I didn't say that exactly,' protested Harris defensively. 'But *you* don't appear to be very disconcerted yourself at what's going on.' He paused, then added: 'Aren't you curious about this place?'

'Curious, yes. But is there any reason why I should be disconcerted?'

'Well, in a way there is, I suppose. Quite a lot of people are, especially if they come at a time like this.' Harris seemed to be studying Chesterfield in turn, eyeing him closely.

'For any particular reason?'

'Perhaps.' The other sounded vaguely non-committal.

'Well, don't keep me waiting.' Chesterfield took out his note pad and laid it on the table in front of him. 'If there's a story here that I could use in my column apart from the bare essentials of what's about to happen tomorrow morning, let's have it.'

The Governor stubbed out his smouldering cigar. He hesitated, clearly waiting for something, then said harshly: 'It's stopped. Listen.'

Silence. A vast hanging pall of it that seemed to press down upon them like lead. It was a deep vacuum, without sound, which came down out of nowhere like the imperceptible pressure of a distant storm.

Quite suddenly, Chesterfield felt nervous, ill at ease, as if something terrible was going to happen at that very moment, and there would be nothing he or anyone else could do about it. He felt a momentary twitch of fear along the muscles of his back. There was a cold, musty smell in his nostrils and his body felt taut. He found himself envisaging all of the inmates, now free from their incarceration, overpowering the guards and sneaking stealthily along the corridors towards them, readying themselves to come streaming into the office and murder them. He shivered, reflecting briefly on how much he hated being here, but this was what he was being paid for, what his editor demanded, and what the public wanted to read about in their early editions. The more morbid and gruesome the details, the more they liked it, and as always, you had to give the public what *they* wanted, not what he'd like to read himself.

This sudden silence after all that noise. It was almost as though someone, somewhere, had given an abrupt signal and each man had instantly stopped shouting and banging.

The deep, unnerving silence continued.

Chesterfield felt crushed and suffocated by it, in spite of the fact that he knew, deep down inside, that there could be no real significance attached to it. Relax, he told himself sourly, relax. The idea that anything could be wrong was utterly ludicrous, totally ridiculous. Yet, whilst the inmates had cried and wailed, the prison had been indisputably alive. Now, in this eerie, haunting silence, it was as though it had died. Suddenly, he felt a little tremor of fear pass through him. It was almost as though there was something – some presence – in the room with them. What-ever it was, it had neither shape nor substance. Rather, it was a disturbing feeling; an impression of looming malevolence.

Harris leant across his desk. 'Every time, it happens like this. Completely inexplicable. This sudden silence.'

'Could it be that there's more to this than meets the eye?' ventured Chesterfield. 'I'll admit I've no psychological background but could it be down to some kind of mass hysteria or perhaps something along the lines of ESP?'

The guard glanced at him with a faint sneer on his lips. 'More of your theories, Mr. Chesterfield?' he asked softly.

'There has to be some explanation.' The reporter turned in his chair. 'Men don't all stop shouting and screaming at exactly the same time like that unless their actions are somehow coordinated.'

'Could be that they've tired themselves out with all of their yelling,' suggested the guard.

'That's no explanation whatsoever, and you know it,' said Chesterfield.

'Maybe not, but it's the only thing I'm prepared to accept. I've heard too many of those stories from the other prison staff. Sheer nonsense.' There was a peculiar expression on the guard's stony features.

'What sort of stories have you heard?' Chesterfield muttered sharply.

The Governor brought his hands together, interlacing his fingers. 'Now then, Brett, I'm sure you understand that this can't go any further than this office. Clearly, I can't prevent Anderson from talking to you about what he's heard, but I must insist that none of these tales be published without looking over them first. It won't do either of our careers any good if word gets around that the prison is staffed by a lot of superstitious fools.'

The guard paused, his eyes fixed on Chesterfield. Then he said: 'Any other time, you wouldn't notice anything out of the ordinary. But on a night before an execution, things are different. Don't try to deny that it isn't beginning to get at your nerves. I can see from the look on your face that it is. It affects everybody like this the first time. I've been here for close on twenty years and even though I don't believe these stories, it still gives me the creeps, sitting here, waiting for the hours to pass, knowing that there's one sorry bastard, sitting out there on Death Row, in the condemned cell, more alone than he's ever been in his life, hoping that the hours will never pass, maybe praying for a last-minute reprieve. Which, certainly for as long as I've served here, never comes.'

'Go on,' said Chesterfield as the other paused momentarily.

'Now, I don't look upon myself as an imaginative man. In this business it pays not to be, otherwise you wouldn't stick at it for more than a month, let alone twenty years. It's something I'll admit that I can't put my finger on but, as for the place being haunted, well that's maybe pushing things a little too far.'

'*Haunted?*' Chesterfield said with a sudden, incredulous surprise.

'That's what some of the others seem to think.'

'But that's ridiculous.' The reporter tried to force conviction into his tone, keeping his voice steady. 'I mean that can't be true, can it?'

'Your guess is as good as ours,' interrupted the Governor, leaning forward over his desk. 'It's not hard to believe that institutions like this might be haunted. Just pause for a moment and look at the facts. We've got the worst of society in here. Murderers, rapists, child-killers, cannibals, Democrats... you name it, they're in here somewhere. Now, contrary to some of the rubbish you may've heard about some of them repenting their sins and finding Jesus, I've got no doubt that they're all bound for that big fire downstairs if you get my meaning. Now, as your cousin, Mary-Sue, may've told you, I ain't a religious man, but I'd have thought that that wasn't the kind of place one would rush to get into. So it seems to me to make some sense that you'd want to try and hang on around here after you'd died for as long as you could.'

'But surely you don't believe that the prison is haunted?' persisted Chesterfield.

'I'm not sure what to believe. Personally, I find it best to keep an open mind. So long as nothing untoward happens, my conscience is clear. So far, the ghosts, if there are any, haven't interfered with the carrying out of the sentence on the following morning and that's all that bothers me.'

'But this *is* interesting as far as I'm concerned. It's something I'd never considered before. *A haunted prison.* The ghosts of all the executed prisoners coming back on the night when another man goes to his death. There's a thought for you, isn't it?'

'Maybe so,' said the Governor sharply, 'but I'd prefer it if you didn't print anything but the facts. We aren't concerned with superstitious theories in a case like this. I hope you'll remember that when you write your report. Don't forget, that it's only because we've got family ties that I agreed to you coming here in the first place.' Without lifting his head, he raised his eyes to meet the reporter's gaze.

Watching him, Chesterfield saw that his eyes continued to flick around the room as though half-expecting to see somebody standing at his shoulder or in the shadows, and being surprised to find nobody there when he looked round. 'Sure. I won't put anything in my column without running it by you first and may I add, once again, how grateful I am to you for allowing me to do this. But, for my own curiosity, I'd be interested in any of these stories you can tell me.' Pointedly, he pushed his notebook away from him. 'Purely off the record.'

The guard near the door smiled grimly. 'There have been a lot of things happen here that nobody has satisfactorily explained. Like the time a couple of years back just after Jack Duffy was executed. Everybody thought they'd seen and heard the last of him. He was lying cold on a slab in the prison morgue when the telephone in the office started to ring. Johnson from C-Block answered it. According to him, a voice that he swore was Duffy's, said that he was coming back and that he was going to get us all. After that the phone would ring at all hours of the day. Two in the morning, midday, late at night when normally there were no calls coming through. Whenever anyone went to lift the receiver there was nobody there at the other end although several of the prison staff swore that they heard breathing and a low voice muttering. Then the line would go dead.'

'Prank calls, perhaps,' suggested the Governor. He had his hands clasped on the desk in front of him, his fingers closely intertwined. There was a tight look on his face.

'That's what I reckon it was,' agreed Anderson quietly. 'But you couldn't tell the rest of the men that. Oh no, they were convinced that it *was* Duffy on the other end of the phone.'

'Anything special about Duffy you can tell me?' Chesterfield asked.

'Well, I don't know if this is anything to go by but he was one of the murderers who died without confessing to his guilt. Even to the end, he maintained his innocence.' Harris looked across at Chesterfield quickly. There was an unspoken question in his eyes. 'They say they always come back to haunt the place on a night like this,' he said suddenly, moistening his dry lips.

'*They?*' Chesterfield asked.

The Governor shook his head as though trying to put

something horrible out of his mind. 'You wouldn't understand,' he said finally, compressing his lips into a thin, tight line. His eyes seemed suddenly round and unnaturally bright in his head. 'You'd have to have been here for the best part of twenty-five years before you really absorbed some of the full horror of it. Many times, I've wished that I could walk from this entire job and all that it entails.'

'If it's getting to you like this, maybe you ought to get away from this place as soon as you can. There's no denying the fact that the atmosphere around here is unhealthy. Why, in the short time I've been here, I've come to the conclusion that something just isn't right. There's something here that, given time, could eat into a man until it changed him completely.'

'I can't leave this place now. This is my whole life. Twenty-five years is a long time.' Harris smiled weakly. 'Another four years and I'll be the longest serving governor of this facility. Obediah Kemp, my predecessor, was in charge for twenty-eight years. Not necessarily a man to emulate in other ways though – one mean, cold-hearted son of a bitch, who systematically abused his position. He had a bullwhip he liked to use. He'd drag prisoners to the yard and flog them for the slightest misdemeanour.'

Anderson chipped in: 'A ruthless bastard, from all that I've heard. They say he flung more than one man in a grave too early.'

Harris nodded. 'There's no denying a place like this needs a strong hand to keep inmates in line but he took it to extremes. It's wrong for a man to derive pleasure from the executions but I'm not kidding you he did just that. They were still hanging them back when he took over but Christ did he see to it that things were done to instil the most amount of fear in the prisoners. On more than one occasion I'm sure he deliberately shortened the rope so that it wouldn't break the neck, leaving the poor bastard to dangle till he asphyxiated. He was ecstatic when they introduced the chair. To him it was just a new toy. I was just a guard back then but I can still see that gleeful look on his face, the sparks reflected in his eyes as he watched.'

'Sounds like a nice guy,' said Chesterfield. 'What happened to him?'

'Well that's a story in itself. One day the prisoners just snapped, started a riot in the yard. We were trying to claw back control when Kemp strode in, all puffed up with confidence. 'You leave this to me, boys,' he said to us. About two minutes later the inmates had overpowered him. Beat him almost to a pulp, but they stopped short of killing him there. They had other ideas. Us guards were outnumbered and the inmates obviously had a plan. A group of them cornered us into the main building and locked the door. By the time we broke out, we found Kemp swinging from his own bullwhip in the execution chamber, but that's not all. We could see they'd put him in 'Old Sparky' and half-fried him first.' Harris took a deep drag on the diminishing cigar. 'He was smoking, his clothes blackened and frazzled. One of his eyes had popped out.'

'*Jesus!*' Chesterfield exclaimed. 'They really executed him? How is it that I've not heard about this before?'

'Do you really think the authorities would let the story out? After the lynching, the inmates calmed down enough to let us get them back to their cells and we called for reinforcements. The high-ups talked for a long time and eventually we were told that Governor Kemp must have suffered a heart attack while on duty. There was no family to send the body to so they were able to hush it up.' Harris looked piercingly at Chesterfield. 'You realise, I hope, that this is strictly confidential.'

'God, yes. Believe me, it's a story I'll try to forget!'

The three sat in silent contemplation for a few moments.

Harris took out another cigar, his dark eyes moving from one point of the room to another, never still, as though he was expecting to see some dark and terrible shadow leap up out of the dimness and pounce upon him before he was aware of its presence.

'I can't help but notice the way you keep looking around the room. You're afraid of something, aren't you?' said Chesterfield.

Harris' face was shadowed as he glanced up. His voice was unnaturally sharp and thin as he said tautly: 'I don't quite understand you.'

The reporter leaned forward. There was a faint look of triumph on his face. 'Now I know that you're scared,' he said slowly. 'I may not be a psychiatrist, but I do know that whenever anybody speaks like that something's got them spooked.'

The Governor looked at him for a long moment with no expression on his broad, unshaven face whatsoever. Then he shrugged. 'So I'm scared. Maybe it's this waiting. Maybe I've seen something that I haven't been able to explain, even to myself.' He drew in a deep breath through his open mouth. 'I'd defy anybody to do what I do and not be affected in some way, knowing that, at the end of the day, you're sending men to their deaths. Obviously, I don't make the state laws but I'm still the one that carries out the final authorisation.' He looked at his watch, counting the seconds. He raised a finger. 'Any time soon.'

There was a brief, uneasy silence, then the yells and howls of the inmates began again. Harsh, almost animal-like screams echoed along the corridors and the loud voices of the patrolling guards could be heard futilely shouting at them to keep quiet.

The next few hours passed slowly, dragging themselves into a dark eternity. The dawn brightened early and gradually, the sounds of the prisoners diminishing in volume, until there was only the occasional high-pitched scream of a man twisting and dreaming in his sleep.

The clock outside chimed the hours with a deadening monotony. The prison chaplain came and said that the condemned man was ready.

It was five minutes to seven.

Chesterfield stood up and felt a strange fluttering in his chest and a feeling akin to panic. He steeled himself deliberately and walked with the others into the small viewing room, the chamber in which the electric chair resided screened by a pale blue curtain.

He took his seat, remembering the tale of Governor Kemp and thinking somewhat macabrely that there were probably still nutcases out there who would pay to witness the forthcoming spectacle.

Ten minutes later, it was all over. He felt a little sick in the pit of his stomach at what he had just witnessed. But he had a story to write and due to his family connections he had been granted access to something many would never see.

Brett Maurice Chesterfield, you have been found guilty of first degree murder and by the power of this court you shall be taken from here to a place of lawful execution. May the Lord have mercy on your soul.'

There was a vague, half-forgotten memory stirring in the back of his mind of events that had taken place almost twenty years ago. They came rushing back, although he couldn't exactly re-member their exact beginnings.

The tiny cell was small and lit by a single bulb set close against the ceiling so that it cast a lot of shadows around the walls. A uni-formed man sat at the table on the far side of the room on death-watch duty, watching him closely, never taking his eyes off him for a single moment. It was well known that condemned men, unable to cope with the dreadful waiting, sometimes resorted to suicide.

Chesterfield lay quite still on the metal cot, staring at the ceil-ing, trying to remember. It was odd how that little thought kept running away into the background of his mind whenever he wanted to bring it out and examine it, see what it was.

Somebody was shouting a long way off and the sound seemed

strangely muffled after it had filtered through the stone walls into his cell. He tried to make out the words, concentrating his mind on them, but finding it impossible to do so, he gave up with a slightly irritated shake of his head.

He hesitated and looked at the man watching him, studying his face to see what he could find there. There was a deep vacuum and a silence inside his mind now and he couldn't think properly because of it. His body seemed to tense on the cot and almost of their own volition, his hands were clenching and unclenching spasmodically by his side. With an effort, he forced himself to relax.

Disconnected thoughts ran through his mind. He felt cold and alone. He dimly remembered being in this place once before; not in the condemned cell, of course, but in an office on the ground floor, talking to the Governor.

He had been just a cub reporter then on his first big murder case. He almost laughed inwardly as he realised just how he had reacted that day. Seeing that man die, it had almost turned him away from journalism altogether. But he had gone on and had gradually made a name for himself in the newspaper world.

Then there was a part of his life which he couldn't remember very clearly. It was as if his brain had put up a defensive mental block and shut the memory off from him. He had a recollection of finding the blood soaked body of his wife, and of their flat being suddenly filled with uniformed cops. The details were a little vague and they didn't seem to fit together to form a coherent story.

'Sure you wouldn't like to play a game of cards, Chesterfield?' asked the guard in a kindly voice.

'No, I'm fine here,' he said quietly.

'It'll be best if you do something to take your mind off it. There may still be a reprieve you know. Best not to give up hope entirely.'

Chesterfield sat up. 'Tell me honestly,' he said, 'do you really think there'll be a reprieve for me? My innocence didn't cut any ice back in the courtroom so why should it now?'

The other's gaze fell and he said lamely: 'There's always the chance. I've seen it happen before. Even at the eleventh hour.'

'Sure,' Chesterfield said sarcastically. 'But only in books or in the films, not in real life.'

'Better come and have a game of cards,' said the other man genially. He took off his cap and scratched the top of his head. 'No sense in just sitting there moping.'

'For God's sake, leave me alone.'

'Okay, okay, relax.'

With an effort, Chesterfield took a grip on himself. He was acting like a coward. But somehow, he couldn't rid himself of the rising tide of black fear that threatened to overwhelm him completely. He ran the back of his hand over his forehead. There was the chill dampness of sweat on his skin and his fingers were beginning to shake uncontrollably. Desperately, he clamped his teeth tightly together in his head and forced himself to breathe slowly. He had to think clearly and steady himself, he thought fiercely, otherwise he would surely go mad with the knowledge of what was to come, of what lay in front of him.

They had taken his watch away from him when he had first come to this place and he had no idea of the time. Mentally he estimated it as somewhere near three in the morning. His brain was humming and his hands jerked spasmodically, his fingers flexing and twitching.

The minutes ticked by slowly and as each fled, his fear and terror began to grow until they could only be contained with an effort.

He wanted to shout out loud. *'I didn't do it. They can't kill me just for that.'* But the words refused to come, sticking in his throat, so that he almost choked as he lay there. Lying back, he closed his eyes. Maybe, he thought wearily, if I don't look for a long time, I'll find that it's all just a dream and nothing more, and when I do open my eyes, I'll be just coming awake in my own room and all of this will be forgotten.

He lay with his eyes closed for several minutes, and then opened them slowly, one at a time. *Had he been dreaming?* He held up his hands and saw the grey tunic which covered his arms and the low ceiling over his head and the screams of the other prisoners shrieking in his ears.

Oh God, he thought wildly, what do *they* have to scream about? *They'll* still be there in their cells tomorrow morning by the time the sun rises.

It'll be me that they'll come for and—

Something seemed to snap inside his brain. A sudden, numbing blackness swept over him and he fell backwards on to his cot. When he came round again, he saw the warder bending over him and he had the vague idea that a lot of time had passed.

'You all right, Chesterfield?' the guard asked in a low voice.

With an effort, Chesterfield moved his head, then sat up. There was a bad taste in his mouth and he felt terrible. It took a long moment for everything to penetrate again. And then he wished that the blackness had gone on forever and he had never regained consciousness.

'Just try to relax,' said the guard. 'Would you like to see the chaplain now? He's been waiting to see you for almost half an hour.'

'What good would that do?' Chesterfield muttered bitterly. 'I wouldn't like anybody to come in and see me like this.'

'That's all right. He doesn't mind. He's done this thing plenty of times before now. He's used to it.'

Chesterfield nodded his head weakly. 'All right. I'll see him,' he said feebly.

The door opened and there was somebody else inside the

125

room. He turned his head slowly and saw the tall, thin-faced man looking down at him. Then he gazed past the other and for the briefest moment, he had the impression that there was someone else, standing near the door.

Wildly, he pushed himself up on to his elbows, blinked his eyes several times, then opened them again. When he could see properly once more, there was no one there but the chaplain and the warder watching him curiously.

'Is anything the matter?' asked the chaplain concernedly.

'No, apart from the obvious,' Chesterfield said roughly to hide his discomfiture.

'It was almost as if you'd seen a ghost,' said the warder. 'God, I never want to see that expression on a man's face again as long as I live. It was unearthly.'

'I'm all right,' Chesterfield said harshly. 'Now if you've anything you want to say, say it, then go away and leave me alone.'

'I'm afraid you won't gain anything like this,' said the chaplain a little sadly. 'A reprieve may come through at any time, of course, but I think you ought to be prepared, just in case the worst happens.'

'Prepared for what?' asked Chesterfield sharply. He glared across at the chaplain. Worthless hypocrite, he thought savagely, his anger inspired more by fear than anything else. What did he know of life beyond the grave, or even if there was one? For all he knew, it was just one long blackness that went on and on forever – and yet they persisted in trying to instil fear into everyone by the threat of a life to come. He felt like laughing harshly in the other's face, then thought better of it. 'If you're hoping to convert me or make me repent for my sins,' he said hoarsely, 'I'm afraid that you're wasting your time. I don't believe in any life hereafter. Once you die, that's the end of it all. There's nothing left but an eternal blackness.'

'There's still your immortal soul to be taken into account,' said the chaplain softly.

'*My soul?* Don't make me laugh,' snorted Chesterfield. 'I hate to think how often I've sat listening to the likes of you, talking about things you know nothing about. *A life hereafter?* You've got no proof of that. They say I killed my wife and now they're determined to kill me. They tell me that's the law. Well, let them administer their lethal injection in the morning, but I don't believe in your Heaven and because of that, I guess I'm a little luckier than most, because you see, I don't believe in Hell or the Devil either.'

'I think you'll find that you're making a grave mistake in this belief, or non-belief, of yours,' said the chaplain soberly. 'I can only tell you what *I* believe and it seems to me that if you don't believe in anything after death, then it must be a terrible thing to have to face. Whereas I think you'd derive a great deal of spiritual comfort if you had some kind of Afterlife to believe in.'

'I believe only in what I can see or hear or touch,' declared Chesterfield stubbornly. 'You'll never convert me.'

After a little while, the chaplain went away, leaving word that if ever the other wished to see him again before the execution, he would be within call.

For a long time after that, Chesterfield lay on his bunk with the light shining directly into his eyes. There seemed to be vague, ill-defined shadows flitting around at the edge of his vision, but whenever he turned his head to look directly at them, they danced away tantalisingly into the darker corners of the room where he couldn't see them properly.

Little shivers of apprehensive fear kept running through his body and no matter how hard he tried to shake them off they still persisted. He could feel time slipping remorselessly by and the knowledge of what was to happen in a few short hours almost drove him insane.

There was movement in the rest of the prison around him. He could sense it rather than actually hear it. The prisoners seemed unusually quiet now. The shouting and banging had ceased and they were now silent, waiting, knowing that what was to happen would not be long delayed.

Little disconnected bits of memory kept coming back of that time, so many years earlier, when he had visited this place. Another man had sat in the same spot where he was sitting now, waiting to die. He had wondered then what it would be like to sit in the condemned cell, knowing that one's life was ticking away very quickly with the night.

Now he knew in no uncertain manner and the thought threatened to drive him insane. He leapt up from his cot, shouting at the top of his voice. To his twisted vision, it seemed that the shadows in the background seemed to grow darker and more intense, to reach out and crowd around him.

Chesterfield turned his head from side to side, several times, trying to see them clearly, to get them into focus. His eyes felt wide and staring in his head and there was a throbbing pain at the back of his temples which seemed to be growing steadily worse with every succeeding second. 'Those shadows,' he said, babbling loudly. 'They're coming at me from all sides. Why can't you keep them away?'

'*Shadows?*' The guard looked puzzled. He came closer towards him and stared worriedly into his face. 'There's nothing here to be scared of. You're just imaging things.'

Chesterfield stood very still and listened to every little sound the room made, every nerve and fibre of his being stretched almost to breaking point. The tension and the horror of what was to come were starting to grow within again. He was afraid to look at the shadowed corners of the room. But with a conscious physical and mental effort, he forced himself to do so. He sucked in his breath, in a great, heaving gasp as the shadows thickened as though a flame had been turned low.

*

When they came for him at five minutes to seven, he was quiet, white-faced, seeming to hold himself in with a tremendous effort. The prison was now deathly silent as he walked between two guards along the short passage.

In spite of the presence of the men around him, he felt terribly alone, more isolated than at any other time in his life. The fear was there, deep down inside, but now, for some strange reason, it seemed to be overlaid with something else which he couldn't quite understand. It was as though this was happening to some other man. Almost as if his mind had wrenched itself out of his body, standing aloof from everything else, looking down and watching himself walking slowly forward to his own death.

It was a strange and terrifying experience.

Then he was in a room and he could see very little. In the background, he could hear the calm, unhurried voice of the chaplain speaking gently; quiet phrases that he didn't understand.

He was scarcely aware of what happened next. For a moment he had the impression that someone was shouting insanely at the top of their voice. It was not until several seconds later that he realised it was his own voice he was hearing.

There was a brief moment of violence. He was vaguely aware of strong arms holding him, strapping him down to a bed. Something pricked his arm and an intravenous tube was fitted. Light faded from his mind and then there was nothing for an instant. It was still quite dark when he opened his eyes again and looked about him.

There was no sign of the chaplain or the men who had been there with him, but there was someone else there, standing in the dimness, watching him.

The man's face was twisted, the lips drawn back in a bestial snarl. The fingers were clawed and flexed as though reaching for him and his sole eye blazed.

A sudden flash of memory came to him and Chesterfield knew

who this was, or had been –

Obediah Kemp!

Slowly, the truth was beginning to penetrate into his numbed brain as he looked at the man in front of him. His features were terrible to see.

'I've got you now boy,' drawled the spectre. 'You ain't gonna escape. There's nowhere to run to. You're condemned to stay here forever,' he said, baring his teeth and drawing out his bullwhip. 'Now it's time I gave you a whippin'.' Sparks and small electric-blue flashes crackled down his smouldering form.

Chesterfield screamed, only vaguely aware of the other pitiful shadows – those who, like him, had died at the John Royce Penitentiary.

Kemp raised his hand, the whip ready to crack down but Chesterfield felt something pulling at him, dragging him away from the sadistic spectre.

He heard a voice, distantly calling his name.

'Chesterfield, come on, wake up!'

More impressions came to him; of light and the feeling of people around him.

In the execution chamber, the doctor was working fast. Luckily they had not administered the final, fatal dose of potassium chloride before the message had come through. Chesterfield's sentence had been overturned at the last moment as a death-bed confession by a known criminal had thrown doubt on the conviction.

'They shouldn't leave it so bloody late,' the doctor cursed. Thankfully he could see Chesterfield's vital signs reviving. He had gone further down the path to oblivion than would be expected having only received the first injection, but the doctor had often wondered if the condemned men actually died of shock or fear at confronting their own demise.

Chesterfield weakly moved his head and opened his eyes.

'Thank God! Lie still. You're going to be alright.'

John Webb, the current Governor, cleared his throat, 'They've given you a stay of execution and you might even get off completely. I'm truly sorry that this has happened. If there's anything I can do for you...'

Relief bubbled up inside Chesterfield as the horror of his near death experience drained away. He could still smell the scorched skin of Obediah Kemp and the reality of what he had seen was something he would never doubt, however long he lived. Some of his strength was returning and he slowly raised his hand to beckon the Governor closer.

Webb stepped over quickly and bent forward.

Chesterfield gripped the Governor's arm more strongly than the startled man could have expected. 'There is something you can do for me,' he said hoarsely. 'Arrange a transfer for me to somewhere else, anywhere else. Then, for Christ's sake, get this bloody place exorcised!'

THE LAST NIGHT OF OCTOBER

When the streets ran red with blood.

THE SUN WAS fast disappearing behind the hills and a cold wind sent the dry leaves hurrying over the road as Edward Haigh changed gears and allowed his battered car to proceed down the steep slope almost under its own momentum. According to his map, nestled somewhere in the gathering gloom below him, lay the village of Kirkwick, an isolated settlement of less than a hundred inhabitants. This part of Northern England, somewhere close to the Cumbrian-Northumberland border, consisted for the main of huge tracts of desolate, undulating countryside; shadow-filled glens, deeply forested valleys and mile after mile of drystone wall, with a few scattered farms lying tucked away behind the tall hedgerows.

Tonight it was All Hallows' Eve. Even the name had a distinctly frightening ring about it. He turned it over and over in his mind as he drove along the narrow, winding road through the darkening countryside. This was the night when, in the old days, every door had been shut against the evil spirits; when jack-o'-lanterns and garlic had been placed on lintels to keep away the dead and the creatures of the night; when it was believed demons rode the night wind, seeking souls.

As an expert on rural folklore, Haigh knew that witchcraft and fouler occult practices had once been rife in these parts. He had done his research, discovering that it was here, in this very village, that the last witch in England had supposedly been burned at the stake. There was a stone in the village square which commemorated this. The sole public house in Kirkwick was even named *The Burning Witch*.

Haigh gazed through the black, lengthening shadows which lay across the road. He seemed to have driven further than he had estimated from the map. Then, as he mounted a low rise and started down the other side, he saw in the distance the church spire rising high above the roofs of the houses clustered around it, as though they were seeking the protection of its proximity. Squinting, he noticed that the tip of the spire was still blazoned with scarlet as the last rays of the setting sun touched it with blood-red fingers.

Five minutes later, he drove into Kirkwick, passed *The Burning Witch* and stopped the wheezing engine of the car. It shuddered for a moment, then died completely. There were few people in the street and those that he saw seemed to be hurrying to get back home.

Getting out of the car, he slammed the door shut and looked about him. Why was everyone in such a rush? One could almost think they were afraid.

Shifting his gaze from the scurrying pedestrians, he scanned the street, noticing the sign of a small, rundown hotel.

He paused for only a moment, then pushed wide the door and strode purposefully into the lobby. There was no one inside, but just as he reached the desk, a door at the back opened and a fat, ugly man shuffled forward behind the counter, eyeing him curiously. Behind him, peering nervously, was an elderly woman, presumably the man's wife. Her skin was grey, the colour of her bedraggled hair.

'Stoddard's the name. What do you want?' said the hotel owner through a largely toothless mouth, emitting a foul waft of halitosis.

'I'd like a room,' said Haigh brusquely.

'None available.' With two fingers, Stoddard burst a lump

below his bottom lip.

'Is that so?' Haigh reached forward before the other could stop him and pulled the register towards him, turning it quickly and scanning down the page. 'Just as I thought. You don't have any guests here at all. I hardly expected any at this time of year, in this out of the way place.' He stared fixedly yet disdainfully at the man.

'Well, I... I guess I was mistaken. We do have two rooms available now that you draw my attention to it. However, you realise that we find it extremely difficult to engage decent staff here, in such a small village and, well, consequently, service is both bad and slow. Take my word for it, this isn't the kind of place you'd want to stay at. There's nothing for the likes of you here.' Stoddard shook his head, his bulldog-like jowls juddering. He dabbed at the bleeding sore on his chin and examined the discharge on his fingers. 'Of course, if you've a car, I'd recommend you drive on to Penrith or Carlisle. There you'll find excellent hotels.'

Haigh eyed the unfriendly pair coldly, his eyes narrowing. 'If it wasn't for the fact that it would be so ridiculous, I'd say that you're deliberately turning away custom.' He planted his palms on the desk. 'Do you always make a habit of this?' He smiled, the action no more than a curl of his lips.

'I'm afraid I don't quite understand.' There was something at the back of the man's eyes which might almost have been fear and his manner and voice showed signs of agitation. Haigh noticed the way in which his gaze continually flicked to the clock on the wall at the rear of the room, almost as if it were slowly ticking away the seconds and minutes of his life, and he was acutely aware of it.

'Now,' said Haigh tightly, beginning to lose his patience. 'I've driven along some of the worst roads I've ever known and this, as far as I know, is the only accommodation in Kirkwick, so I'm afraid there's nowhere else I can go. You've spare rooms, you admitted that yourself and I'm willing to pay any reasonable sum for somewhere to spend the night.'

'It isn't that. Any other time we would be delighted to have you here. We get so few strangers in these parts. But, tonight – well, things are a little different. You understand?'

'I'm afraid that I understand nothing of the kind,' remarked Haigh angrily. He went on: 'Either you tell me exactly why I shouldn't stay here tonight, or give me a room.'

Stoddard sighed and shrugged his weighty shoulders resignedly. 'Very well. If that's what you wish. But don't say I didn't warn you. We don't do food so if you're after something to eat you'll have to go to The Burning Witch just along the road. They stop serving at eight so you've plenty of time.'

Haigh signed the register with a flourish, then took the key which the other reluctantly handed to him.

'Your room is the first on the left along the corridor at the top of the stairs.'

The room, Haigh discovered, was as small as he had expected, but well furnished, and the bed was soft and looked comfortable. Not that he intended to sleep.

After depositing his overnight bag, he left the hotel. Twilight was now giving way to full blown darkness. He strode the short distance to the public house, pausing for a moment to examine the curious sign which depicted an unfortunate woman tied to a stake, flames licking at her lower half. Even though the street lighting was poor, he could see that the manner in which it had been done was quite impressive. There was a certain dynamic quality to it which fascinated him. The best part of a minute elapsed before he tore his eyes from it and went to the door.

His entrance went largely unnoticed by the dozen or so locals.

If there should be anything here which might prove interesting to him, perhaps he could get one of these villagers to talk. They might be reticent about talking to a stranger, of course, but he had met their kind before on many occasions, and he knew that he would be able to handle them.

The meal which the landlord provided a quarter of an hour later proved to be little more than adequate. It was while he was eating that one of the locals got up from his seat in the corner of the room and came over, standing beside the table, looking down at him curiously, a glass of whisky in his hand. He was a chubby, bald-headed individual, who, from the visible dog collar, was clearly the village priest. From the way he swayed it was obvious that he had been drinking for some time.

'You're a stranger here,' he slurred.

Haigh nodded. 'Your observation is correct. Although I've been to Kirkwick before.'

'Then you should've known better than to come here a second time.' Unsteadily, the priest sat down.

'I've come here looking for something, and I don't intend to allow you or anyone else in this village to put me off.'

The other drank deeply from his whisky, then set the glass down and stared at it for a long moment. 'You've come here to find out something about the witch, I suppose.' He seemed to have sobered up slightly.

Haigh smiled a little and felt a slight tremor of excitement pass through him. He hadn't expected the other to talk so frankly. Perhaps he might find something here in this little, out-of-the-way village after all – something to make up for all of the disappointments he had experienced in the past.

'You're a witch-hunter, yes?' queried the priest after a brief pause.

Haigh looked him dead in the eyes. 'Does that surprise you?'

'Why, no. I suppose you know what you're looking for?'

'Perhaps,' Haigh admitted cautiously. 'Naturally I'd heard about her when I came through here some years back. I know that there's a stone in the square commemorating where she was burned at the stake.'

'That's right. Whenever we get anyone here they always ask about her and almost invariably they go away satisfied and suitably horrified by the story.' The priest paused, took up his drink again and peered at Haigh over the brim of his glass. 'Well I'm sorry to disappoint you but there's nothing that should concern you behind the story. Most of it's just fabricated nonsense – a gruesome little tale passed from father to son, which, over the years, has become... mythologised.'

Haigh drained his glass, pushed his empty plate away into the middle of the table. 'So there never was any truth in the tale after all? Is that what you're saying?' Deep down inside, he felt the sinking sensation of defeat which he had known many times before. So it had been nothing more than idle gossip which had been spun by these villagers into a semi-legend, obviously for their own avaricious purposes when they had realised that something like this, some half-forgotten mystery, could help to put their otherwise insignificant village on the map, and bring in interested tourists during the summer months.

'Oh, there was an old hag burned here several hundred years ago, there's no doubt about that. But she was no witch, believe me. In those days, as you probably know, any old woman who lived alone came to be regarded as a witch sooner or later. She only needed to make one enemy in the village and she would be denounced, and witnesses would swear to the vilest things to get her tried. That's what happened then. She insulted the village baker who brought an accusation of witchcraft against her. According to the reports of that time, which I have read, she made no effort to defend herself against the charges made. Perhaps she'd been drugged before the trial had begun – that sometimes happened – and after she was found guilty of being in league with the Devil, she was burned in the square.'

'But you're quite sure that she was no witch?' Haigh put the question directly to the other.

'Quite certain. She was nothing more than a poor old woman accused of witchcraft on the flimsiest of evidence.'

'I see, so it seems I've come all this way for nothing.'

'Well, maybe not for nothing, you see —'

At that moment the landlord came over with a second bottle of wine and placed it beside Haigh. 'I trust Father Wilfred isn't annoying you,' he said quickly. There was a strange look on his face. 'But sometimes, he talks too much. His mind is befuddled and the more he drinks, the more he imagines he tells the truth.'

'He was telling me that the witch who was burned here was merely an innocent old woman.'

For an instant, a look of relief flashed over the landlord's features, as he nodded swiftly: 'That much is true. All this talk of witches and witchcraft is bad for us all. They used to say that it would bring in tourists, people with money to spend, and that Kirkwick would become rich in a very short time. A bit like that 'Last Drop' attraction they've got down Pendle way. But it never did and the sooner we all forget about these things, the better for everyone concerned.'

'Ah, but you're forgetting about Amelia,' exclaimed the priest, sitting up straight in his chair. 'And if our friend here is to remain in the village tonight, then he must be told.'

'Be quiet, you old fool,' snapped the landlord hurriedly. 'I'm sure he isn't interested in your stupid tales and rumours.' He turned to Haigh. 'I apologise. Our village priest's old and now lives too much in the past and at times, his mind...' He left the remainder of his sentence unsaid, but the implications behind it were perfectly clear.

'Old am I? Simple in the head, is it?' With an effort, the other was on his feet, scraping back his chair. 'Perhaps it's because you're all so afraid of what's going to happen tonight. Yes —' He looked down swiftly at Haigh, eyes flashing fiercely. 'Tonight is All Hallows' Eve. The pagan festival of Samhain.'

'I know that,' began Haigh. 'But I don't understand, you said that—'

'There's nothing whatever to understand,' interrupted the landlord quickly, a trifle too quickly. 'These are nothing more than the ravings of a madman.'

'Nevertheless. I'd like to hear them,' said Haigh slowly.

The landlord threw the clergyman a warning glance, then turned abruptly on his heel and walked back to the bar.

The priest watched him go with a faint sneer on his face. 'Fool!' he said harshly, spitting the word out. 'You must forgive him, but like all the others in the village tonight, he's afraid.'

'Of what?'

'Of Amelia; the horror in the church.' If the other had leaned forward and said the words melodramatically, Haigh might not have believed him; but the casual, simple manner made it more credible. 'Tonight is the one night a year she gets out.'

'Sounds intriguing.' Haigh looked at him closely, then poured himself another glass of wine. 'Would you care to tell me about it?'

There was a momentary hesitation on the priest's part. Then he nodded. 'You'll no doubt find out most of it for yourself very soon. But perhaps if you were to know something about it, before anything happens, it may help you to understand. Amelia Cranswell lived in Croglin, a village not far from here. Legend has it that in 1685 she was attacked by a vampire whilst she lay in her bed. Her screams awakened her brothers who chased it from the grange, out towards a disused crypt in the nearby graveyard. Allegedly, once they had cornered the fiend, they shot it, drove a stake through its heart, chopped off its head and burned the body.'

'And what became of the woman, Amelia?'

'She...'

'She became one of the undead?' Haigh's eyes were suddenly drawn to a nearby window as a figure carrying a flaming torch passed by. From the shadowy movement and the sounds it appeared that something was going on outside.

The priest noticed the other's curious look. 'That'll be them getting ready for the street party. The villagers have one every All Hallows' Eve even though, every year, I warn them to stay indoors. But they don't listen. It's as though they forget the annual horror that befalls Kirkwick.'

'You're beginning to interest me,' said Haigh quietly. 'This Amelia. I take it she came here?'

'Yes. Originally it was claimed that she was taken to Switzerland in order to recover from the shock of her ordeal but her brothers, once they discovered she was cursed with vampirism, were unable to bring themselves to destroy her. She was brought here, to the church instead, when they realised nothing could be done to save her. For nigh on three hundred years she's been kept in the vaults below the church. Neither myself, nor any of my predecessors or anyone else for that matter has been able to destroy her. All of the conventional methods; the stake through the heart, beheading, burning, mouth-filled with garlic cloves, dousing in holy water, have proved ineffectual. Which leads me to doubt that the original vampire was destroyed by her brothers.'

'Why do you let her out?'

'What makes you think I let her out? I don't let her out,' Father Wilfred said, shaking his head with indignation. 'Do you think I would willingly let such a creature loose? It's just that on this night, when the forces of darkness are at their strongest, she re-awakens and there's nothing that I, or anyone else, can do to prevent it. That's why I come here. In order to get away from the church. I get drunk and stay here till sunrise. It's safer that way. I've been doing this for the past thirty-five years. It's a pity that none of the villagers heed my warning. But as I said, it's as though they've fallen under some kind of a spell—a curse, perhaps—for in the morning, you can be sure that she'll have claimed several victims. Yes, they'll be mourned but within a week or two everyone will have forgotten what happened.'

All of the villagers, except the priest, seemed to be there in the chill darkness; torch-bearing figures, their faces covered by grotesque masks and wearing hideous costumes. A large float moved slowly and ponderously along the narrow, winding, cobbled streets, pulled by a pair of large, strong horses. On the float, which had been draped with growths of black ivy, was a witch on a broomstick, soaring high against a painted, circular moon. The face of the witch was not that of a wizened crone as Haigh had expected, but that of a beautiful young girl. However her features had been subtly distorted so as to make a horrible and crazy caricature of real beauty. A dozen young children, six on either side, had been done up to resemble mediaeval plague victims, their grey-green faces covered with leaking boils and filthy bandages. There was an unsettling eeriness to the scene which was compounded by the relative silence which accompanied its passing. None of the children laughed or spoke, almost as though they really were victims dying from some horrible condition. The fact that those on the float numbered thirteen – the unholy number for the witch's coven – did not go unnoticed by Haigh.

Carrying lanterns and flaming torches in their hands, holding them aloft, the villagers crowded around the slowly-moving float as it paraded the whole length of the village street. The young and the old followed closely behind the ghoulish procession, their uncanny, inhumanly-masked faces glowing weirdly in the flickering light.

'Don't you think they're rather like children, playing a strange game that they don't really understand?'

Haigh whirled at the croaky voice, peering into the darkness. He had not heard anyone approach but told himself that the creaking wheels of the float would have drowned out the sound of footsteps. The old hunchbacked man was standing a few feet away, in a doorway, peering up at him through rheumy eyes like an aged mole. Like himself, he did not wear a mask.

The old man shrugged his shoulders disdainfully. 'They're all fools! What do they hope to gain by all this? Is it because they're afraid of what will happen and they hope that this display will ward off the evil hour?'

'Perhaps,' Haigh answered. 'And who are you?'

'I'm Victor Crowmarsh, the sexton. You're a stranger here, aren't you? I could be wrong but I get the impression that you're secretly longing for something to happen. Something other than this pathetic masquerade.'

Haigh nodded. 'For many years I've been examining reports of witchcraft, hauntings, and any other supernatural phenomena; but they have all turned out to be either elaborate hoaxes or there has been a quite natural explanation. I came here several years ago and first heard of the witch then. I thought that, perhaps tonight, I might see or hear something which I couldn't possibly explain. So far, I've heard only dark rumours and seen this.' He waved his hand in the direction of the procession.

'Perhaps this is all there is,' suggested the sexton with a sly laugh. While they had been speaking, the floats had drawn up, halting in the village square. From a makeshift stall, a pig-masked villager was handing out bottles of local ale and portions of pumpkin pie.

Haigh stared up, to where the church brooded over everything, dark and sombre against the night sky. There was a moon low down, and it was just possible to make out some of the details. 'I don't think so,' he said thickly 'After all that I've heard tonight, there has to be something in these old legends.'

Crowmarsh grinned. 'Then if you think that, take a look about you. Study the faces of these people — closely. What do you see?'

For a moment, Haigh stared at the sexton in surprise. There had been an odd intensity in his voice which seemed oddly out of place. Then he turned his head and glanced at a bearded man who stood a few feet away, watching the floats, his head turned away a little. The mask which the other wore looked incredibly lifelike, almost as if it had been painted on. The goat horns, sprouting from the forehead, pointed and curved, might almost have grown out of the bony ridge of his skull. The bearded man turned, the goat's lips drew back in a fiendish sneer, revealing twisted, brown-stained teeth. A baying neigh came from the open mouth. Now that the drink was flowing, everywhere he looked it was the same. Weird, inhuman creatures, dancing and cavorting around the floats, men and women with the heads of beasts.

'I think you'd better come with me.' Crowmarsh tugged at his sleeve. 'Away from all this madness. I'll take you to what you came here to find.'

Haigh found himself unable to answer. His mind reeled slightly, but was oddly clear. The hideously warped beings before his eyes melted back into normal, mask-wearing people. It had just been a phantasm; an illusion. A terrible laughter bubbled up from the darkness directly ahead of him and he realised that the old man had been leading him away from that demoniacal scene of horror in the street, up towards the church which towered broodingly over everything. 'Where are we going?' he asked.

'I thought you wanted to see everything,' Crowmarsh said softly. 'Well, I'm the only one who can show you that.'

Then, with almost startling abruptness, the huge black shadow of the bell in the church tower began to boom the hour. Nine deep, shuddering echoes that rattled eerily through the darkness. A mist came and went about the steeple, momentarily erasing its stark shape and the outjutting stone gargoyles that stared down with sightless eyes.

The wind was soft, whimpering a little bit, a lonely sound between the headstones that reared on either side. Every few minutes, it would mutter and grumble under the shadow branches of a gently-bending elm, right up to the vast stone shape of the church itself.

There was a sudden pressure in Haigh's chest. His arms were tingling. As he climbed the narrow, twisting stairway leading up to the top of the church, he glanced back over his shoulder and saw the flickering cluster of lanterns were still there, like a lot of corpse candles clustered around the village square. All was quiet and there was only the faint sound of their own feet on the path. Presently, they reached the summit. The moon had risen above the horizon now and flooded everything with a weird bilious glow. He paused and looked about him, then turned to face the sexton.

For a moment, the other regarded him in silence, a curiously malevolent look on his face.

Haigh slowly shook his head. Something dark and terrible seemed to be lurking out there, very close. The sense of excitement had not faded once they had left the village behind and climbed up into the still blackness and in a fearsome instant of deeper darkness and understanding, he remembered how the landlord back at the hotel had warned him. His legs were stiff, his arms remained at his side, fingers clawed, nails digging into the flesh of his palms. Some invisible force seemed to be clamping itself about him, holding him there, trying to root him to the spot.

The white face of the moon was blacked out for several seconds by the racing, scudding clouds. A black shadow-pattern lay across the quietude. The graves were no longer white stone faces that leered at them hungrily through the mist. Instead, they were dark blocks of granite and carved stone and silence; evil, menacing fingers of night that ringed them around. The influence on him eased gradually and he managed to shake it off.

'Around the back of the church is a door to which I have the key.'

'I see. And I take it there's something inside that you think I will find of interest?'

'Oh, without doubt.' Crowmarsh reached into a trouser pocket and removed a large rusty key. 'I'll admit that being up here on a night like this isn't for the faint-hearted, but believe me what you're about to see will make it all worthwhile.'

'And what exactly is that may I ask?' questioned Haigh tensely.

Crowmarsh turned. 'Ah, you'll see soon enough. I wouldn't want to give the surprise away, now would I?' He had led Haigh to a place where a flight of stone steps descended into darkness. From inside a coat pocket he removed a torch and switched it on, shining the beam down to where the stairs ended at an ancient-looking door. He then panned the torch over the near wall of the church, illuminating a large stained-glass window. 'If you look carefully enough,' he said, taking Haigh by an arm and steering him so that the other could be in a better position, 'you can see a very strange depiction of our Saviour. There! In that far left corner.'

Hands in pockets, Haigh stared up to where the other pointed.

It was at that moment that the heavy torch came crashing down on his head.

Haigh had been neither hurt nor surprised by the violence that had been directed towards him. He had been dragged down the stairs, had heard the door being unlocked and then he had been pushed inside. It hadn't been the most ceremonial of entrances but he knew that he would not have been able to enter the church of his own volition.

It was perfectly clear that the sexton had lined him up as a sacrificial offering to Amelia. No doubt it was all a necessary part in reawakening her – so that she could indulge in her once a year orgy of destruction. Although it was highly feasible that the festival of Samhain provided her with the unholy strength to permit emancipation, it was also possible that the villagers colluded in this, aware, perhaps, that this annual bloodfest at least satiated her and kept her from attacking at whim. They would rather feed her once a year than live in constant fear.

It was as black as midnight down here but to one such as he that posed no problem at all. Looking around him, Haigh could see that he was in a stretch of passage, its walls adorned in places with faded murals. He edged his way deeper into the bowels, the air becoming colder with each step.

Soon, he came to the yawning mouth of yet another flight of steps, pausing for a moment in order to look at the malign and deviant images which stared out at him from the crumbling brickwork all around.

Slowly and carefully, he began down the steps. Deeper and deeper he went, into the very foundations of the church. Had he still been in possession of his soul, Haigh would no doubt have felt the unholy chill which gusted throughout these nightmarish catacombs. Stepping into a large, vaulted chamber, he saw the many stone sarcophagi which lay to either side.

Striding down the central aisle of this dreary mausoleum, Haigh was strongly aware of the hatred which, like a dark flood, seemed to spew out in waves from some of the carved granite and black marble coffins, channelled by the deceased priests who were interred herein. Yet he knew they were impotent, unable to harm him or the one he was about to invoke. That she had not arisen was undoubtedly due to the fact that she hadn't sensed his presence. Had he been a hapless villager then there was little doubt that he would be dead by now.

In the hushed silence, he knelt before one particularly grimly-carved tomb. 'Amelia, my love. I have come to awaken you, to free you from this foul place,' he intoned. 'Even though your brothers staked me, beheaded me and reduced my body to ashes I vowed I would return to make you mine. It has taken me nigh on three hundred years to reform, during which time I have shared your torment. Together, we will wreak our vengeance on those who have kept you here.'

A dark bluish light began to appear in a beam around the sarcophagus, bathing the stone funerary container in an indigo glare. Shadows slowly coalesced into rigid, discernible shapes. Haigh watched as the glow began to shift and transform.

A young woman's spectral face blurred into view. She looked utterly terrified, identical almost to how she had looked three centuries ago when he had first set eyes on her, peering in through her latticed window. Slowly her expression changed to one of intense evil. Her eyes blazed with recognition and a hunger that made even his dead heart leap.

The next morning, Father Wilfred woke slowly, with a cold autumnal sunlight pouring in through the wide window, and an opaque pattern of frost-crystal on the pane. He reached out for his coat and shoes and dressed hurriedly. At the back of his mind was a tiny little thought, a sensing that something horrible was going to happen—or had happened. It had been a long night, one filled with screams and shouts that had stretched like a dark eternity—a nightmare in which he had imagined all sorts of horrors. He had heard the sounds of frantic hammering as though someone had been battering at the door to get in but he had been both too drunk and too frightened to answer their calls.

Then he remembered. Last night had been All Hallows' Eve. That evil, indestructible thing—that accursed vampiress from Croglin, the abomination from the church—would have been abroad. The memory still left remnants of fear and madness inside him. He called out, surprised not to find the landlord or any of his helpers. A savage, pounding headache beat remorselessly at his temples as he approached the door. Fear bubbled up inside his brain, frothing over, foul with the thoughts that came boiling to the surface. Panic was back, building up thickly in his throat. His hands clenched tightly, his palms suddenly hot and clammy.

A rivulet of blood seeped from beneath the door, congealing in an obscene puddle.

Grimacing, the priest stared down. Reluctantly, he reached out for the handle, twisting it in nerveless fingers before pulling the door towards him.

With a suddenness that made him jump, he found himself having to leap clear as a ravaged corpse which had been slumped against the door fell over the threshold. Despite the brutal degree of mutilation, he recognised Henry Jarvis, the school teacher. One of his arms had been torn out at the socket and his bloody face and torso bore deep lacerations; claw-marks. The hideous mask he had worn lay shredded beside him.

He felt sick. The sight, the scale and the savagery of the carnage brought his supper to his throat. Lurching to one side, he vomited, reaching out with a shaking hand to support himself. He felt his legs weaken and quiver beneath him, while his eyes were glued to the grisly remains that lay spread-eagled before him. Fear thickened until it paralysed his thoughts. He could feel his pulse racing. He had to get out—to leave this place of madness. To run, and run, and not stop running. In stumbling movements, he stepped over the body, leaving *The Burning Witch*.

The village of Kirkwick had become the sight of a massacre, its streets awash with blood.

In the village square, the dead—young and old alike—were strewn all over the place. A scattering of unsightly body parts lay near the overturned float. Even the horses hadn't been spared from this murderous rampage, their disembowelled corpses glistening wetly in the morning sunlight and sprawled upon the witch's memorial stone was the gory, headless remains of the sexton.

PALE LILAC

A stranger with a strange obsession had come to Harvest Wood...

IT WAS A WET Tuesday evening and Maggie's Bar was quiet, empty almost, with only a few regulars and old-timers inside. Some dull country and western track was playing on the jukebox and in the corner, near the bar, a black and white television was showing a late-night boxing match, the commentator failing to arouse any kind of passion amongst the handful of viewers inside.

Sheriff Rod Hooper was off-duty. Peering along the length of his pool cue, lining up his shot, he made a deft forward thrust, cursing as the white ball missed the remaining black.

'Looks like your luck's run out.' Maggie Brennan, the owner of the bar, screwed back and potted the eight-ball. 'Guess that'll be five bucks, sheriff.'

Hooper laughed. 'Ah well, maybe next time.' Returning his pool cue to the rack, he picked up his beer from a nearby table and took a swig. He delved into his pocket for the cash and handed it over.

'Do you want another game?'

'Just so as you can beat me again and show me up in front of all these...' Hooper looked about him, wondering how exactly, and more to the point, politely, he could describe the uninterested aged patrons, '...fine folk? Besides, I can't afford to play you any-more.' He turned to Maggie and smiled, liking what he saw.

Thirty-three years old, auburn haired, bright blue eyes and one hell of a figure. Admittedly, she wasn't the brightest of women but she was by far the prettiest in town. He himself was in his mid

151

-fifties with two divorces under his belt and a considerable belly above it.

'Suit yourself.' Maggie went behind the bar.

'Say, Maggie. You heard of anything recently? Anything I need to know about?' This was something Hooper asked her every time he came in. It had become a routine. Like nearly everyone he knew he had lived in Harvest Wood, the small town ten miles south of Crawford close to the Nebraska-Wyoming border, all of his life and he knew that all local gossip eventually filtered its way through to the bar. He found out about more things that were going on in here than he did on his police radio.

'I hear tell that Old Jed's dog died the other day. That damn mutt must've been nearly as old as he is.' Maggie began cleaning some of the glasses. 'Do you want another beer?'

'No, I'll just have this one and then that's me.'

'Suit yourself.' Maggie began stacking some of the glasses away. Suddenly she stopped and turned. 'Gee, I nearly forgot, but I don't suppose you've heard the news about Aubrey?'

'Aubrey? Aubrey Penton?'

'Yeah. Seems that he's managed to shift the old MacPherson place.'

Hooper raised his eyebrows in surprise. 'God, I didn't think anybody would ever buy that place. Certainly not after, well, you know.'

Not surprisingly, the MacPherson farmhouse had lain abandoned for close to fifteen years after its previous owner, Danny MacPherson, had murdered his entire family. His three sons he had killed with a chainsaw, his two daughters he had hacked to death with a wood-axe and his wife he had shot at point-blank range with a double-barrelled shotgun before dousing himself in petrol and setting himself alight. Even the family cat had not escaped his murderous rampage for it had been found hanging from a beam in one of the outlying barns close to its owner's cremated, smouldering remains.

'Well, it seems that someone has. Aubrey was in the other day and he said that the buyer was some English guy. Talked all sophisticated. I can't see him fitting in well around here. My guess is he'll be gone before the end of the year, maybe by the end of the month.'

'Did Aubrey say anything else? Like what this man does for a living? Does he have any family?' Hooper was curious. They didn't get many strangers in Harvest Wood. In fact, he couldn't remember who the last one had been. Sure, they got drifters from time to time, but those folk were transitory, seen one day and gone the next. They sure as hell didn't buy property, especially places like the MacPherson farmhouse with its bad reputation.

'According to Aubrey he's a retired scientist or something. I think he said he was into plants; flowers and things. As to family, I'm pretty sure he hasn't got any. I'd say that's probably for the best, considering where he's going to be living. That ain't no place to bring up children, now is it, sheriff?'

'You're right there.' Hooper finished his beer. 'Well, I guess I'd better be leaving. I might see about paying this English guy a visit in the morning. Introduce myself and try to make him feel welcome.'

'Be sure and find out what he's up to.'

'I'll do just that. If it's flowers he's into, I can't see him being any trouble. I might see if he's got any spare roses I can bring back for you.'

'My, that'd be sweet.' Maggie smiled. 'But what would Mrs. Hooper think?'

'She needn't know.'

'Come on sheriff, in a town as small as Harvest Wood news would soon get around.'

'Maybe you're right. Besides, as I keep telling myself, I'm too old for you.' Hooper fastened up his jacket, sucked in his stomach and put on his sheriff's hat. 'Well goodnight, Maggie.' He strode for the door, left the bar and went to his parked car.

It was still raining the next morning and it was also slightly foggy with a light mist lying over the gloomy-looking fields. It had rained heavily all night and the backwater road leading out to the MacPherson place was partially flooded, making the going hard for Hooper. Driving slowly, negotiating the worst of the deep puddles, he made a left turn, the dark farmhouse outbuildings — the half-collapsed barns, the abandoned silos and the tumble-down weather-vane tower—now becoming visible on the ridge ahead, silhouetted forebodingly against the slate-grey sky. Miles and miles of neglected wheat field stretched as far as the eye could see in almost every direction, the uniformity of the landscape broken only by the dark forest of Harvest Wood—after which the town was named—barely visible to the north.

A pall of dreariness hung over everything.

Thunder rumbled in the distance and from somewhere nearer at hand could be heard the sound of crows cawing.

Hooper brought the car to a stop. He got out and stretched, staring up at the buildings, the rain pattering off his hat. The last time he had been out this way had been some two years ago when a local boy had gone missing. He had led a group of volunteers in the search, finding nothing. The boy had never been found.

Everything was dark, shadowy, grey. The wind gusted all around him blowing the swirling mist into ghost-like formations.

On his right, twenty yards away, Hooper could see a ghastly-looking scarecrow made from stuffed sacking and the sight of it caused him to shudder. Here, there was something more than ordinary, earthly cold.

Something more deep and intense. It was like a dampness in his heart. He looked about him, warily, alert.

His mind was beginning to race inside his head and blood was pounding in his veins.

Why anyone would want to live out in this godforsaken place, almost five miles out of town, he had no idea. Getting back in the car, he threw a sideways glance at the scarecrow, ensuring that it had not moved or disappeared, satisfying himself that it was not sat in the backseat ready to grab him around the throat and throttle him with its twiggy hands. His heart rate quickened, fearing for one moment the sight of its torn, sack-like face with its button eyes and ripped mouth in his rear-view mirror.

Get a hold of yourself, sheriff, he told himself. This wasn't like him.

It was this place though. He was sure of it. There was something about the MacPherson farmhouse that just wasn't wholesome. Evil and murder had been committed here. It was a place of madness—at least it had been, and possibly still was. The events of fifteen years ago still clung to area, blanketing it like a funeral shroud. The sooner he introduced himself to Harvest Wood's newest resident and got back into town the better.

With that thought, he drove the remaining two hundred yards up to the farmhouse. It looked very much as he remembered it; tumbledown and partly ruined, its walls in desperate need of a coat of paint. Several of the windows were smashed and in the drive-way lay a large rusting farm vehicle of some description; all vicious, curved spikes and upturned plough shears.

In one of the barns over to his right, he could see a much more modern-looking car, no doubt belonging to the current owner. A shiver went through him. It was in that barn, fifteen years ago, that he had found the incinerated remains of Danny MacPherson.

He parked up and got out, slamming his car door, hoping that he'd made just the right amount of noise to attract attention. He bent down and tied his shoelace and was just about to head up to the front door when it opened.

In the doorway was a tall, spindly, white-haired individual

wearing dark sunglasses. There was the pallid look of a dead-fish's underbelly about him and his face was sunken, almost cadaverous. His narrow, pencil-thin lips were blue-black. He wore a full-length dark-brown leather apron that was covered in unsightly damp stains and he had similarly stained yellow rubber gloves on his hands. It was obvious that he suffered from albinism.

Hooper hadn't known what to expect but the sight that greeted him was certainly not it. He faltered slightly and gulped nervously. This man looked as though he had just stepped fresh from the County Morgue.

The stranger stood staring at him through his dark glasses.

Maybe he's blind, thought Hooper. He found his voice. 'Good day. My name's Rod Hooper. I'm the local sheriff for these here parts and on behalf of the inhabitants of Harvest Wood I'd like to welcome you to our little town.' He didn't extend his hand. The last thing he wanted was to shake hands with this slime-spattered individual, besides, if he was blind, he wouldn't notice.

'Why thank you, sheriff. I'm Sebastian Rutherford.'

Despite his appearance, the man's words were clipped and cultured, very English.

'I trust you're settling in alright, Mr. Rutherford?'

'Yes, yes. A few problems here and there but nothing that can't be dealt with.' The white-haired man removed his gloves and stuck them into the wide apron pockets. 'Please, I'm forgetting my manners. Would you care to come in for a cup of tea? Or perhaps a coffee?'

'Sure, I'd like that.' Hooper took off his hat and followed the other into the house. As he got closer he couldn't help but be struck by the repellent smell that came from his host. It was like rancid meat mixed with freshly chopped garlic. It bordered on the overpowering.

Surreptitiously, he wafted at the foul air with his hat. What had the man been doing, he wondered — skinning squid?

The interior of the house looked as though hardly any work had been done to it since Hooper had last been here. The wallpaper was peeling from the walls and huge damp patches spread throughout. The floor was largely uncarpeted and creaked audibly as they went down a dimly-lit passage before entering the lounge.

The furniture inside was crude and basic; stuffed and ripped armchairs, old tables and cabinets, out-dated ornaments on the walls and mantelpiece. He reckoned it had to be the original MacPherson stuff. He couldn't help but shiver, thinking it ghoulish that these personal effects were still here. Heavy curtains were drawn across the shuttered windows, the only light coming from a small lamp in the far corner.

'Do take a seat.' Rutherford removed his apron and carried it into another room. He walked woodenly yet without the stumbling carefulness of someone who was blind, leading Hooper to the conclusion that he probably could see. 'I take it you would like a cup of tea, sheriff?' he called.

'If it's no trouble, I'd rather have a coffee.'

'Very good. Just make yourself comfortable. I'll only be a few minutes.'

Hooper couldn't help but feel uneasy. Perhaps it was due to knowing what had happened here fifteen years ago or the overall sense of weirdness Rutherford exuded. He found himself staring around him, trying to establish just what kind of room he was in but it was so damned dark and shadowy. Admittedly, it was grey and overcast outside but surely a normal person would have opened the shutters and the curtains in order to bring in more light rather than keep them drawn and although he could see more lamps none of them were lit.

Rutherford returned with a cup of steaming coffee. 'Here's your drink.' He passed it to the sheriff and took a seat by an old dresser.

'Thanks.' Hooper took a sip, scalding his lips.

'Now then, would you care to tell me the purpose of your visit?' Divested of his apron and gloves, Rutherford now looked slightly more normal. His jacket was old-fashioned but stylish and that horrendous stench had lessened noticeably.

'I just thought I'd come out and introduce myself. You know, a bit of public relations.' Hooper rested his cup on a nearby table. 'I understand that you're a scientist and that your field of expertise, if you pardon the pun, is flowers, is that correct?'

Rutherford leapt from his chair in anger as though he had been tugged upright by invisible ropes. '*Flowers*!? Flowers! Don't take me for some lay botanist who doesn't know his Eumycota from his myxomycetes and oomycetes!' He was shaking all over as though someone had just passed a low electric current through him. 'I'll have nothing to do with flowers, thank you very much! What outrageous nonsense! Whoever told you that should be strung-up from the nearest telegraph pole.'

Hooper was taken aback by the man's extreme reaction and his bizarre, unwarranted behaviour. 'Steady on, I only —'

'*I'm a mycologist!* I study fungi—the alluring, mesmeric, fascinating, biologically diverse and adaptive world of fungi. Flowers!' Rutherford spat the last word as though it befouled his mouth. 'What perverse lie has fed mankind the belief that fungi are repulsive, slimy, undesirable things; bulbous organisms to be shunned and feared by the ignorant? What beauty does a rose possess that cannot be bettered by that of a common basidiomycota? Have you or they ever gazed upon the wonders of a microscopic mould, awestruck by the principles of decomposition, or taken delight in the discovery of a hitherto unidentified microcellular smut, enraptured by its delicate spore-releasing capabilities? Well, have you sheriff? Have you?'

The man was clearly unbalanced.

158

Hooper shook his head. 'No. I can't say that I have.' He straightened in his seat. 'Look, Mr. Rutherford, I apologise if I've caused you any offence. It's just that we're all a bit ignorant of things like that out here.'

'Apology accepted.' Rutherford sat down. He seemed to have regained some of his self-composure. He was no longer trembling.

The sheriff cast around for a topic that might calm the man down. 'So can you tell me what brings you out here? I mean, are you doing some kind of scientific research, writing a book, perhaps?'

'Well, seeing as you've asked, I may as well tell you. I am carrying out some rather fascinating experiments. I would tell you more, but alas I'm still at the very early phases. Indeed, I can't go ahead until I receive some laboratory equipment, which I'm hoping will arrive in the next day or two. Come to think of it, I will be needing a strong back to help me with some of the more manual tasks, so if by chance you know of anyone reliable in town who is willing to earn an honest wage, I would appreciate it.'

Hooper thought for a moment. 'There's Butch Langford. He's always on the lookout for a bit of work and he's pretty trustworthy. And I believe he used to work here as a farmhand here back in the days before—' He paused. 'Anyhow, if I see him I'll have a word, tell him that you're interested in taking on a hired hand.' There was something else that he wanted to ask but he was rather uncomfortable about asking it. In the end, he decided to just come right out with it. 'I understand that you bought this property from Aubrey Penton, the real estate agent in town. I don't suppose he mentioned to you anything about the history of this place, did he?'

'I take it you're referring to the murders? Yes, he did raise the subject.'

'And, you weren't put off?'

'No. Not at all. Why should I be? Those events, although indisputably tragic, happened a long time ago. Now, if you're trying to imply by the nature of your question that perhaps the house is haunted or something similar, tainted by that terrible incident, then I'm not interested. You see, I'm a man of science, not some ignorant-minded, superstitious fool. There are no such things as ghosts. Similarly, there is no such thing as the soul or spirit. Humans are but organic, biological constructs; a conglomeration of chemical elements given a rudimentary semblance of animation via electrical nerve impulses.'

Hooper was feeling more and more out of his depth. He was more used to dealing with drunken, foul-mouthed truckers; breaking up the frequent bar room brawls or apprehending teenage delinquents over acts of petty vandalism or other forms of criminality. This eccentric, toadstool-loving weirdo was something completely different. Something way beyond his expertise.

'So you see, sheriff, you needn't be concerned that I'll come running for help in the dead of night claiming that I'm being harangued by ghosts. Because they simply don't exist. Now, if there's anything else you'd like to ask I'd appreciate it if you were quick about it. I've got some fresh samples of the most peculiar saprobic myriostoma that I am currently cultivating in my make-shift laboratory downstairs and I'm sure they'll be missing me.'

'Missing you?' Hooper spilled some of his coffee. He wasn't sure whether he had heard right.

'Why yes. Almost certainly. I talk to them, you see. I found out long ago that communication stimulates and enhances growth. Don't look so surprised. Certain genera have been known to respond exceedingly positively to the voice of their cultivator. Although I doubt whether they derive actual nourishment from sound, it is evidently highly beneficial. My discoveries will open an entire new world regarding saprobic phenomena.'

'Right, I see.' Hooper slowly nodded his head. He didn't understand a word of what the other was on about nor did he believe much of it. It was sheer bloody nonsense as far as he was concerned. That man was off his rocker. 'Well, thanks for the coffee. I think it's time I was going.' He got to his feet. In this darkened room he was beginning to feel like a mushroom him-self—in the sense that for the past fifteen minutes or so he had been kept in the dark and fed on the proverbial.

Five days later the sun was shining and the skies were blue. Sher-iff Hooper was just leaving the police station when he saw Butch Langford crossing the street. Hailing him, he waited for him to approach.

Butch was tall and well-built, good-natured but exceptionally dim-witted. He was a damn good labourer however and three days ago he had taken Rutherford up on his offer of helping him with some of his heavy work.

'Say Butch, how are you finding working for Mr. Rutherford? Are things going okay?'

'Yeah, sure are sheriff.' Butch grinned revealing a largely tooth-less mouth. 'I've been helping Mr. Rutherford move some of old Danny's stuff. You remember Danny, don't you?'

Hooper didn't know how to answer that question. He doubted whether he, or anyone else in town for that matter, would ever forget Danny MacPherson. 'Sure, I remember Danny. He did some bad things up there, didn't he? Anyhow, do you think Mr. Rutherford's getting rid of the furniture?'

'I don't know about that, sheriff, but I've been clearing out the chairs and the tables, even a couple of beds from upstairs. Mr. Rutherford got me to set up these big lamps that arrived only a day or two back in several of the rooms and he's put in a new generator. You should see them, sheriff. They don't half make a funny noise when they're all powered up. And the light! I ain't ever seen nothing like it. I reckon they must be brighter than the floodlights they have down at Casey Park.'

Hooper gently chewed his bottom lip. 'Are these all part of that experiment he's doing?'

Butch shrugged his broad shoulders. 'How would I know? To be honest, I don't know what he's saying most of the time. I can't understand him. He's from England, you know. That's on the other side of the state. All I do is lift and carry. He said he was waiting for some last bit of equipment and then he'll be able to start his work. I finished early the other day so he had me out looking for mushrooms. I told him that my pappy told me not to touch those things on account of some of them being deadly poisonous.'

'What did Rutherford say to that?'

'Why he just laughed and told me to wear a pair of gloves.'

'That's good advice. So, is that you done working up there now?'

'Mr. Rutherford said to call back in a couple of days. By which time he should've got whatever it was he was waiting on. I've just been to the hardware store, seeing if they sell any acid. Do you know where I can get some acid, sheriff?'

'Acid? What do you want acid for?'

'It's for Mr. Rutherford. He told me to buy some acid. Said something about it might being needed if anything bad were to happen. Here, have a look.'

Butch reached into a pocket of his tattered dungarees and took out a slip of paper, which he handed to the sheriff. It was a shopping list of miscellaneous bits and pieces, mundane necessities and provisions for the main part. Two things at the bottom of the list stood out however—a large carboy of industrial strength sulphuric acid and a shotgun with two boxes of shells.

*

Something very peculiar was going on at the MacPherson place. Of that, Hooper had no doubt. After his conversation with Butch he had become increasingly suspicious as to just what it was

Rutherford was up to. He had deliberated over whether or not to pay another visit in order to satiate his curiosity, to make up some false pretence in order to have a snoop about.

In the end, he had decided to wait until Butch went up next time and to accompany him. The only snag was that Rutherford had told Butch not to arrive before sundown—an odd detail that had set off little alarm bells within Hooper's brain. Consequently, as extra support—not that he reckoned it would be required, but if there was one thing he had learned during his years as sheriff it was always better to be safe than sorry—he would also take along his deputy, Jim Bexley.

Bexley was a thin-faced thirty year-old. A no-nonsense kind of guy who did everything by the book. His only vice was the foul-smelling cigarettes he constantly smoked.

'So when're we meeting Butch?' asked Bexley. He was sat in the front passenger seat of the patrol car playing idly with his handcuffs.

'He'll be along any minute. I told him that I'd give him a lift. I've had to make some space in the boot 'cause Rutherford needs a carboy of acid. He also requested a shotgun, but I'll be damned if he's going to get one. Not while I'm sheriff of this town. Hell, the guy's as crazy as a coot with a red-hot poker up its ass if you ask me.'

'What d'ya say he does again? Talks to mushrooms?' Bexley had to fight in order to contain a laugh.

'That's what he told me. Can you believe it? First time I heard him talk I didn't know what to think. He's a real oddball. I was in two minds about informing those folk at the mental unit up in Crawford.'

'I used to know a guy at school who talked to trees.'

'Ah, shut-up, would you?' Hooper had had enough of this stupidity. In the streetlight, he spotted Butch coming towards them pushing a wheelbarrow in which was the carboy. 'Here's

Butch now. Why don't you get out and give him a hand instead of sitting there and talking rubbish.'

Five minutes later they were heading out towards the MacPherson place. It was dark now and in the car headlights everything seemed eerie. Hooper began to feel a tightening in his stomach and there was a cold film of sweat on his face. There was a vague throbbing at the back of his eyes and some inner voice seemed to be reaching out to him, trying to make him turn round and stay well clear. The feeling of danger kept intruding on his mind and it was only with a great deal of willpower and mental reserve that he managed to remain focused and drive carefully.

They made the turn-off and started the approach to the farm-house.

'Say sheriff, what the hell's that light?' Bexley began unrolling his window. He stuck his head out to get a better look.

'You what?' Taking his eyes off the road, Hooper looked up and saw something so weird that he rubbed at his eyes before looking again. From numerous windows there shone a pale lilac light. There was an otherworldly quality to its strange effulgence; a certain abnormality in the way in which it bathed virtually all of the MacPherson place in its alien radiance.

'That's the light from them lamps I was telling you about, sheriff. Only it was more orangey the time I saw it,' said Butch excitedly. 'My, sure is pretty all the same.'

Hooper didn't think it was pretty. It was ghastly, eldritch. It was certainly not normal. He didn't think that Rutherford was breaking any known laws but he sure as hell wasn't going to let such outlandish activity go on in his town unchallenged. There would be some serious answering to do and if the mad scientist — as he had come to think of him — proved uncooperative then he would make life difficult for him. Hell, Rutherford had been made aware of the terrible events that had happened here. So why on earth was he exacerbating that bad memory that had plagued

Harvest Wood for the past fifteen years by perpetuating the insanity? He was convinced something fiendish was going on. Why the acid? Why the shotgun?

'Are we going in there?' Bexley asked nervously.

'We sure as hell are,' replied Hooper. 'It's high time we found out just what this guy is up to.' He parked the car, got out and strode purposefully towards the front door of the farmhouse. That strange light seemed to come from everywhere and he could hear the sounds of a running generator coming from somewhere. Looking to his right, he could see that the glow was even present in the outlying barn where Danny MacPherson had taken his own life. He knocked vigorously on the door. 'Open up, Mr. Rutherford! This is Sheriff Hooper.'

For a moment or two there was no answer and he was about to knock again when the door was opened.

Rutherford looked ghastly, his pallid skin given an even more unnatural tone due to that unearthly pale lilac glow. 'Why, sheriff, I wasn't expecting you.' His words came out tremulously—like the explanation of some misdeed by a guilty schoolchild. 'I thought it was only going to be Mr. Langford.' He peered over Hooper's left shoulder. 'Ah, I see he is here and I do believe he has my acid. Excellent.'

'Yeah, but I'm afraid no shotgun.' Hooper found the light was now painful on his eyes. It made them sting and he was beginning to feel the onset of a headache. In addition, there was something about it that made him feel nauseous. Or maybe that was down to the foul reek that was prevalent once more. 'Just what the hell are you up to out here?' he asked, aware that Bexley and Butch had now joined him.

'Why, just a little experiment. I can assure you that there is nothing illegal or otherwise with what I'm doing. In fact, I would be more than happy to allow you and your friends to stay and watch. Believe me, this is ground-breaking scientific research. I've already been able to actually attune the lamp-filters to the correct settings in order to find the hotspots, to accurately pinpoint the precise locations. I knew it would have to be something outside the normal wavelength spectra. U.V. wouldn't do it.'

'Can you talk in plain English? Just what are you on about? Hotspots? Precise locations?'

Rutherford appeared genuinely dumbfounded. 'The exact locations where the murders occurred of course. My lamps have been able to detect, with one hundred percent accuracy may I add, where each death took place. The negative residual energy from the corpse of the freshly deceased leaves an imprint that can be discovered using certain filtered chromatic light waves. It was a phenomenon I first became interested in when I read a paper on Kirlian photography. I have taken it one stage further than merely investigating the observable coronal discharges visible in moisture. By applying it to the examination of —'

'What the hell are you on about?' Hooper interrupted. He was fast losing his patience.

'I can see that you're somewhat confused, sheriff.' The mycologist pushed his dark glasses back on his face. 'Come, let me show you. Then all will be made clear.' He headed off down the corridor and into the large farmhouse kitchen.

The others followed.

The room they entered had been stripped of most of the furniture. Two large tripod-mounted lamps, like the kind used by professional photographers, had been installed in the room and Hooper had to shield his eyes so intense was the pale lilac glare that came from them.

'There! On the floor. That's one of them. A patch of residual death, for lack of a better term.' Rutherford proudly pointed to a black stain on the ground. It was roughly child-shaped in outline. A dark indigo moss-like growth in which unsightly forms of fungi grew sprouted from it. 'As you can see, I've already initiated cultivation on this one like the one in the barn and I'm —'

'Just what the hell is this?' asked Hooper, looking down with distaste. That feeling of nausea grew stronger. 'Are you telling me that you've found all the places where MacPherson's victims were killed and that you're planting your bloody mushrooms there?'

'Not mushrooms or any other form of gilled Basidiomycetes, but otherwise yes. That's it exactly! A touch of genius, wouldn't you agree? My specially genetically-modified species certainly seem to be deriving nourishment —'

Hooper swung out and struck Rutherford with a solid right fist busting his lower lip and sending him reeling back against the sink. 'You sick son of a bitch!' He turned to his deputy. 'Cuff him and get him out of here. I don't know what charges we'll pin on him but I'm sure I'll think of something. Gross weirdness, springs to mind.' He looked down with alarm at the obscene bristling moss on the floor. It seemed to have grown considerably within the space of a few minutes. 'Might be for the best if we dissolve this in acid while we're here.'

Forcibly, Bexley grabbed the stunned Rutherford, spun him around and slapped his handcuffs on him.

Hooper and Butch brought over the reinforced plastic container filled with acid.

'Okay, you mind yourself, Butch. I'll warrant this is strong stuff. Stand clear.' Hooper unscrewed the lid and took a backward step in order to withdraw from the released acrid fumes. Carefully, he then tipped the carboy, sloshing out some of the acid. Instantly, it began dissolving the black carpet of unsightly fungi that was now close to a foot in height.

The growth began screaming!

Was it just Hooper's imagination or was it trying to pull itself upright on appendages that remotely resembled legs?

'No! What are you doing?' cried Rutherford. 'You're killing it!'

'Sweet Mother of Mercy!' shouted Bexley. 'Those screams! For

God's sake stop it screaming!'

Hooper was horrified but determined to finish the job. Whatever this thing on the ground was—this thing that even now seemed possessed of some kind of animal sentient awareness that made it writhe and slither in an attempt to escape—he knew it had to be destroyed. It was an unholy abomination. Something that looked vaguely like an underdeveloped hand started to emerge from the middle of the grotesque puddle. It was a monstrosity engineered by one man's madness. He kicked the carboy over and completely doused the terrible thing in acid.

Smoking and sizzling, the bulbous growths began to dissolve further. Nodules popped and burst, and nightmarish puff-balls scattered a cloud of spores. Steaming and bubbling, the black patch became more of an ooze, more liquid, like an oil slick. Suddenly the dreadful screaming sounds stopped.

'Do you think it's dead?' queried Bexley.

Shaking his head in disbelief and disgust, Hooper looked down one final time at the smouldering blob on the ground. He turned to Butch. 'Go and switch off the generator, would you? We'll get Mr. Rutherford into the car.'

'Sure thing, sheriff. I know where it is. I can do that.' Butch headed back along the passageway and out the front door.

Hooper punched Rutherford a second time. 'That's for coming to the wrong town and thinking you could start your madness here, you goddamned freak. I knew the MacPhersons and what you've done here tonight is despicable. If I have my way, you're going to be inside for a long time. Hell, there's a big patch of mould growing next to the toilet in the cell you'll be spending time in. Maybe you two could become the best of friends.'

Bexley chuckled at that.

'Come on. Let's get him into the car. The sooner he's behind bars the better.'

The two policemen frogmarched Rutherford outside.

At the car, Bexley opened the back door, pushed his prisoner's head down and forced him inside. He slammed the door closed and then got in the passenger seat. Hooper got in beside him and started the engine.

They waited a couple of minutes. The lamps remained switched on.

'What's taking Butch so long?' asked Bexley.

'You know him. He probably can't find the off switch. Either that, or—' It was then that Hooper glanced to his right and noticed that the barn door was now hanging on shattered hinges. It was as though something immensely powerful had smashed it open. Fear was a tangible lump in his chest. 'Bexley...'

'What is it, sheriff?'

Suddenly Butch's blackened and dripping body came hurtling out of the darkness. It smashed off the windscreen, rebounded and fell to the ground.

Hooper and Bexley yelled in shocked surprise.

Lumbering into the lurid lilac light came a loathsome nightmare. Stomping on trunk-like legs it stood well over seven feet high, its main body formed from a thick, glistening, fungoid stem from which two stumpy fingered appendages extended. Its overall appearance was as though a man had become engulfed within the form of a giant toadstool. There was a huge gilled cap, which flopped and sagged. Oily secretions dribbled from it.

'You've got to be kidding me!' Hooper stared wide-eyed. He then did the only thing he felt he could do under the circumstances. Pushing the car into gear, he slammed his foot on the accelerator and sped straight for it.

There was a loud crumpling sound and the hideous thing fell under the wheels. Tar-like fluid splattered over the cracked windscreen. Hooper felt the car bounce and heard a horrible squelching sound as he drove over it. He was reminded of the time he had accidentally ran over two of Old Jed's piglets when he had

169

been leaving his farm several years back. Then there came a terrible screaming sound and in his rear-view mirror he saw a sight that would haunt him for the rest of his days.

Getting to his feet, illuminated all too clearly in that hellish lilac aura, blackened, slime-covered, naked and with an evil glow in his eyes, clearly revelling in his fungoid rebirth was Danny MacPherson!

DEATH AFTER DEATH

'I'm going to take you back to a time before you were born,'

'D ARLING, WHATEVER'S THE matter? You look awful.' Anthony Harris rubbed at his bloodshot eyes and tried to focus on his wife who was seated at the kitchen table. This was the third morning that week he had woken up screaming. He now stood wobbling slightly, his face pale and sickly-looking. His hair was wild and he was still dressed in his pyjamas. He cursed as a barefoot came down painfully on a discarded plastic toy.

One year old Alfie Harris let out a bleat of laughter from where he sat next to his mother and waved his arms, accidentally knocking over a bottle of milk.

'Are you —?' Pauline Harris got to her feet.

'Oh my God!' Unsteadily, Harris stumbled forward and managed to reach a chair. Using the table as a support, he sank down, his head in his hands. He was shaking noticeably. Twisting his face, he screwed up his eyes momentarily as if trying to shut out the memory of something that was too horrible to contemplate. Then he shook his head and took a tight grip on himself.

'What is it?' Pauline moved towards him, placing a comforting arm around his shoulder. 'Was it another bad dream?'

For a moment Harris was silent. He seemed to be suffering from one of the worst hangovers imaginable. He began tugging gently at his ruffled hair. 'That was the worst so far. It was... horrible'

'Let me get you a coffee.' Pauline prepared to move away.

'It was so real. So bloody real... with an emphasis on the

bloody. It was as though I was actually *there*. I feel as though—'
Harris quickly reached out for his wife's now empty cereal bowl
and threw up into it. A cold shiver went through his entire body
and he began to shake convulsively. Wiping strands of sick and
spit from his quivering lips, he slumped against the table, his
breath coming out in great wracking heaves.

'I'll phone Doctor Yates.'

Now that he had been sick, Harris felt marginally better. 'No…
that won't be necessary. Besides, I've an appointment with him
this afternoon.'

He leaned back in his chair and began to regulate his breathing. The sight and smell of his fresh vomit in the bowl almost triggered a second bout of nausea but he managed to force it down.
'I'll have that coffee though. Black and extra strong.'

'Sure.' Pauline gathered up the bowl and made for the sink.
After disposing of the vomit and rinsing clean the bowl, she
began boiling the kettle.

Harris tried his best to smile at his son but succeeded only in a
grimace. He knew he had to keep down the horrible images that
had plagued him in the last few minutes before waking. The very
thought of the vileness which his subconscious had conjured in
his brain sent a further jolt through his body. He felt like tilting
his head back and screaming to the ceiling. For in his nightmare
he had seen himself looking down on his own torn-apart body.
His broken, severed limbs lay scattered around his blood-
drenched torso and yet he could see he was still alive, his mouth
working madly, yelling insanely, his eyes filled with blood and
terror.

'Will you be all right going to work this morning?' Pauline
asked, pouring his drink. She came over and rested the steaming
cup by her husband's elbow.

'Yes. I think so. Besides, it's only a half-day.' Harris worked as
a technician at a large industrial research centre some ten miles

away. 'I'll finish this drink, then I'll go and have a shower.'

'Do you feel up to having any breakfast?'

'Just some toast.' Harris sipped at his coffee. He was trying to put things into perspective; to come to terms with his horrendous vision and to deal with the insanity of what he had witnessed some half an hour previously. It was just a dream—a particularly vivid and nasty dream—but a dream nonetheless. He pinched his hand, feeling the pain register, ensuring to himself that this was reality. It had been unlike anything he had— He stopped himself. There had been something once... something similar. But that had been long ago. Very long ago.

A fresh bout of confusion and madness threatened to seize him as he sought to untwine the dark vines now growing in his mind.

'Here's your—' Pauline stopped, seeing the ghastly look on her husband's deathly pale face. 'I'm going to phone Doctor Yates right away.' She put down the plate on which were four slices of buttered toast and raspberry jam and made for the hall.

'No!' Harris looked up. 'I'll be all right. Honestly. All I need is—' The sight of the lumpy dark-red jam almost triggered another bout of sickness. He stared at the sticky preserve, half-expecting it to suddenly liquefy and seep over the plate. He turned away quickly. Gulping, he staggered like a cripple to his feet.

'Take my advice and go back to bed. I'll phone your boss and say you won't be—'

'I have to go in today. There's an important job on this morning.'

'Don't be a fool, Anthony! You're sick. Anyone can see that. I'm sure that Mr. Burgess will be very understanding. It's not as though you've ever missed a day before.'

'I...I'm feeling better already.' It was a lie but Harris knew he had to say something. It was imperative that he went to work today. 'Maybe I'll feel better after a quick shower.' Ignoring his

173

wife's protestations, he somehow made his way out of the kitchen and climbed the stairs to the bathroom.

Forty minutes later, after Harris had showered, dressed and drunk two more strong coffees, he got in his car, ready to go to work.

It was a fine morning, the bright early Spring sunlight warm and pleasant.

He switched on the car engine and put it into reverse. He backed out of the drive and turned on to the main road.

Mercifully, he was now genuinely feeling better. Now that the initial shock was fading, dissolving from his mind, he felt that he could properly tackle the day ahead. He focused on driving, pleased to have something grounding to divert his troubled mind. The details of the nightmare were now hazy; little interconnected pieces of horror that were gradually evaporating—a troubling smoke that was becoming a mist. If he managed to stop thinking about it perhaps it would soon vanish completely. In time, it might become something he could laugh at.

He settled back in his seat.

Houses flashed past as he stepped on the accelerator. Soon he was out in the countryside. He turned on the car radio. It was tuned to a classical music station and some loud, operatic piece, filled with gusto and bravura, blasted forth. It was not anything he had ever heard before but it was rousing stuff all the same.

The music finished in time for the eight o'clock news.

After the broadcaster had introduced himself he went straight into the main story

'Police were this morning called to an address in Croydon where they discovered the dismembered body of a man. The butchered remains of forty-four year old Anthony Harris were found...'

A shockwave blasted through Harris' mind. His hands left the steering wheel and the car swerved dangerously. Raging thoughts crashed through his brain. Fear was a black cloud about him, choking and suffocating, stifling his breath and threatening to stop the thudding of his heart. At the last moment he regained control of the car and steered it back from disaster. Through the insanity, he managed to take in the closing news item.

'...*the deceased's wife, thirty-five year old Pauline Harris, has been taken into custody. The police are not looking for anyone else in connection with the grisly murder. In other news, the supermarket giant —*'

Heart thumping, Harris switched the radio off and brought the car to a stop. He sat there, gazing absently through the windscreen, his fingertips gently patting his damp forehead. His brain was rambling, descending through a veritable host of dark and senseless possibilities, trying to pull an answer from the irrational thoughts and half-formed ideas that ran chaotically through his mind.

Was he on the verge of going insane?

His surroundings darkened as clouds gusted in from the north. Everything about him was suddenly ominous, filled with a dread that was impossible to overcome. It was as though dark claws were reaching for him, tearing into his psyche, attempting to rip his very being to pieces.

'No!' he screamed, bringing his fists down heavily on the dashboard. 'It can't be!' He looked up at his reflection in the rearview mirror and for a second he was convinced that the man that looked back at him from the reflective surface was someone other than he. Then his familiar visage reappeared. There was a haunted look in his eyes and perspiration sheened his skin.

There came a sudden rap on the side window.

Harris jumped in his seat. He turned and saw a young police constable gazing in at him. He wound down the window.

'Good morning, sir. I take it everything's all right?'

Harris nodded. It was the best he could do at the moment.

'I must say, your driving back there was a little erratic. You're very lucky there was no oncoming traffic when you veered across the road.'

'I... I had a fright. That's all,' replied Harris.

'A fright?'

'Yes... I've not been sleeping too well of late and I—' Harris paused. 'Do I look all right to you?'

The police constable stood confused. 'Why... yes.'

So at least I'm not lying chopped-up in a black body bag in the back of an ambulance on the way to the morgue.

Harris let out a long sigh of relief. 'Well, I do apologise for my driving back there, constable. I assure you it won't happen again. A momentary lapse, that's all.'

'Very good. Seeing as there was no harm done, I suppose I'll let you off this time but please be more careful in future.' Satisfied, the police constable prepared to move off.

'There hasn't been anything major reported in town this morning, has there?' Harris asked. 'No, well, murders or anything?'

'Not that I'm aware of, sir.' The policeman looked at him curiously. 'Why do you ask?' There was a touch of suspicion in his tone.

'I thought I heard something on the radio. That's all.' Harris smiled and tried to look more normal than he felt. 'Maybe it was somewhere else. Well, if it's all right with you, constable, I'd best be getting to work and I can assure you I'll take it more carefully.'

That news item had been nothing more than his feverish imagination playing tricks on him, he tried to convince himself as he pulled into the research centre. He drove up to the main checkpoint and fumbled with his security pass. Slowly the barrier was raised and he turned off the avenue, heading for the staff car park.

It was then, just as he was about to park the car, that he felt a peculiar tingling in his wrists. It was as though a hundred hot little needles were pricking into his skin. He stopped the car in a parking bay and rolled up his sleeves, alarmed to see that both forearms, from about halfway down to the wrists, were now covered with a mysterious blue-red weal.Fear surged through his brain as he stared in puzzlement and horror, not knowing just what had happened. Was it some kind of allergic reaction? He felt like screaming. 'What the hell?' he asked himself as, removing his wristwatch, he began to rub at the strange marks in the vain hope that he could wipe them away.

Things were now becoming very sore. There was a tightening sensation and he began to lose all feeling in his hands. He tried to flex his fingers but found it excruciating.

Biting down his pain, and using his shoulder and his elbow, Harris somehow managed to open the car door. He had no sooner clambered out when he felt his arms being raised as though they were being pulled by invisible ropes. He no longer had any control over his own body. Matters were made worse when he felt a similar sensation around his ankles. There was an agonising squeezing.

For a fleeting second he was lifted a couple of inches off the ground.

A car door slammed shut nearby.

Harris' feet landed back on the tarmac.

'Morning, Anthony!' called out a deep voice. 'I take it you're all set for the testing of the new —' Edward Burgess, the chief director of the site and Harris' boss came striding forward, fixing his glasses to his face. 'Are you feeling all right? You look a little peaky, if you don't mind me saying.'

Harris looked worse than peaky. He looked downright awful but at least he was back on the ground and the pain in his wrists and ankles had all but vanished. The marks on his arms were still plainly visible. They were now beginning to turn an ugly, bruised blue-black.

'There's a nasty bug going around just now.' With no further talk, Burgess started for the main buildings.

Harris watched him go. Had the man not seen what had just happened? And as for the discolouration on his arms – surely he would have noticed.

Now that the pain had finally gone, he found himself getting dazedly back into his car. Taking in some deep breaths, he tried to regain some element of composure. As a scientist, he had always sought to explain the world about him in a clinical, logical manner. Yet he knew that there was something seriously wrong with him. For even if he had just imagined all that had happened to him so far this morning, there was no denying the reality of the marks on his arms. They stood out livid and stark.

Yet his boss had failed to see them.

He examined them again. He ran his fingertips over the wounds, feeling the rough abrasions on the damaged skin. If this was all some kind of delusion, perhaps brought on by a sickened mind, then why were they tangible?

Confused, he opened the car door, stuck a trousered leg out and rolled up the hemline, not particularly surprised to see the same red raw weal just above his sock.

That was it. Coming swiftly to the conclusion that he had to seek professional help, Harris pulled his leg back inside, slammed the car door and drove off. His determination to get to work seemed ludicrous to him now. His appointment with Doctor Yates was scheduled for later that afternoon but surely what he was experiencing called for immediate assistance.

A disturbing sensation of impending disaster began to take hold of him, stirring deep in the vaults of his mind. There had been times in the past when a kind of warning bell had rung, alerting him to danger long before it actually materialised and he knew from instinct never to ignore it. The thought made him grip the steering wheel tighter, almost convulsively, his muscles tautening themselves of their own volition.

With a conscious mental effort, he forced himself to think clearly. He had to put things into some kind of perspective. He was undoubtedly sick; suffering from some mental disorder. The sooner he could be diagnosed by an expert and given proper medication the better.

The traffic up ahead had slowed down. A tailback had formed and Harris could see the cause—a slow moving tractor. However, he failed to notice the sign on the verge informing motorists of the hedge trimming taking place five hundred yards ahead.

The country road was narrow and full of hidden twists and turns which made overtaking treacherous. Seizing their opportunity, the two cars ahead of him pulled out and made the manoeuvre, each nipping back into lane before a sudden bend.

Harris edged his car forward so that he was now directly behind the tractor. He could see the mud being kicked up by its huge, deep-treaded tyres and even with the windows down he could smell the cow dung it emitted. Small clouds of black, noxious exhaust fumes belched out.

Tattered fragments of the nightmare were returning unbidden and unwelcome to Harris' memory. Terror raced through his body and there was a dull throbbing at the back of his temples, behind his eyes. Wiping a sheen of damp sweat from his forehead, he shifted the car to the right slightly, gauging the road ahead, wondering if he could overtake.

There were no turnoffs and he knew that in all likelihood he would be behind this frustratingly slow-moving vehicle for a good time for its driver showed no sign of pulling over. To make matters worse there were now two cars behind him and in his rear-view mirror he could see the impatient look of the motorist following him.

Harris was a confident driver and under different circumstances he would have probably overtaken by now, but today things were very different. There was something holding him back, a heightened awareness perhaps of his own mortality.

The driver behind hooted his horn.

'Okay! Okay!' Harris veered out further. The road ahead looked clear but he would have to be quick for there was a curve to the right coming up. Shifting gears, he decided to take his chance. He pulled out and sped forward.

Spraying a cloud of leaves and twigs and screeching like an operating saw-mill, the hedge-trimming vehicle lumbered out of a concealed farmyard entrance on his right.

The huge mechanical arm of the machine swung into view before his windscreen. A lethal blur of rotating, scything blades flashed before him.

A blast of car horns erupted in his ears.

At the last moment, Harris managed to swing the car over, narrowly avoiding a gruesome death. His heart was thumping wildly as he fought to control his vehicle. For a split-second, he saw himself lying diced and mangled; his body lacerated beyond recognition, his car windscreen smashed to pieces; the vehicle, a sundered wreck.

Then, the danger over, he stepped on the accelerator and sped off unaware that he was holding his breath until it hurt in his lungs. He heard it gasp harshly as he released it suddenly. There was a peculiar salty taste in his mouth where a thin trickle of blood was flowing from his bitten lower lip.

This was proving to be the worst day of his life but there was worse to come. Much worse.

On the drive back Harris had decided to call in at home first, to inform his wife of his altered plans.

But she's being questioned by the police over your brutal murder, muttered an insidious little voice inside him.

Fiercely shaking his head, he pulled into his drive and parked the car. Everything was just as he had left it little under an hour ago. There were no policemen stood outside; no crime scene investigators sealing the place off with their lengths of tape.

Nerves tingling, he got out and went up to the front door. With a shaking hand, he removed his key from a pocket, opened the door and went inside. There was no sign of his wife or son and he suddenly remembered that today was the day they went to her sister's on the other side of town. They would be well on their way there by now.

Taking off his jacket, Harris closed the door behind him and went into the lounge.

The domestic normality and familiarity of his surroundings were doing wonders in restoring his peace of mind. He switched on the television, sat on the sofa and waited for the local news to come on.

Ten minutes later, having heard no mention of any dismembered corpse having been found in the vicinity, he forced himself to accept that it *had* all be purely delusional. Of course it had — after all he was still here with all his limbs intact. Even the marks around his wrists and ankles had all but vanished. There was a residual puffiness and they were tender to the touch but apart from that they looked more or less normal.

It had just been a bad morning.

Still, Harris thought a stiff drink would help calm his nerves. He got up from the sofa and paced over to the drinks cabinet. There was an unopened bottle of single malt whisky which he had been keeping for his birthday but right now he thought his current need was greater. Unscrewing the lid, he poured himself a generous measure and went back to the sofa.

The first sip was heavenly. He followed with another, the raw liquor pleasantly warming the back of his throat and soothing his nerves. He leaned back and closed his eyes.

Aaaaaagggh!

A tortured scream burst from his mouth as instant, agonising pain wrenched through his entire body. The whisky glass fell from his hand on to the carpeted floor as he leapt to his feet like someone who had just been subjected to an immense electric current. The pain was intense yet fleeting and he knew that had it lasted a moment longer he would surely have passed out, such was its ferocity.

'What's happening to me?' he yelled to the empty room. 'What the hell's happening to me?'

The bizarre rash was coming back to his wrists. He could see it spreading before his very eyes. The pain in his ankles now flared up again. It was as though he had been manacled by a sadistic torturer who was taking great delight in tightening his leg irons. Invisibly fettered, he somehow staggered into the hallway, the pain biting deeper with every stumble. Frantically, he reached the phone and managed to call for an ambulance. He had just finished when the pain became a dark blinding sheet of fire that tore through his body, rendering him unconscious.

Harris' return to consciousness was slow and forced. The sensation was more than a little alarming as his mind, stimulated in part by the mental images carried over from that truly terrible nightmare, conjured up a myriad of dark, unanswered questions. There was a swirling fog inside his brain and his eyes ached. He was lying in a bed which was screened off. Disorientated and unsure of his surroundings, he panicked for a moment then sat up.

'Help! Will someone tell me where the hell I am?'

A male nurse parted the curtains and peered in. 'Ah, Mr. Harris. I'll go and let the doctor know that you're awake.' He disappeared as quickly as he had appeared.

Stifling the cry that threatened to burst from his lips, Harris freed his arms from the blanket, horrified to see that both wrists now had crude bracelets made of rope wrapped around them.

The curtain was pulled back on its rail and a tall, bespectacled doctor stepped into view. 'Good afternoon, Mr. Harris. I'm Doctor Andrews and I'm pleased to see that you're finally awake.'

Pitifully, Harris held out his arms. 'Help me,' he whimpered. 'For the love of God, help me! Take these things off!'

Doctor Andrews walked forward uncertainly. '*What things?*'

'These ropes! They burn and I can feel them tugging at me.'

'But there are no ropes.'

'The pain. Make the pain go away. Please, I'm begging you!'

'Mr. Harris. Having been in touch with your treating psychiatrist, Doctor Yates, I'm of the view that the pain you claim to be experiencing is purely psychosomatic.' Doctor Andrews briefly consulted a medical clipboard. 'You've been X-rayed and thoroughly examined and I'm pleased to say that there's absolutely no signs of trauma to either your arms or your legs. I can also assure you that there are no ropes. Now—'

'Does…does my wife know I'm here?'

'Yes. I believe she should be along soon, but in the meantime may I suggest that you get some rest.'

'I need painkillers! Give me the strongest you've got. Morphine, something like that.'

'I'm afraid not.' Doctor Andrews shook his head. 'I don't want to prescribe a strong dose of analgesics until we can really assess the true problem here. If indeed there is one at all.' He looked sceptical. After all there was no evidence to support his patient's claims. Quite the opposite in fact.

'Doctor, I woke this morning having seen my body torn limb from limb! Then something hauled me off the ground and, believe me, I'm definitely in need of painkillers. So don't you stand there and tell me there's no problem.'

'I'm sorry, Mr. Harris. Now if you'll just—'

'To hell with this!' Harris swung his legs out of the bed and got to his feet.

'Please, calm down and—'

'No! I've had enough of this! If I am cracking up then I want to see Doctor Yates.' Harris fought to regain control of his limbs. With difficulty, he managed to hobble his way down the ward, heading for the exit doors. They opened and he saw his wife. 'Pauline,' he called. 'Help me get out of here! Help me get these ropes off!'

There was a grave look on Pauline's face as she rushed to assist her troubled husband.

Ignoring Doctor Andrews' pleas, they both headed out of the hospital.

There was an excruciating agony in Harris' extremities as his wife drove down the high street, searching for somewhere convenient to park. He felt like screaming as he watched the bindings on his wrists constrict, crushing the delicate bones under the skin and cutting off the circulation to his hands. His fingers were turning blue. There was a wrenching in his shoulders and such was the severity he expected he was going to be torn limb from limb at any moment. The rending pain in his ankles was just as severe.

It was how he imagined an unfortunate being wracked would feel. That was it! He was being subjected to some form of mediaeval torture.

Gonzalo Barabas!

The name flashed through his mind. He felt himself slipping in and out of consciousness. A dark hold came over him as the all-out agony tore through his body and the last sight he witnessed before passing out once more was of a fat, jolly-looking butcher chopping meat in a high street shop, his cleaver coming down heavily, separating the cuts of beef.

Out of the darkness shone a pencil-thin beam of intense white light.

'Hello! Is there anybody in there?'

Harris could feel pressure on his right eyelid. He was lying flat on a low couch.

'Mr. Harris. Can you hear me? This is Doctor Yates.' The words were soft and mellow, pleasing on the ear. 'I'm going to give you an injection. You'll feel a little scratch.'

Harris mumbled something. He felt his shirt sleeve being rolled up and then the fleeting stabbing sensation as the hypodermic pierced his skin. Thankfully, it was the only pain that registered at the moment. He felt some of his energy returning and a few minutes later he sat up, noting immediately that the ropes and marks on his arms had vanished.

'I must say you're looking better than you did ten minutes ago.'

'Where's Pauline?' asked Harris, looking around.

'Your wife's gone to collect your son from her sister's but all I want you to do at the moment is relax.' The psychiatrist returned to his desk. 'I know that we've been over this several times before but I really think if we want to treat what's plaguing you we'd better go over it once more. So, these nightmares you've been having. When did they first begin?' He sat on the edge of a chair, a pad resting lightly on his right knee. He held a pen poised above it expectantly.

Harris stared vacantly at the ceiling for a long moment then licked his lips. 'Several weeks ago.'

Doctor Yates nodded and jotted something down on his pad. He eyed his patient observantly. 'I see that you're constantly examining your arms. Your wife mentioned something about *ropes.*'

'There were ropes fastened around my wrists.'

'And... these ropes. I take it they're no longer there?'

'They've gone…for the moment. As has the pain.'

'Good.' Doctor Yates eased his tall body into a more comfortable position. 'I take it the pain is always associated with your seeing of the ropes?'

'Not at first but it seems to be now.'

'And this, shall we say physical dimension to your dreams has only come on today? No indications of this before?'

'Just this morning. It first happened when I got to work. I was lifted off the ground.'

The psychiatrist's eyebrows raised. 'Interesting.' He scribbled something else on his pad.

'Well what is it, doctor? Am I mad? I guess I must be.'

'Of course not. However, with your permission, I'd like to perform a little experiment. It's quite simple really, but it should give me an insight into your mental processes.'

Harris smiled weakly. 'What sort of experiment, doctor?'

'Nothing elaborate. Merely an association of words. I'm going to say a word and all I want you to do is tell me the first word that you think of. Whether or not it seems to make sense at the time is of little consequence. Are you ready?'

'Yes.'

'Very well. Here's the first word... day.'

'Night.'

'Good.'

'Eee... evil.'

'Life.'

'Mmm... muerte.' Harris struggled as the Spanish word for *death* blurted from his mouth.

Yates sat up. 'White.'

'Nnnn... *negro*.'

'Fear.'

'Mmm... *miedo, miedo*... what's happening?' Harris exclaimed. 'I don't know that word!'

'Try to relax, just say whatever comes to mind.' Yates spoke calmly. 'Torture.'

'*Para! Para por el amor de dios!*' Harris suddenly shrieked. The room seemed to be melting and swirling in front of his eyes and the tightness was beginning in his wrists and ankles once more.

'You're safe, Anthony. Nothing is happening to you here in my office,' Doctor Yates insisted gently, his voice level and with little variation in tone. 'You need to speak in English. Your native tongue is English, not Spanish. Tell me what you are feeling.'

Harris fought to make his eyes focus but he felt as if he was falling sideways, that the room was tipping. He could feel an intense heat and heard the sound of many people close by. The ropes were back on him and he felt himself lift off the ground, on his back. There was red, rocky sand beneath him. Sweat stung his eyes and there was blazing sunlight on his face.

Terrified, he thrashed his body from side to side and started shouting: 'Anthony Harris! I'm Anthony Harris! *Me llamo Gonzalo Barabas!*' He was vaguely aware that the psychiatrist was bending over him and pulling his head round.

'Look at me, Anthony! You are here, in Croydon. It's March the twenty-ninth, 1972. Look at me!'

Harris gradually felt the sand beneath him turn to carpet. The heat faded and the pain subsided. He was lying spread-eagled on the floor of the psychiatrist's office and sweat was prickling all over his body. He tried to speak but found he was terrified at what might come out of his mouth. Painfully, he pulled himself up into a sitting position.

Doctor Yates brought him a glass of water. 'Drink this and listen...no, don't talk for a minute, just listen.' He brought his chair over, opposite Harris. 'I believe that we are finally getting somewhere. Your speech just now, your panic as if you were in mortal danger...it all points to one thing – you are remembering a past life or perhaps I should more accurately say, a past *death*.'

Harris stared at the man in confusion.

'Many people, many religions, believe that the human soul is re-incarnated and lives through many different lifetimes before achieving peace. Normally, the soul has no memory of the other lives but I have heard of cases where the barrier between one life and the next becomes weak, especially if the individual in question suffered a very traumatic death. People start to have glimpses of other lives they have lived and this can bring huge problems with it.'

Harris had to say something. 'You can't really believe that surely? It's nonsense; religious claptrap!'

'How can you be so sure?' Doctor Yates countered. 'I too was sceptical when I first heard about this concept but I've seen too many patients over the years who have had no basis for their neuroses and aberrations that can be pinpointed in their past. At least, not in their current lives. I've done my best to give them coping strategies but I've never felt satisfied. You, however...' He looked more animated than Harris had ever seen him. 'You may actually be able to access the memories of your former life and if so, can move past the trauma you experienced. The fact that you are experiencing such a strong manifestation of it shows that it needs to be acknowledged. If you do not, then it will continue to torment you.'

'But this is ridiculous, impossible!' Harris protested, wiping sweat from his face.

'What was your name?' Doctor Yates suddenly demanded, grabbing Harris by the wrists and squeezing hard.

Harris gasped at the pain. '*My name?* You know my name. I'm... I'm...' He was struggling to shape the words in his mouth. There was an inner conflict taking place, a battle of wills. Inside his head he heard a chorus of voices screeching and shouting in Spanish, their words unintelligible.

Doctor Yates steered his patient back to the couch where he sat him down. He began waving his pen torch from side to side. 'Focus on the light and answer my questions. Who are you?'

There was a vacant look in Harris' eyes as he began to talk. 'I'm

Anthony Brian Harris.'

'Where were you born and in what year?'

'Retford, Nottinghamshire. 1927.'

'What date?'

'April the twelfth.'

'Who were your parents?'

'Jack and Betty Harris.'

Doctor Yates was swinging the light faster. Back and forth. Back and forth. 'You're feeling very sleepy, Anthony. Close your eyes and let your mind drift. Imagine you're falling down a long, dark tunnel, spiralling away. Down. Down. I'm going to take you back to a time before you were born.'

Spitting and cursing, Gonzalo Barabas—thief, bandit, murderer and rapist—was frogmarched through the jeering mob of spectators out into the dusty arena of the converted bullring. The noon day sun was like a furnace which struck at him without mercy, pulsing down at him in great waves of heat, burning and stinging his shirtless, freshly lashed back. With each step, the sand beneath the soles of his bare feet grew hotter. Blood from a rifle butt wound—a farewell present from one of his gaolers—trickled down the side of his rugged, unshaven face. Like a stream in a gulch, it dribbled down a furrow in his cheek, collecting on a swollen, split bottom lip. His tongue tasted it, relishing the moisture, no matter its source.

The horses were waiting; four large, powerful creatures that champed and neighed, their flanks flecked with sweat. Stout wooden yokes were being fastened to them by two uniformed men.

There was no time for fear. Fear was for the weak.

Defiantly, Barabas, his face scarred, cracked, bruised and blistered, gazed up at the fiery disc in the sky, the intense brightness burning his piercing green eyes. For a moment, he managed

189

to discern its shimmering outline. Then he was roughly pushed forward. He fell to his knees before being hauled upright by the hair.

Half a dozen steps and then he was manhandled to the ground. The sand burned his back.

Someone was screaming and it was only after his hands had been securely strapped to the metal bars attached to the lengths of thick rope that he realised it was him. Frantically, he kicked out, landing a scuffing blow on one of his captors. Then his feet were being clamped, bound as were his hands. Out of the corner of his eye he could see the array of butchering tools spread out on the ground; knives and hatchets – bladed implements that would be called for if the horses failed to —

There was a blinding flare of agony as his body was lifted from the sand, raised by the sudden movement of the horses. Then the beasts were being whipped and the true pain began.

Harris screamed and sprang upright. His eyes were staring wildly and sweat boiled from his face. There was a dryness in his throat and he found it hard to swallow.

Doctor Yates had stopped the pendulum-like motion of his pen torch. 'Are you all right, Anthony?' he asked.

'What happened?' Harris gasped.

'Under hypnosis I successfully regressed you to a past life. You were living the last moments of a previous existence. From what I could make out it would appear that you were once a notorious Spanish criminal named Gonzalo Barabas who was sentenced to death sometime in the late-seventeenth century. The method of your execution was quartering by wild horses.'

Harris got to his feet. 'No! This can't be happening.'

'You can't hide from your past, Anthony, no matter how much you may want to. It's all embedded here, in your brain,' said Doctor Yates, tapping his temple. 'You were, and to some extent still are, *Gonzalo Barabas.'*

'No! This is madness!' Harris made for the door. 'Complete and utter—'

'Don't fight it, Anthony. Better to accept and work through the memories.'

'Never!' Harris flung the door wide and lurched out into the waiting room. 'You're the one who's mad! You're the one who needs a doctor!' he shouted over his shoulder. His mind was reeling and his heart was palpitating furiously in his chest. His whole being fizzed and hummed with fear and disbelief; unable and unwilling to accept what his psychiatrist had just told him. Crashing against a door, he stumbled out into the main street.

A man walking his dog cursed as he was bumped into.

Oblivious to the strange looks he was getting, Harris staggered up the street.

You were, and to some extent still are, Gonzalo Barabas. The words preyed on his mind, fastening leech-like to his brain. With each hurried step, he could feel them gnawing away at him; the psychological pain now becoming physical once more as the sense of fugue—of separation from his own self—grew greater.

'Hello. Are you all right?'

A face he thought he knew swam into vision before his eyes.

'You're not looking too good.'

His left leg buckled beneath him and he half-fell into the road, an outstretched hand reaching for the bonnet of a parked car in order to support him.

'You're not drunk are you? Come on, pull yourself together man.'

Pull yourself together – something's trying to pull me apart! Unsteadily, he edged back on to the pavement.

You were, and to some extent still are, Gonzalo Barabas.

With a cry of utter horror and pain, Harris was dragged over the car bonnet. There came a terrible ripping sound and, accompanied by a thick jet of blood, his left arm was wrenched from his body.

People screamed as the limb was sent flying across the road.

The gentleman in the now blood-spattered suit who had tried to help Harris stared, wide-eyed and horror-stricken.

His yelling and screaming drowning out that of the horrified bystanders, Harris was now suspended in the middle of the road, his back horribly curved. He was beginning to unravel. There came a further tearing noise as the bones and sinews of his right arm were stretched to breaking point. Then, with a pop and a wet-sounding splatter, the limb was ruptured, torn from its socket. It went spiralling into the air, hit a shop window and, leaving a messy smear down the glass, landed on the ground whereupon a dog quickly snatched it up and ran off with it.

His arms having now been reduced to unsightly stumps of bone, blood and gristle, what remained of Harris was dragged by unseen forces down the centre of the road. Still very much alive, he felt every moment of excruciating agony as first one leg, then the other was torn from his body.

And then a darkness began to descend.

There were people standing over him, looking down in fearful, morbid curiosity. In the distance he thought he could hear the sound of an approaching siren.

'Jesus Christ! I've never seen anything like it.'

'Poor bastard! His eyes are still moving!'

'Anybody know who he is?'

It was just as death finally took him that he heard the last voice.

'His name is Gonzalo Barabas. He is—or rather *was* – a wanted man in Spain.' Doctor Yates looked down indifferently on the messy remains of his patient, wondering if he had finally perfected his method of murdering by past-life regression and psychological suggestion—and the occasional surreptitiously administered drug. There were a few more test subjects he was working on but this trial, as he considered it, had proved demonstrably successful. Smiling to himself with satisfaction, he turned and walked away.

THE NIGHTMARE FROM THE SWAMP

In the deeps of the Russian taiga, far from civilisation, something lurks.

IGOR VHIRINOVSKY CURSED savagely and ran a hand down his unshaven chin. A heavy rain shower had just passed and his murky surroundings were dismal shades of grey and green. 'Aren't they ever going to stop? Just what the hell is it all in aid of?' He stood just inside the opening of a crudely-built hut, dampness glinting wetly on his harshly chiselled, hit-man's features. In this godforsaken place, somewhere on the West Siberian Plain, deep within the taiga, he found himself sweating and cursing as incessantly as the thudding of the drums of the nomadic Lyushukan people—an offshoot of the better-known Ket. It was stiflingly humid and airless, yet he knew that, once the brief summer was over, this place would become a glacial, frozen land. He glared past the figure of his companion, at the village itself. It was compact and small, necessarily so, because of its impermanence. At times, the floodwaters of the fast-flowing river came rushing over its banks, prompting a move to higher ground.

'Who knows? One of their dammed rituals, probably,' muttered Vyacheslav Blokhin. He took his cigar from his mouth and blew out a cloud of strong-smelling smoke. He was an ex-mercenary turned treasure hunter; a big, balding man with broad, fleshy features. 'I was in Mozambique two years ago and I'm not kidding you, the drumming went on for a whole month. It was worse than the flies. Drove some of the guys I was with to the brink of madness. That was one hellish expedition, I can tell you.'

'What happened?'

'Lots of things. Things I'd rather not talk about.'

'As you wish.' Vhirinovsky's steely eyes narrowed, taking in the preparations the tribal shamans, in their hideous furry headdresses, were engaged in; cleansing the central area with a peculiar ritual known only to themselves. He swore angrily to himself. All this would no doubt mean more delay, more frustration. For days now, it had been like this, while they waited impatiently for a guide to take them up-river, deeper into the fetid, taiga swamplands. He swore again, louder this time.

'I can't stand this constant waiting,' complained Blokhin. A red blaze of anger flared up inside him. 'Have you any idea how much longer?'

Vhirinovsky shook his head. There was a certain hardness about him that was like steel below the surface. He was the kind of man who needed little reason to commit murder and had indeed done so in the past. An ex-Red Army general, as a young man he had served under Khrushchev at Stalingrad but years of disillusionment had burned the patriotism from his heart. These days his motives were purely self-serving. During his military career he had heard rumours, provided largely by the Siberian forces, who talked in hushed voices of a forgotten ruin alleged to contain tremendous wealth.

'To hell with this! There's a treasure somewhere out there that will set us up for life and knowing that we're now within spitting distance of it is driving me crazy,' Blokhin vented his frustration.

'Then what do you suggest we do about it?' Vhirinovsky was deliberately sarcastic. 'They won't stop the ritual just for us you know and venturing into the interior without someone who knows the way would be suicide. Men have tried in the past. None have ever returned.'

Blokhin scowled and threw away his cigar butt. Deep inside, he knew that what the other said was true. The nomads were a superstitious lot. For them, the supernatural was just another facet of reality. It was something that not only existed among the darkness of the crowding trees, just over the spilling torrent of the river but which dwelt among them. All around them, everyday, lurking darkly in the night.

Their journey here had been long and arduous. By rail, by car and by foot they had made their way from Omsk, crossing some truly desolate and lawless parts of Russia. Into this vast, unfriendly wilderness, in which only the hardiest of people eked out an existence, they had ventured, following in the footsteps of previous doomed expeditions in search of a legendary secret treasure.

Like an annoyed bear, Vhirinovsky throatily grumbled his frustration and impatience. The presence of something far detached from the sane world he knew was beginning to get at him now. He tried desperately to relax his mind as well as body. Here, in the stinking waterlogged forest, several hundred miles from anything that remotely resembled civilisation, it was impossible. The dark, evil forces were always present, tangible almost. Only the very foolish, or the very brave dismissed them as mere fantasies.

Suddenly, the drumming ceased.

The village became strangely silent. There was only the heavy liquid gurgle of the water in the distance beyond the fringe of pines and larches and the eerie sound of the wind over the marsh.

If only there wasn't the damp – and the eternal stench of rotting, half-decayed weeds in the river. It was too still, unnaturally so. From somewhere, an animal screamed; a harsh, thin shrill of bestial rage.

Vhirinovsky grabbed his Kalashnikov assault rifle from where it stood, propped ready against the wall of the hut. 'I can't take any more of this. It's time we made a move. Come on, let's find out just what the hell's going on.'

Blokhin reached for his own rifle, checking it with a smooth automatic movement, his face tight. 'Have you any idea what's going to happen to us if we haven't got these negotiations figured out right?' he asked.

'What do you mean?'

'Well, what if they decide to turn against us?' Blokhin swatted a mosquito that had landed on the nape of his neck.

'Then it will just be too bad for them,' answered Vhirinovsky with a savage grin, a mere skinning of his teeth. He patted his rifle meaningfully. 'You should know me by now. I've got no compunction about killing anyone that gets in my way.'

Together, they walked purposefully between the squat shapes of the ramshackle huts and crude tents. Step by step, not looking round, with the eyes of the hidden villagers on them, they trudged across the muddy opening. An evil-smelling wind sighed in the mournful trees, rustling the branches ominously.

The chief's hut stood in the centre of the village, slightly larger than the rest, as befitting his position. From a wolf hide-covered throne bedecked with furs, bear pelts and other forms of exotica, the hut's sole occupant, an ancient, wizened being, watched their steady approach with a sly gleam in his dark eyes. His long, tangled grey hair was draped over his knees.

'Chief Kazlak,' Vhirinovsky began. 'I would see the man who is to act as our guide on the journey through the swamplands. It is important that we begin as soon as possible. You know as well as I how treacherous and inhospitable this place will become if we delay too long.' With an effort, he kept all trace of impatience out of his tone.

Kazlak regarded him wearily. 'There will be no guide.'

Vhirinovsky felt a sick feeling inside him. Days of promises and now this... His grip on the rifle tightened. He decided to try bluff as a sudden idea came to him, one that he was sure would have the desired effect and one which he cursed himself for not having thought of before. 'You *will* provide us with a guide or you will regret your rash words. We do not wish to cause trouble, but if that's the way you want it—' He left the remainder of his sentence unsaid, but his unspoken words hung quivering in the taut silence.

Kazlak's eyes narrowed. And there was a cold and emotionless look about those inhuman eyes; strange eyes, black and unblinking, filled with an empty gaze that was difficult to meet directly.

A group of villagers entered the hut, forming a ring around them; muttering to themselves, encompassing them in a large circle. Sharp-bladed knives could be seen in the hands of some.

Vhirinovsky was worried. If the worst came to the worst, he and Blokhin could no doubt kill Kazlak but that would be scant comfort when they turned and found themselves facing an angry horde of murderous, vengeful nomads.

'You say you want to go south, upriver, deeper into the swamp, towards the Hidden Lands?' asked Kazlak solemnly. He nodded his head slightly. 'It is an evil place you wish to visit. A cursed place. A land of evil spirits. Why do you wish to go there?'

The air was thick with tension.

Vhirinovsky felt his throat suddenly dry. He moistened his lips nervously with a quick movement of his tongue. His mind was ticking over madly. He thought fast. It would be foolish to tell the real reason. No, this was a time for lying. 'We are environmental agents of the USSR. It is our duty to prospect for new sources of natural gas, raw materials and as yet undiscovered areas of geological importance. Failure to comply with our demands will result in the forced upheaval of your people.'

Kazlak uttered a harsh laugh that wobbled through his emaciated body. 'You think that won't happen anyway? Moscow has already forced out many of our tribes. It will do them no good and you are fools if you go there. You will never return. Not even your bones will be found.'

Vhirinovsky straightened his back and squared his shoulders.

'We will return,' he said tightly. 'But first we need a guide who knows the trails through the marsh. As I've already told you, we can pay well for your services.'

'I would like to help you,' mumbled Kazlak, shuffling his skeletal frame into a more comfortable position on his throne. 'But none of my men will go into the Hidden Lands.'

'What are they afraid of?' asked Blokhin uneasily.

The old chief waved a scrawny hand and one of the shamans hurried over. After a few moments of whispered conversation in their own dialect, Kazlak nodded and, arthritically, rose to his feet. 'The inhabitants of the Hidden Lands are not like you or me. They are an ancient people who care and know nothing of the outside world. My people have never seen them though they are known in our myths. They live in a world of nightmare.'

Vhirinovsky hesitated. *A world of nightmare!* Several times, that phrase had cropped up during his travels. Even now, he didn't know what to make of it. A chill fear coursed through his veins. Angrily, he threw it off. He smiled but there was no humour in his face. 'We're afraid of no stupid superstition,' he said finally, wiping a thick sheen of grime from his forehead. That was the way to look at it. Once these folk thought you were afraid, that was the end.

'Tell them,' interrupted Blokhin suddenly, 'that every man who goes will receive payment enough to last him for many days. They will be well recompensed by the state if any significant discoveries are made. In my short time here I've noticed that none of your men have access to a gun... this can be remedied upon our return.'

Kazlak's eyes gleamed at that. 'I will tell them,' he promised. 'Now leave while I talk to my people. I will reach a decision come first light tomorrow.'

Vhirinovsky bowed his head a little. Gripping his companion by the arm, he steered him outside. Once clear of the hut, he turned round, a savageness in his eyes. 'What makes you think we can afford to give away rifles, just like that?'

'What makes you think we're ever going to come back here?' countered Blokhin, an evil glint in his eyes. 'Once we get our hands on the treasure, we'll kill the guide and bypass this place. All we need to discover is how to get to these so-called Hidden Lands.'

'Fair enough.' Vhirinovsky nodded to himself. Of one thing he was sure. He would be watching Blokhin during the days that were to come, otherwise, he wouldn't be coming back either. There was no way of telling how the sudden possession of so much wealth would affect a man. Perhaps Blokhin himself could be conveniently removed. It would be so easy in the trackless wilds. A hundred different ways in which a man could die. Quickly, or extremely slowly, so that he screamed and pleaded for death. He pushed the dark thought away into the background of his mind. There would be time enough to think about that when a suitable opportunity presented itself.

Slowly, they moved through the village, heading back to their allocated hut.

All was quiet. There was no one else to be seen.

Vhirinovsky watched Blokhin out of the corner of his eye, walking silently beside him. Something was troubling the other. He could tell that at once. Blokhin had his head cocked a little to one side, as if listening for something – or *to* something that was almost out of earshot. He opened his mouth to speak but, with an abrupt movement, the other suddenly darted inside the shadowy opening of one of the smaller huts. For an instant, Vhirinovsky thought he heard a dull murmuring, a dry voice intoning words and phrases that were meaningless. A strange chanting, mumbled in a peculiar monotone that sent the blood racing through his veins though he didn't know why.

Then Blokhin was crying out. 'So it *was* you! I thought so. Well, this is the last time you'll work your spells on me.'

Something thudded dully inside the hut. An ugly, horrible sound that was repeated twice. After that, there was a long pause.

Then Blokhin staggered out of the opening, his eyes bright. He held his rifle limply in his right hand, and there was a dark staining of blood on the heavy wooden butt. 'She won't cast her damned curses on me anymore,' he said shakily, his voice a racking gasp.

'What do you mean?' Vhirinovsky asked worriedly.

'I mean I just killed the old witch. What do you think I mean?'

Vhirinovsky threw a swift glance into the dimness of the hut. At first he could see nothing. Then, he managed to make out the still figure of an old woman, lying face down on the floor. Her arms and legs were twisted beneath her body. Blood leaked from her battered head, pooling on the coarse timbers.

A single glance was sufficient to tell Vhirinovsky that she was quite dead. 'You bloody fool, Blokhin! Why the hell did you have to do that?' He choked the words out as if they made a bitter taste in his mouth. His lips twisted. He glanced nervously around, hoping no one had seen his companion enter the hut.

Blokhin held out something. 'It's only due to my experiences in Africa that I knew what she was up to. See what she had. Go on, take a good look for yourself.' There was a rising note of hysteria in his tone. 'That pain in my chest I felt the other night. I knew it wasn't a normal feeling. This old hag has been watching us ever since we arrived.'

Then, all thought of what had happened fled from Vhirinovsky's mind as he saw what it was the other was holding in his hand. A crude figure of twigs and rags – a primitive doll in the image of Blokhin.

'Damned magic,' said Blokhin thinly. He seemed to have a little difficulty in speaking. 'I had an idea she might have been the one who was doing it.'

'But why? Surely she had no reason to —'

'Perhaps she had every reason,' muttered Blokhin. He threw the figurine into the bushes. 'You see, she wasn't of this tribe. I spotted that almost as soon as we entered this village. My guess is that she originally came from somewhere further south, deeper in the interior, from these so-called Hidden Lands And if she had some awareness of what we're looking for, isn't it just feasible that she would do her utmost to stop us?'

'Maybe you're right.' Vhirinovsky felt his brain reel under the sudden impact of the knowledge. It had never entered his mind that their mission might be known. That made things more awkward. They would have to be on the lookout for similar devilry every single minute from now on. He threw another quick glance at the dead woman sprawled on the floor of the hut, her upturned face seemingly grinning in an unsettling, sardonic manner. Was it just his imagination or was there an expression of malicious amusement on her face, even in death? He shuddered. 'We can't just leave her lying here. We're going to have to hide the body.'

'As you wish,' agreed Blokhin. He crouched down and got his arms under her, lifting her up.

There was an odd strained grin on Vhirinovsky's face. 'Still, you didn't have to kill her. These damned villagers won't move if they sense there's a curse hanging over either one of us. You know what they're like.'

'Providing we hide the body well, they'll never know.' With a grunt, Blokhin hefted the dead woman over his shoulder. 'We'll take her outside and throw her in the swamp,' he said grimly.

Mile upon mile of seemingly endless marsh, broken only by stretches of half-submerged forest lay before them; several thousand square miles of unexplored, trackless quagmire. The taiga was an inhospitable wilderness through which they wound their lugubrious way slowly and arduously, their eyes wary and restless in their heads.

Vhirinovsky's hands strayed nervously towards the rifle slung over his shoulder. He marched wearily, listlessly.

Chief Kazlak had been as good as his word. A guide had been provided for them, Ychev, who knew a little true Russian. Vhirinovsky could see the other's tall, muscular figure striding ahead, hacking his way through the tall reeds that barred their way.

The terrain grew wilder and more impenetrable as they progressed, cutting and wading their way through the unforgiving wilderness.

Poisonous, choking mists from the deadly swamps curled like an impenetrable wall between them and the invisible horizon. It was agony to drag oneself along, but they did, step by step, mile by painful mile, fumbling over creepers that clutched upwards with writhing coils, and other things that slithered away with a warning hiss.

On the morning of the sixth day, the drums started again. But this time, there was something different about them. A menacing, blood-curdling undertone of insidious warning that sent dread washing strongly over Vhirinovsky's mind. Fear seared through him – a stark, unreasoning terror that was like a physical thing, lancing into his brain. He lurched into the sticky mud of the swamp that lay a couple of feet on either side of the narrow trail. There was a moment of sheer blinding panic in his brain. Then his foot came free with an ugly, squelching sound. He turned to speak to Blokhin, then stopped as Ychev came towards them.

'We must proceed with caution. We now stand at the edge of the Hidden Lands.'

'Do you think we've been spotted?' asked Blokhin. His eyes flickered to the trees and the dense undergrowth, the swamp around them. He knew that at any moment their surroundings could suddenly swell full of death.

'It's possible,' muttered Ychev. 'They're all around us at this very moment.'

'I don't see them,' muttered Vhirinovsky in a quiet whisper.

'They are there.' There was a note of finality in Ychev's voice.

Vhirinovsky nodded. He hefted his rifle into his right hand. There was fear in the pit of his stomach, but it was beginning to abate slightly. After all, whoever these people were, they could die just as other men. And he knew that they wouldn't have access to the kind of firepower he and his companion were carrying.

'What do you suggest?' inquired Blokhin, his eyes wide and staring.

'We keep going,' said Vhirinovsky sharply. 'They don't seem to be either suspicious—or particularly hostile. Probably they're just curious. Could be they've never seen outsiders before which is why they've made no move to attack us on the way in.'

A few moments later, they reached a clearing in the swamp, a vast area that had been gouged out of the dense undergrowth, filled with huts fashioned from reeds.

The swamp-dwellers were gathered all around them in a vast semi-circle, waiting.

Vhirinovsky ran his judgemental gaze over them uneasily. There must have been two hundred or so of them; men, women and children—far more than he had expected from the size of the village. Their swarthy skins were painted with white and red tribal markings and many of them had applied powder and pigments to their faces in order to give them a somewhat ghoulish, skull-like appearance. There was a blankness; an emptiness to their eyes that he found deeply unsettling. He had expected them to be curious or even overtly hostile but this vacant staring was somehow worse. Much worse. It was as though they were regarding him and his expedition members as nothing more than meat.

'Looks as though we were expected,' hissed Blokhin, walking warily forward. 'I guess that's the chief, over by the central hut.'

He inclined his head slightly. 'They seem friendly enough.'

'*Friendly?* You've got to be kidding.' Vhirinovsky looked to Ychev. 'What do you think?' he asked quietly. 'Think they mean trouble?'

The guide shrugged uncertainly.

Vhirinovsky waited tensely. There was a threatening tension in the air that he could almost feel, touching subtly at his nerves. He stood very still, fighting within himself to keep the expression of uneasiness from his face. The vast majority of the natives were armed with short, stabbing spears. *How the hell could Blokhin consider them friendly?* He knew they were helpless here, utterly outnumbered. If they miscalculated, played their hand too quickly, or rashly, they would pay the price of their foolishness. He didn't know whether this tribe was cannibalistic but—

The skin covering of one of the huts was thrown aside with a suddenness that was almost numbing. Someone—something— came leaping into the centre of the clearing. A weird figure, small and hideously grotesque, the face hidden behind a death-mask, draped with the bones of slain enemies, and festooned with coloured feathers and pointed, yellow fangs.

Wicked little eyes glared at them with a red malevolence from behind tiny slits in the mask. It was obviously the shaman of the tribe. A sudden chill swept through Vhirinovsky's body. For a single, horrible moment, there seemed something familiar about the shrunken creature. His finger tightened on the trigger of his rifle. The death mask was suddenly thrown aside. He saw the other's face for the first time. Lined and wrinkled and —

It was the face of the woman Blokhin had killed back at Chief Kazlak's village!

Vhirinovsky recoiled. The whole clearing was spinning and swaying insanely and there was a shrill, high laughter sounding in the air above his head. His brain shrieked at him amid the bubbling sounds. The circle of natives began moving slowly forward, pressing quietly around them. With a piercing cry, he opened fire, gunning four down in a vicious spray of bullets. Had he been thinking straight he could well have held his ground and blasted them away before they got near but instead he spun on his heel, and raced madly away, only vaguely aware that Blokhin was behind him. Close on his heels, was the huge shape of Ychev.

The roar of the villagers was becoming louder now. Then there were knives flashing in the watery sunlight and the swish of spears arcing through the air.

A war whoop sent a tingle of fear along Vhirinovsky's nerves. Something hummed over his shoulder like a flash of frozen flame. A spear stuck quivering in the tough bark of a tall tree a foot above his head. Then there was the cold bite of a knife against his arm and the warm slickness of blood flowing over his wrist. He pitched himself forward, crashing into the trees and fallen branches, climbing up, and racing on.

The trees thinned.

There was firmer ground under Vhirinovsky's running feet and he was outdistancing the bloodthirsty horde. He was out in the open, and darkness was coming up out of the far horizon, and there were tall trees in front of him. Uttering a barrage of expletives, Blokhin came splashing towards him, Ychev at his heels.

There was a pause in the wild shouting behind them.

'We've given them the slip,' gasped Vhirinovsky. He forced himself to breathe quietly. Gradually, the mad hammering of his heart lessened and slowed to a more normal pace.

'It's not that,' Ychev panted. 'They won't come any further.'

'Why not?' asked Blokhin, looking back to ensure they weren't being followed. Blood trickled down his face from where he had run into a branch. He had lost his rifle.

There was a curious expression on Ychev's face. He was silent for a moment. Then, with a shaking hand he pointed before him. 'Look!'

Vhirinovsky and Blokhin turned to follow his pointing finger.

From out of the swamp rose a huge mound of hardened earth ringed with a copse of hideous, straggling trees. Atop the hill was a ghastly structure. It was a ramshackle hut festooned with weeds in which could be seen the discoloured bones of the dead. Stakes had been driven into the ground each one surmounted by a rotting head. Posts carved with eldritch sigils leant at strange angles and large, bat-winged creatures flew around them.

A foul stench polluted the air.

'The legends are true!' cried Ychev. 'The house of Baba Yaga!'

'There's no such being,' snapped Vhirinovsky. 'She doesn't exist. It's just some stupid superstition, invented to keep thieves away. An old legend, handed down over the centuries.' He glanced back, ensuring none of the villagers were approaching. 'Still no sign of them,' he said with a nod of satisfaction.

Blokhin twisted his head and looked about him. There was a menace in the silence that clung about them, squeezing itself around them with hidden, sadistic fingers. 'Let's hope the legends are true regarding the treasure. If so, it will be up there somewhere. Come on, let's move!'

Ychev was too frightened to go up so they left him on watch at the base of the mound informing him to holler a warning at the first sign of trouble.

The very soil, silt and mud of which the mound was formed seemed infected with evil, as though it possessed a malign, mischievous force which seemed to trip, cling and sink with every boot which fell on it. Filthy water, laced with what looked like blood, bubbled, squelched and flowed in rivulets from the befouled ground. In places, ragged skeletons protruded from the earth.

'It's one massive corpse heap,' said Blokhin, staring at the ground with disgust. 'A midden filled with the dead. And that stink. It's horrendous.'

Fighting back his revulsion, Vhirinovsky ploughed on, focusing on the wicked looking structure at the summit. The terrible, corpse-saturated mud was now up to his knees.

As they struggled higher they could see that there were numerous sinkhole-like openings here, dark cavernous mouths that gaped out of the slope like soulless eyes, black and empty.

Vhirinovsky shivered in spite of the tight hold he had on himself, fighting against the growing feeling that there were things inside this cursed barrow. Dim, vague things, that were evil. Made and born of that same horror that had fashioned the unbelievable nightmare back in the village. His grip on his rifle tightened.

A noisome green mist began to rise from the ground.

Suddenly the earth beneath them subsided and they found themselves sinking deep as, with a loud slurping sound, they were sucked down. One moment they were up to their waists, then their chests until, within a matter of seconds, they were pulled under completely. Panic and horror threatened to overcome them as everything darkened and breathing became impossible. The nightmare went on for the best part of a minute until, accompanied by a ghastly assemblage of bones, they splashed down into a huge, subterranean pool of rank water.

Surfacing, Vhirinovsky took a deep breath and swam to one side, pulling himself free of the underground pond. He heard splashing and cursing and then Blokhin emerged.

It was pitch dark.

Vhirinovsky unslung his pack and rummaged around for his torch. Switching it on he was surprised to see the hewn stone walls of the huge chamber they were in. Wiping away the worst of the mud, he panned the torch over the water, seeing if he could find his rifle which he had dropped on his passing through the ground and into this stygian hell.

'Where the hell are we?' asked Blokhin, looking around

incredulously.

'I've no idea. I'd guess this place must be a thousand years old. Maybe older.' Vhirinovsky was scared although he tried not to show it. 'Come on, we have to get out of here. Let's see if we can find a way up. He started for a shadowy opening visible at the extremity of his torchlight.

To their dismay they found that the passage beyond sloped down.

Darkness fell around Vhirinovsky like some evil, ominous cloak. The ground was smooth beneath his boots, dipping downwards and away into a black nothingness. The walls dripped moisture and somewhere there was the dull splash of something slithering away. He played the beam of his torch around in a wide, sweeping arc. Black shadows scurried away into corners of ebon silence.

Slowly, they inched their way along. It was difficult to keep upright and at the same time to keep their hands sliding along the wall because the floor of the cave was slipping and sloping away from them.

Vhirinovsky began to feel physically sick, the light from his torch chasing the little midnight shadows momentarily out of his path. But always, they came back and closed in behind them as they progressed; like an endless wall of blackness that stretched for an indeterminate distance before and behind them.

'How much further does this go?' Blokhin's voice was a floating murmur.

'No idea.'

Blokhin snorted at that, but said nothing.

'The treasure must be down here somewhere. This has to be the place. A ruined temple perhaps...' Vhirinovsky pulled his body forward. There was an outjutting corner of stone in front of him. He rounded it with an effort, then stopped. Glancing down, he found emptiness beneath him; black and awful. A seemingly bottomless abyss. For a mad moment, he teetered on the brink, straining desperately to maintain his balance. In his mind's eye, he could visualise himself falling through that blackness, down, down, down—dying of dehydration before he struck the bottom. Then, abruptly, the vertigo passed. He swallowed and looked across at Blokhin. The other's face was a dim white blur in the torchlight. And there was a faint gleam of fear in his eyes, but it faded almost at once.

'I wonder how deep it is.' Blokhin picked up a small rock from the ground at his feet, and dropped it over the side.

For long moments, they could hear it, crashing against the sides of the pit with a hollow, wailing clatter that was horrible to hear. Slowly, it drifted away to the edge of silence, then stopped altogether. After that, there was nothing.

'Hell!' muttered Blokhin. He swayed back. 'It goes down a long way.' Fear edged his voice, showed once more in the half-shadow of his face.

With a conscious physical effort, Vhirinovsky forced steadiness into the muscles of his arm, and shone the torch over the edge. For an instant, he could see nothing. Then, gradually, he was able to make out details.

Below the jagged lip of the pit, some thirty feet down, another cave showed vaguely as a dark opening, a gaping mouth in the side. There was a narrow ledge of rock below it.

Blokhin had seen it too. He pointed a shaking finger. 'Looks as though there's something down there,' he said sharply, wincing a little as the distant walls flung back faint echoes of his words.

'Think we could reach it with the rope?' asked Vhirinovsky.

'You're determined to go down there, then?'

'Of course. Do you know any other way? Maybe it'll lead to a way out.'

Blokhin unstrapped his pack and took out a second torch and a coil of rope which he dropped to the rough floor, casting about for a suitable place to anchor it. Finally, he looped it over an upthrusting needle of rock, then threw the other end into the unbroken blackness of the pit.

Vhirinovsky glanced down. Nausea was strong in him now. He had no more fear of heights than any other man, but that emptiness beneath him did something to his nerves.

'I'll go first if you want,' said Blokhin, slinging the torch over a shoulder. He crouched down and lowered himself over the edge.

In the torchlight, Vhirinovsky watched him go, a black, squat figure climbing down the sheer wall of the pit.

Blokhin reached the top of the narrow ledge, threw a swift glance upwards, then vanished inside.

Vhirinovsky waited. The silence grew long and the shadows seemed more evil and menacing, living things of the dark that almost *breathed* on his neck. Slowly, the minutes lengthened. Leaning far out, he saw the ledge. But there was no sign of his companion. The rope was still there, dangling freely against the dark. He leaned out, snatched at it wildly, feeling it suddenly rough and burning between his fingers. He caught a tight hold of the rope, feeling that awful drop beneath him, pulling subtly at his swinging body. Fastening the torch to his belt, slowly, hand over hand, he lowered himself down. Terror clutched at his brain and cut like a knife into his racing heart.

He was suddenly quite sure there was something as black as the pit and twice as awful waiting down there to strike up and tear him down, to rend him apart. But there was no way back now. He would have to go on. Even if he could talk himself into going back, he doubted whether he had that much strength left to pull himself up again. There was a dull roaring in his ears and a peculiar tightness behind his eyes. His arms felt as if they could hold on no longer. He couldn't breathe. He was caught in some vast web of blackness, held fast, and there was no way out. It was no use screaming. He felt sure of that. Because the loudest sound in the whole of creation would be swallowed up and lost in the great void around him.

Something hard and sharp struck against his feet. He had reached the ledge. Carefully, he swung himself in. The cave was larger than he had expected; a cold chamber of chill quietude. The floor was oddly smooth, unnaturally so, and covered was something slippery that shone with a dull gleam in the light of the torch. He looked about for Blokhin. But there wasn't the slightest trace of— Something moved at the back of the cave. There was a round opening that obviously led through to another cave at the back. It filled suddenly. He swung his torch.

'Blokhin?'

Suddenly his mind was a screaming turmoil. For the first time, he saw what it was. A vast, obscene creature, forty feet or more in length that slithered forward on its belly with a tortuous motion as if it were trying to move several times faster than a perverse nature had intended. The mouth was a nightmare slit of drooling horror. A deep triangular travesty of a mouth, rimmed with gaping, brown fangs and beslimed tusks that spilled a torrent of gelatinous fluid in front of it, lubricating the rocky floor. A single red eye glared balefully from out of the centre of the great, veiny, bulbous head. It had arms – strangely human arms; massive and leprous white, at the end of which were huge taloned hands. One claw crushed Blokhin's body in its murderous grip before cramming him into its gaping maw and biting him in two, gorily gulping down the man's upper half.

Vhirinovsky's mind screamed at him.

Still, the creature came on, dragging itself like a burrowing mole on those hideously human hands.

For an instant, he stood still, paralysed, rooted to the spot. Beyond the horror he could see an exit from the cave. Then something seemed to buckle inside him. With a piercing cry, he fled for the opening, leaping clear as it brought its slavering bulk towards him, reaching with one of its outstretched hands.

And then he was running as the horror slid behind him, his heart threatening to explode in his chest. Leaping over ravaged skeletons and weaving through slimy heaps of reeking excrement, he dashed into the darkness, taking small comfort in the fact that he was now going up.

From the diminishing sound he knew he was outdistancing it. Still he ran on. For an unknown time he made his way up until he came to a place where the way ahead was blocked by a heap of contorted skeletons. Frantically, he set about clearing the grisly obstacle, heaving the slime-covered bones to one side. Beyond, the tunnel ran for about thirty yards before reaching a dead end.

Vhirinovsky's heart sank. There was no escape.

Madly, desperately, he staggered forward, searching for a way out. He was becoming dizzy with fear and exertion. The walls were cold and damp against his palms. Something seemed to infiltrate his mind; a dark, insidious laughter the came from everywhere—yet he could see no one. And far-off, yet getting nearer, came a loathsome slurping as the nameless abomination, that thing from the subterranean depths, dragged its way towards him. As he began to pass out he thought he heard a peal of horrible laughter.

It was all a nightmare, Vhirinovsky told himself as, accompanied with a loud hammering, he regained consciousness, the sound of Ychev shouting and beating at the wooden door of the horrendous room he was in breaking through the darkness. With a crash, the door flew open, spilling a meagre amount of grey daylight into the dismal confines. In the doorway stood the guide, his face a mask of absolute horror.

Now that Vhirinovsky could make out his surroundings better, he felt bile rise to his throat. He lay, bound with rope, in the corner of a small room that was filled with thousands of fragments of bone. Mouldy hip bones, femurs, rib cages and skulls lay scattered all over the floor. Some of the piles were knee-high in places. Bones hung from the ceiling like ghoulish ornaments. A huge black cauldron in the fireplace was crammed full of them.

The stink of the long-dead pervaded everything. It was visible as a brown mist that hovered near the raftered ceiling.

'Help me!' Vhirinovsky yelled.

Ychev cried out something in his own language before dashing over to where the other lay. He withdrew a knife and cut the thick bonds. 'Come on. We must get out of here before she returns.'

Massaging his wrists, Vhirinovsky got to his feet. He rushed for the door, fearing that it would suddenly slam shut, closing off that sane rectangle of daylight, plunging them both into an abysmal darkness. He reached the threshold and saw that he was at the top of the dreadful hillock. Below him, and in every direction, the swamp extended for as far as the eye could see.

Suddenly a gangrenous, clawed hand burst from the earthen floor, grabbing Ychev.

The guide screamed and frantically tried to pull away but the grip was vice-like.

Dislodging clods of dirt, a corpse-like figure began to pull itself upright. With a supernatural strength, it tightened its hold and then twisted, snapping the unfortunate guide's leg at the shin.

Ychev hollered out his agony and fell backwards, crashing into a heap of skulls.

With an obscene gargling laugh, the horror emerged fully from the grave-like pit. It was a hideously shrivelled and emaciated entity. Stained and torn linen and fur garments were wound around much of the ghoul but the exposed parts were brownish-green revealing glimpses of leather-hardened, desiccated skin. Bone amulets and tarnished bracelets had been incorporated into its wrappings. Its face was stretched, the skin lumpy and mottled. Tufts of black, ragged hair sprouted from its head and lambent red fires burned in the depths of its otherwise empty eye sockets.

Although the guide had risked his life in order to save Vhirinovsky, he felt no obligation to reciprocate. Instead, he turned and fled, bounding down the slope, plunging through the deep sludge in which the dead festered. Streaked with mud, he was now laughing insanely. Tripping, he fell face first into the morass.

There came a loud creaking, slurping sound from behind.

Terrified, he turned to look over his shoulder and what he saw finally broke his mind.

The strange, weed-festooned hut was rising from the ground!

On a pair of long and spindly, reptilian legs, akin almost to those of a giant chicken, the structure rose fifteen feet into the air. In the open doorway was the cadaverous witch, hurling her curses. The bizarre construction started down the slope towards Vhirinovsky.

In a few lurching strides it overtook the doomed man and he felt a large splayed foot push him to the sodden ground where the foul swamp mud suffocated him as he struggled helplessly. The last sensation he knew was the agony of his spine breaking.

Some indeterminable time later, Vhirinovsky opened his eyes. He could see the anaemic sun beginning to rise beyond the horrible swamp. He had made it! Somehow he must have escaped. Then he noticed that he was some distance off the ground and could not feel his legs, in fact, he realised he could feel nothing below his neck. There was a groaning noise to his right and he swivelled his eyes in that direction. The bloody head of Ychev had been placed on a stake and he saw the man's eyes begin to open. Frantically looking around him, Vhirinovsky finally understood the dreadful truth.

The screaming of the severed, but alive, heads tore through the forest as the sun rose over the Hidden Lands.

DEAD ON ARRIVAL?

A night in the morgue just got a lot livelier...

THERE WAS SOMETHING very puzzling about this whole affair, thought Doctor Nathan Webb to himself as he sat in the small office annexed to the hospital morgue and read through the notes on the two corpses—a man and a woman—that had been delivered a couple of hours ago. Through the glass window, he could see the covered, lifeless forms lying on the operating tables in the adjacent room. Neither had, as yet, been formally identified, something which the police were currently trying to rectify. However, the cause of death was as grotesque as it was mystifying and he would love to know the circumstances behind the discovery.

The dead man was in his mid-thirties and perfectly average from a morphological point of view with no discerning marks, scars or tattoos. Something – probably some kind of wild animal, perhaps a large canine – had torn his throat out. There was even a large bite, inflicted by undoubtedly the same fanged creature, on his right arm, where, it was reasoned, he had tried to protect himself.

However, the woman—

Webb read through the medical notes again – notes which had been written in Doctor Chris Laidler's spidery handwriting. Had they been produced by anyone but Laidler, his highly respected superior at the hospital, he would have been compelled to check the findings himself.

For the woman, brown-skinned and perhaps of Thai or

Malayan origin, had been decapitated in the most brutal fashion. The brief forensic tests that Laidler had performed prior to reaching the decision to continue his investigations in the morning, revealed that most of her internal organs were also missing, along with her head; her chest and abdominal areas now empty cavities. It was, as he wrote in his report: '...as though her head has been torn off with such violence that her insides have been withdrawn as well'.

Webb shook his head in disbelief. He had spent ten years working down here, in a part of the hospital commonly referred to as 'Frankenstein's Laboratory', and had never known anything like it.

To the best of his knowledge, the police were 'keeping an open mind' as to the cause of death but he had little doubt that they were linked. It was all so strange. Bizarre and unsettling. Still, it was not for him to speculate what could possibly have transpired. All he had to do was sit his shift out and wait until Laidler arrived in the morning.

Unbeknownst to him it was going to be the most nightmarish few hours of his life.

Webb was going through the medical notes on some of the other cadavers they had in cold storage when the phone rang. Recognising the caller's number on the screen, he picked up the receiver and, doing his best Vincent Price impersonation, said: 'Frankenstein's Laboratory. Igor speaking. The Master's out at the moment. Is there anything I can do for you?'

'For Christ's sake, Webb. How many times have I told you to stop doing that? It might have been funny the first time but it ain't anymore.'

'Lighten up, Charlie. Just having a bit of fun with you. Hell, you need to have a bit of a laugh now and then down here or else you'd go nuts. Anyway, what do you want?'

'There's a cop from the NYPD at reception looking for you. Well, when I say looking for you, I think he wants to talk with whichever doc's working the graveyard shift in the morgue. He says that he was here earlier with old Laidler. His name's White. Detective Bill White.'

'Oh yeah. I met him just as he was leaving. Did he say what he wants?'

'Not to me. Should I send him down?'

'Yes, I suppose you'd better.'

'Okay.'

Webb put the phone down and went to the entrance of the morgue, wincing slightly as a sudden vinegary tang, distinguishable from the numerous other chemical smells, struck his nostrils. The morgue was at one end of a long, strip-light lit corridor from which many other doors gave access to other rooms and passageways. Halfway along were the stairs which led up to the ground floor and he waited in silence for the echoing footsteps which would herald the arrival of his visitor. He did not have to wait long before Detective White appeared on the scene – a short, stocky man dressed in a damp, black raincoat.

White raised a hand when he caught sight of the doctor. He began marching down the corridor.

'Detective. Nice to see you again,' greeted Webb. 'I see you don't get much sleep either.'

'It's all part of the job,' replied White. 'Do you mind if we have a talk? There's some things that just aren't adding up and I can't afford to wait till morning.'

'By all means. Come on in.' Webb held the door open permitting White to enter. He ushered the other towards the office, noting the strange manner in which the detective glanced at the two recently brought in corpses. One could have been forgiven for thinking that he was scared of something.

White took a seat.

'Would you like a coffee?' Webb asked from where he stood by the small vending machine. 'I go through half a dozen cups—'

'Has anything strange happened?' White interrupted. 'Anything...out of the ordinary?'

For a moment Webb was at a loss for words, uncertain how to respond. He took his seat opposite the detective. 'Strange? What do you mean?'

White scratched his head. 'I dunno. Anything...*weird?*' He looked over his shoulder, through the glass window into the operating theatre.

Webb could clearly see the man's reflection in the glass and it was the face of a man in fear. It was almost as though he was half-expecting to see something ghastly emerge from the shadows or for the cadaver-lockers to slide open debouching their zombie contents. The doctor shook his head. 'Nothing unusual. Why do you ask? Are you expecting something? Something I should know about?' He asked this last question with some measure of concern, suddenly reminded of the time when a psychopathic, violent drug dealer had caused mayhem searching for a body in which were stashed bags of dope. He had not been on duty that night but one of his colleagues had spent days in one of the wards upstairs after having been badly beaten.

White turned round. 'You've probably guessed it's to do with those two stiffs that were brought in earlier. The two you've got lying out there.'

'The man and the woman?'

'Yes. Mr Henry North and... Miss Boon-Mee.' White struggled to get the woman's name out.

'So you've managed to identify them?'

'Yes.' White reached into a pocket of his coat and removed a small black book. 'This was found in Mr North's jacket pocket. Now...I can't with any honesty say that I'm a religious man, nor do I believe in the supernatural, however I've spent the last hour or so going through this, which, to be honest with you, proves extremely hard reading.'

'You've got me interested. What is it?'

'First, may I ask if you're aware of the Staten Island child abductions?'

'Of course. It's been on the news and in the papers for months. How many kids have gone missing so far? Ten? Eleven?'

'Eleven,' White answered sharply.

'Why do you ask?'

'Well, it's just possible that the culprit's lying in the room next door.'

'Jesus!' Webb's mouth hung slackly open.

'Is it me or is it hot in here?' Loosening his tie, the detective then dabbed at his forehead with his fingertips, wiping away a sheen of sweat.

'It's not cold, that's for sure.'

White shifted in his seat.

'When you say the culprit, I take it you mean the man. This Mr North?' Webb's eyes were drawn to the black book.

'No. I mean *her*.'

'Miss Boon-May?'

'Boon-Mee,' White corrected. He turned round in order to look into the morgue once more. 'Although I doubt if that's her real name. I doubt if—' He gave a sudden startled cry and sprang out of his chair, his hand going for his gun.

Webb got out of his seat. 'Detective?'

'The... sheet. Did you see it? Did you see it move?'

'What are you talking about?' Webb went to the office door and pushed it open. The operating chamber where he and Doctor Laidler had performed hundreds of autopsies was bathed in a sharp actinic light which did little to make the morgue look welcoming.

White held his revolver in a shaking hand. He pointed towards the closest sheet-covered body, that of the decapitated Oriental woman. 'It moved.'

'Eh?' Webb was unsettled. Had this been Halloween, and had this been one of his colleagues telling him this, he might have put it down as a sick joke but for a NYPD detective to make such an observation bordered on the downright macabre.

'I saw it. I saw the sheet move.'

'You're kidding me, right?'

'I'm telling you. I saw it move.'

A sickly knot of fear was tightening in Webb's stomach and he could almost hear his heart thudding against his ribs. His mind screamed at him and he found himself gulping nervously. Death was his business — the examination of the dead something he had lived with for over ten years but never had he been faced with anything like this. In his well-ordered, sane world, the dead stayed dead and even though he had read of one or two very rare cases when someone mistakenly pronounced dead had been brought in with the DOA toe tags, this woman's head and guts were missing. There could be no mistake. Horrible thoughts boiled within his brain, conjuring terrible images which were no doubt given substance by the countless horror films he had watched over the years. Was it just his imagination or did the sheet twitch a little? It was impossible, he tried to tell himself.

White was backing away towards the door. It was obvious that he was ready to make a dash for it if anything out of the ordinary were to happen.

This was crazy, Webb told himself. Absolute madness. Managing to put things back into perspective, he dismissed his earlier notion that the cover had moved. Pacing over to the corpse, he dragged the sheet clear.

Boon-Mee's headless remains were motionless; seventy or so pounds of dead, naked flesh — gutted like an animal.

That unpleasant vinegary stink was stronger and seemed to be coming from the corpse itself.

Webb did the respectful thing and covered her up again. He turned to the detective. 'She's still dead. I guess you must have imagined seeing the cover move. Believe me, I've spent many a time down here on my own and I'll be the first to admit it can get a little creepy. The mind can play havoc if you let it.'

'Are you sure... she's dead?

'Absolutely.' The very fact that she was headless was surely evidence of that.

Slowly, White edged his way back from the exit.

'Do you think we can go back to the office so that you can tell me more about what's going on?' asked Webb. His own thoughts were gradually returning to normal although he would be the first to admit that he had, for a minute or so, been more than a little frightened.

'Okay.' White's eyes were constantly on the covered cadaver as he made his way back into the small room. He took his seat.

'Are you all right?' The doctor asked concernedly as he too returned to his chair.

White smiled and nodded unconvincingly.

'I believe Doctor Laidler keeps a small bottle of the hard stuff lying around somewhere if you're in need of a drink.'

White waved a hand. 'No. That won't be necessary.' He reached out for the book which still lay on the table before him. 'From what I can gather, this was written by Henry North who was the father of one of the missing youngsters. The first dozen or so pages are concerned mainly with his own investigations into the disappearances and from a cursory skim through it's pretty obvious that he didn't think much of how the police were handling things. Anyway, he mentions covering all the areas where the kids vanished, conducting door-to-door inquiries, talking to several of the other parents and so on. However, it's in the second half of the book that things —'

The phone rang causing Webb to jump. He did not recognise the caller's number. He picked up the receiver. 'Doctor Webb. St Michael's Hospital.'

'Is... is she still...'

It was a woman's voice but the words were heavily accented. Maybe Spanish, thought Webb. The line was not too good either. 'Sorry, I can't—'

'Is she still there?'

'Is she still there?' Webb repeated, unsure if he had heard correctly. Calling a morgue at half-past one in the morning to ask if someone was still there was one hell of a prank to play. It was not as though those in his care were likely to go anywhere. With that thought a tingle of ice crept along his spine. 'Who? Who do you want to speak to? This is Doctor Nathan Webb.'

'Is she still there?' The voice was stronger now, demanding.

'Look, I don't what you're talking about. I think you've got the wrong number.' Webb put the phone down.

'Who was it?' asked White.

Webb shook his head. 'I've no idea.'

The phone went again.

Webb picked it up, somewhat relieved to see it was the number for Charlie at the main reception.

'Doctor Webb?'

'Charlie?'

'I take it you got your call?'

'Yes. Any idea who it was? Did she leave a contact number?'

'No, a foreign-sounding woman phoned about ten minutes ago asking for your private number. I take it that was her. I tried to tell her that she should wait until morning but she was very persistent. She said it was a matter of life and death. Something about a friend of hers having been in a terrible accident. She'd been informed that she'd been brought here.'

'I see.' Webb felt a pang of guilt. 'Well put her straight through if she calls again.'

'Will do.'

Webb put the phone down. 'The mysterious caller claims to be a friend of the deceased woman.' He looked at White questioningly. 'I notice from the notes that there's no information whatsoever regarding how the injuries were sustained, estimated time or indeed location which I find highly unusual. Perhaps you can fill me in.'

'One of my officers was alerted to what at first was assumed to be a break-in at an abandoned property off Fedderson Avenue in the Bronx. A passing member of the public reported hearing 'unearthly' screams and shouts coming from one of the upstairs windows. Inside, the officer came across a scene of absolute carnage. North and Boon-Mee were found in the hall and...and several other bodies, mostly children, I'm afraid to say, were found in the basement.'

'Bloody Hell!'

'The dead kids have been sent to Saint Vincent's but it appears as though they've all been drained of blood.'

'Christ! There's some sick bastards out there.'

'Anyway, back to the book for this is where the really interesting clues lie.' White flicked through several pages. 'As I said, I've only skimmed through it but either it's the ramblings of a madman; a man perhaps driven mad with grief over his lost daughter and the obsessional search he undertook to try and find her or... well, I'll let you decide.'

'Before you go any further I've a question for you, detective.' Webb leaned forward, resting his elbows on the desk and interlacing his fingers. 'If I get you right you're theory as it stands runs something like this: For reasons that have still to be established, Mr North, believing he had found the whereabouts of the child murderer, stole into Boon-Mee's house in order to confront her? Yes?'

White nodded.

'Yet, that doesn't explain the nature of the injuries. This man's been savaged by a ferocious creature and if he murdered Boon-Mee, why and more to the point *how*, did he do it in such a barbaric way? There's a lot here that just doesn't make sense.'

'This is where the book comes in. But you're not going to believe what I'm about to tell you. Hell, I don't know whether I believe it, however it's apparent that Mr North did. To the extent that it cost him his life.'

'Well, what is it?'

White flicked through several pages. 'Here. This is it.' He handed the book over.

There was a crude drawing of a long-haired woman's head, her eyes mad and staring, her mouth wide-open and fang-filled. From the severed neck dangled an unsightly mass of tangled insides complete with lungs, heart, stomach and intestines. It was incredibly repulsive yet as a medical professional, Webb had to acknowledge its anatomical detail.

'North refers to it as a *penanggalan*,' said White, seeing the confusion on the doctor's face. He read directly from the book: 'A South-East Asian female vampire-like creature which feeds on the blood of the young. By day it appears as a normal woman, attractive, the kind of person you could easily pass in the street but by night, and when on the hunt, it transforms into a most horrible entity. The head detaches itself from the body complete with digestive tract and flies—'

Webb shook his head. 'Sorry, I'm...I'm not fully with you. Are you saying that—?'

'I'm just telling you what North believed,' White interrupted. 'Whilst at the same time trying to get to the bottom of this case. This was no ordinary murder, of that I'm certain. Amongst North's possessions was a bag filled with broken bottles. Glass shards. Now in the book it states that one way to kill one of these things is by stuffing the headless corpse with glass thus preventing the—'

'Will you just listen to yourself for a moment, detective? Hell, I thought you guys were supposed to be, well, if you don't mind me saying it, rational. You're making this sound like something from a bloody horror film.'

Tiredly, White rubbed his head. 'Yeah, I guess you're right. Maybe I've been working too damn hard. Everybody's been putting in the hours trying to apprehend this dreadful child-snatcher.'

'The best thing you can do is go home and rest. No doubt in the morning you'll feel better and you can go over this with Doctor Laidler.' Webb sniffed the air. That acetic acid reek was getting stronger.

'I guess you're right.' White stood up. 'Well, I'll be going but if you need to get me here's my number.' He handed over a small white card. 'If you can leave a message for Doctor Laidler informing him that I'll drop by around ten I'd appreciate it.' He turned and left, obviously eager to be going.

It was only after the detective had gone that Webb noticed that he had forgotten to take the book. He picked it up and began reading. He had only got to the third page when the door to the morgue crashed open and White rushed in, his gun in his hand.

Webb opened the office door. 'Detective?'

'She's here! That bitch is here!'

'What?'

'Your receptionist's dead and so are two nurses. Boon-Mee's come back for her body!' White was on the edge of hysteria, his eyes darting in every direction.

Fear bubbled in Webb's mind as he stared at the detective, his mind spinning madly.

'We've got to get out of here!'

'What?'

'Do you want to die?' asked White pointedly.

With wooden steps, Webb stumbled forward. *What the hell was going on?* There was a sudden tightness in his throat and he swayed for a moment, unable to come to terms with everything that was unfolding. 'No, of course not, but—?'

'Then let's go. Let's get out of this place.'

'Okay, okay.' The last thing Webb wanted to do was get on the wrong side of a man whom he now believed was mentally unhinged. More so as the man in question had a gun.

'Come on then.'

A riot of chaotic thoughts were swirling around in Webb's brain as he left the morgue and stepped out into the corridor.

'I've already called for back-up,' said White.

'That's—' Webb stopped. Up ahead, lying face down in a puddle of blood was one of the late-night nurses—an attractive young woman called Stacey Hopkins with whom he had shared many an intimate moment. He broke into a staggering run and knelt down at her ravaged corpse. 'What the hell?' There was no pulse. She was as dead as dead could be.

White screamed.

Webb looked up from the mangled corpse.

From around the corner, where the stairs led up to the ground floor, floated a truly nightmarish vision—the penanggalan. Its gruesome appearance was, more or less, as North had depicted it in his book. The head was that of a dusky, red-eyed, Oriental woman, her facial features twisted and bestial, her black hair long and parted down the middle. Like a jellyfish's tentacles, from the stump of her neck trailed a grisly growth of unsightly entrails and organs. The thing hissed, exposing its sharp fangs as it saw the two men.

Webb cursed volubly as he scrambled back to his feet. Now that he had seen that unearthly, utterly horrendous thing in the flesh it would be unlikely that he would ever sleep comfortably again.

White raised his gun and shot off three bullets.

With an unholy screech, the penanggalan sped forward.

Screaming, both men turned and fled.

Webb was the faster. He flung the morgue door open and leapt inside.

The detective was close behind. He had only just crossed the threshold when the disembodied head reared high above him and launched down, its maw agape. A second later, White roared in agony as the fanged mouth clamped down on his throat.

Webb stared helplessly as the penanggalan sank its sharp teeth deeper, latching itself firmly on to its victim. To his horror, he saw the thing's dangling innards take on a life of their own, coiling around the unfortunate detective, entwining him like some terrible vine, drenching him in blood. Despite the fact that its now heavily bloodied mouth was otherwise occupied, sucking the life from its prey, an evil sounding laugh was coming from it.

Struggling violently, the detective was dragged away from the morgue entrance. His feet skidded in a pool of blood and he went down. Still the fiend bit into him. Blood sprayed from his severed carotid artery. Ferociously, he was shaken like a rag doll in the jaws of a vicious Rottweiler.

Webb dashed forward and slammed the morgue door shut. He snatched up a nearby chair and wedged it. Frantically, he searched for anything that might prove of use — anything he could employ as a weapon. His eyes fell of a bone saw.

The door juddered but held firm. Blood seeped from beneath it, trickling along the tiled floor.

Snatching up the saw, Webb pulled back further from the door. A dark wave of adrenaline surged through him as he mentally wrestled with all that he had seen. Breathing heavily, he stood, transfixed, staring at the closed door, a cold sweat bubbling to the surface of his skin. *This was not happening,* he tried to tell himself. His mind suddenly lurched and for a moment his vision swam, then darkened. He felt incredibly dizzy as a bout of nausea threatened to overcome him. Reaching out for a nearby wall, he managed to support himself.

All was quiet.

Nerves afire, Webb somehow staggered back to his office. Mind reeling, he sank into his chair. He felt unnaturally cold but there was a filming of sweat on his face. A peal of hideous laughter gurgled in the depths of his mind. There was the sensation of evil around him, crowding in from every direction.

There came a sudden clatter from the operating theatre.

Webb sprang to his feet and rushed to the office door. With grasping, ugly claws, horror tore through his brain as he saw the headless, disembowelled cadaver of Boon-Mee, having fallen from the operating table, get clumsily to its feet. A sudden madness took hold. Yelling insanely, he rushed out and, gripping the bone saw, hacked down at the decapitated zombie, the serrated edge of the heavy surgical instrument embedding deep into the thing's left shoulder.

The decapitated corpse stumbled, pale arms, which should have succumbed to rigor mortis, reaching out, trying to grab the one attacking it.

A clawed hand flashed before Webb's face. He withdrew the bone saw and savagely hacked down a second time, enlarging the wound at the shoulder. With a cry of rage, he pulled, slicing through flesh and bone.

The stench of vinegar was almost overpowering.

Something thumped heavily against the door, the loud bashing accompanied by a wailing scream.

Boon-Mee's headless body fell to the floor. It was trying desperately to get to the door, to let its other body part in.

Webb sat astride the fiercely bucking corpse. A blood-crazed madness had now taken possession of him for he was now hacking with abandon. Blood streamed from his face and there was a mad look in his eyes as, like a butcher with a carcass, he repeatedly chopped down. He then began sawing at the arm.

Soul-wrenching screams accompanied a frenzied battering at the morgue door.

Frantically cutting through the bone, Webb severed the cadaver's left arm. The chair which he had blocked the entrance with went flying. His heart almost stopped beating as he looked up, his gaze rising from the trailing intestines and leaking innards to the monstrous head which perched at the top. Madly, he sprang forward and slammed the door on the advancing horror. Unaware of the sounds of his own screams, he applied his strength to keeping the penanggalan out.

The one-armed, acephalous body began crawling forwards, its actions weakening.

Webb could see that around the neck stump a milky, white liquid was frothing and dripping. It was this secretion which exuded the pungent, almost lachrymatory stink of vinegar. Even in his maddened state, he was drawn to the conclusion that this lubricatory fluid was being released in readiness for the re-attachment process of head and body.

Still the horror banged at the door, butting it, needing to get in.

There came a scream from outside—a man's scream.

The pressure on the door ceased and Webb could only assume that another doctor had arrived on the scene and that the penanggalan had gone in pursuit. Poor bastard, he thought. Still, it gave him a few moments. Knowing that to venture outside would be fatal, he looked for somewhere to hide. He could just lie on one of the spare operating tables, pull a sheet over himself and hope or —

His eyes were drawn to the morgue lockers.

Hurriedly, he ran over to the twenty or so metal cabinet doors and, like a contestant in some warped game show, began opening them. But these did not contain prizes just the cold, white-grey faces of dead men, women and children. All of those on the bottom row were filled. Heart thumping, he finally found an empty locker. Next came the awkward procedure of getting inside. Feet first, on his back, he pushed against the walls of the locker.

The storage compartment slid forward.

It caught on something, refusing to go any further.

Webb was now half-in, half-out. He cursed, suddenly remembering that several of these lockers did not close properly. Frantically, he pushed. Still the metal tray on which he lay would not budge. Then it gave a little, sliding forward on its rollers. It was now just his head and shoulders that stuck out. If his situation was not as deadly serious things could have been farcical.

The door to the morgue burst open.

A moment later, Webb gave a final heave and the locker slipped mercifully into place, plunging him into darkness. He felt like a lump of meat going into an oven. He lay there, hoping against hope that he had been quick enough. If not…

A terrible caterwaul-like screech shattered the silence.

Webb dared not breath. There came another scream and he had a mental image of the penanggalan staring down at its one-armed, autopsy-scarred body. There came a series of loud crashes and he knew that in its rage the foul being was wrecking the place in its search for him.

After a minute or so there fell a disturbing silence.

It was during this time that Webb feared the most for his life and sanity.

This was assuredly worse, far worse than being buried alive; knowing that at any moment the locker in which he hid could be slowly drawn back and that he would find himself staring up at that unbelievably hideous abomination. In such a position he would be vulnerable, unable to move, trapped, completely at its mercy.

He could envisage the loathsome creature floating around the morgue like some grotesque fairground balloon, its horrible, hanging, looped viscera the string.

The sound which followed was truly disgusting. A wet, squelching noise. There was a final pop and then the faint sound of bare feet running.

Five, then ten minutes passed.

Straining every sense, Webb lay motionless. All was quiet. Dimly, very dimly, he thought he could hear the sound of police sirens. He waited a while longer. Then, when he reasoned the coast was clear, he gave a gentle push.

The locker door was jammed.

Webb cursed. He pushed harder. The tray on which he lay did not budge. A ripple of insane laughter came to his lips as he realised he was now well and truly stuck.

His lab coat blood-spattered, Webb was still laughing to himself when the locker was eventually forced open by two obviously apprehensive cops. He was rolled out and helped upright.

'All right, buddy. Would you care to tell us what happened here?'

'You wouldn't believe me if I told you,' Webb answered, only vaguely aware that there was at least one gun levelled at him. He could see that Boon-Mee's mutilated cadaver was no longer on the floor and, as he was led away, gibbering and giggling, he noticed that Detective White's coat was also missing.

ANGELS OF DEATH

Their music was far from heavenly.

*A*PRIL 1945
The sounds continued to beat at the composer's ears, building with terrible intensity to the finale that he knew was close at hand. The screams and sobs, the animalistic outpourings of grief and fear from the doomed people in the room below were being drawn through him and into the electronic monster he had been wired up to. He prayed with all his might that he would die before the machine was able to capture the distilled pain and despair. If his heart gave way it would stop the psychic transfer on to the recording device and this dreadful use of his gifts would be over. Ever since he had been captured, he had feared death but now he wanted nothing more than for his torment to end so that others might be saved. Tears, mingled with sweat, ran down his face as the sounds reached a crescendo and then abruptly cut off in a mental death cry that echoed through his mind and broke the flimsy barrier of his sanity.

The recording equipment continued for a few more seconds before a black-gloved hand reached out and turned it off. The owner of the hand regarded the shrieking wreck of a man with some satisfaction before ordering his execution. He had what he needed although it would take a while to perfect. The priority now was to get out of the country and keep a low-profile. A smile creased his lip as an idea came to him.

November 1978

Bespectacled, forty-seven year old private investigator, John Salford, got out of his car, retrieved his briefcase from the back seat, locked up and stood for a few seconds appraising the large, detached red-brick house before him.

Clearly he was in the wrong business, he reflected, for such a property, especially in an area like this, did not come cheaply. Shivering a little in the cold morning air, he lit a cigarette and took several much needed puffs before throwing it to the pavement and stubbing it out under the heel of a highly-polished shoe.

Straightening his tie, he then pushed open the garden gate and walked along the short stretch of flower-bordered drive, noticing the figure at the downstairs window. The front door was opened a moment later by his prospective client, the recently-widowed Mrs Sally Parker.

'Hello, I take it you're Mr Salford.'

'Yes, that's me.'

'Please, come in.'

'Thank you.' Salford entered the house. 'It's a nice place you've got here, Mrs Parker. Very nice.' Noticing the slightly haggard look in the late middle-aged woman's face and the weariness behind her eyes, he could see that the sudden death of her husband had, naturally enough, hit her hard.

'May I first offer you my deepest condolences. Obviously I didn't know your husband but from what little I've been able to find out so far he was clearly a well-liked individual. I'm sure he'll be sadly missed.'

'He will indeed.' Sally gave a half-hearted smile.

Fully aware that this would have to be handled delicately, yet knowing that sometimes the best thing was to get down to business, Salford reached into an inner suit pocket and removed an envelope which he handed over. 'This is just a standard contract letter. It contains all the information relating to my fees, expenditure, what I can and can't do and all the other admin stuff.'

'Very well. I'll read it later.' Sally placed the letter on a small stand. 'Shall we go into the lounge? And would you like a drink?

Tea? Coffee?'

Salford shook his head. 'Not for me, thank you.'

Sally led the way into the well-furnished room. She had obviously prepared things for this meeting for two chairs and a desk had been set up at one end, atop which rested several large binders and two box-files.

'You said on the phone that your husband, Michael, was an accountant,' said Salford. He sat down and removed a pen and a small black notebook from the same pocket from which he had extracted the contract letter.

'That's correct.' Sally sighed and collected her thoughts. There was no doubt it was going to be hard dredging through Michael's documents in such detail.

'He worked in the City at the private accountancy firm Harrington's for twenty years before deciding to go freelance. Although I never met any of his clients, Michael called them his 'luvvies' for they were comprised in the main of retired actors, over-the-hill performers and the like. Eccentrics mostly. The kind of people who may have been famous forty years ago but are now largely forgotten. You see, Michael's grandfather had been a turn of the century entertainer; a magician I believe. Consequently, he'd always had an interest in things like that. Old variety acts and such. Anyway, he'd obviously found a niche for himself, dealing with such people.'

'Interesting.' Salford sat back in his chair, interlacing his nicotine-stained fingers. 'Now, I hope you don't mind me speaking candidly, Mrs Parker, but I suppose we'd better try and establish just why it is that you think that your husband did not…well, take his own life.'

Having done some research in order to find out the 'back story', he had read that Michael had been seen by several witnesses clutching his head before purposefully throwing himself in front of a London bus. A post-mortem examination had ruled out anything like a seizure or drugs, which only left suicide. Case closed.

Sally choked back a tear. 'My husband had absolutely no reason to kill himself. We were happily married. As you can see, we have a lovely house. He had just received a glowing endorsement from the highly regarded Board of Independent Accountants. Everything was going so well and then I came home from a brief stay at my sister's to find the police here. It just doesn't make any sense.'

'Is there any history of mental problems in the family, Michael's family, that is?'

'None that I'm aware of. Of course his parents have been dead a long time now.'

'No… suicide note?'

'Nothing. Nothing whatsoever. Had Michael left some form of explanation I might be able to come to terms with his death but as it is I'm in limbo. I'm haunted, not knowing if it's something I could have prevented. I feel guilty in so many ways, unaware if there's more I could have done.'

Salford was beginning to get out of his depth. He knew how to track down missing people and he could muddle his way through the ins and outs of tax evasion but he had never had reason to console a grieving widow before. 'I take it you're getting some help in this matter, friends you can talk to?'

Sally seemed to ignore his question. She picked up one of the heavy account ledgers. 'I knew everything about his home life and there was nothing wrong there. That only leaves his work. He never mentioned any problems but there must be an explanation contained in here somewhere. There has to be.' She opened a page at random.

Unsure as to how much good it would do but coming to the realisation that he had to do something, Salford rose from his chair and walked around the desk so that he could look over the woman's shoulder. On the open page was a meticulously ordered list of dates, names and figures, all contained within neat margins.

Sally turned a page, revealing more of the same.

It was filled with invoices, expenditure sums, amounts and financial facts that Salford knew would take hours, if not days, to sift through. 'Clearly your husband was very detailed in his work.'

'I want you to go through all of this. I can pay you well, more than your normal rate, whatever that is.'

Salford winced. It was not so much the prospect of having to face such a time-consuming task but what he considered to be the likely futility of it.

'Mrs Parker.' He removed his glasses and gave his eyes a quick rub before putting them back on. 'Forgive me for speaking bluntly, but don't you think you're searching for explanations which may not exist? I mean, tragic as your husband's death undoubtedly was, I fail to see how it can be attributed to anything *but* suicide. As a professional, the last thing I want to do, especially at a time like this, is to prolong your pain. I know this can't be an easy time for you but the last thing you need is for the likes of me to cash-in on your suffering.'

'I believe Michael was murdered.' Sally closed the thick ledger. 'There! I've said it.'

'*How?*' Salford asked incredulously. 'The police—'

'Yes, yes. I know the police think it was suicide. But, deep down, in my heart, I can't accept it. Something or someone drove him to kill himself.'

Technically that was still suicide, Salford thought, but he understood what she meant. If someone intentionally drove Parker to take his own life then surely they were morally, if not legally, culpable. He was unsure where the law stood on this. He nodded, mentally resigning himself to accepting the case. He had to at least attempt to bring some measure of closure to the poor woman. And, at the end of the day, he would be getting paid for it.

He reached down and picked up one of the leather-bound ledgers. 'Well…I'll look into these accounts for any inconsistences if you want, but please don't get your hopes up.'

After stubbing out his tenth cigarette of the evening, Salford paced over to his drinks cabinet and poured himself another whisky. Glass in hand, he stared down at the account files he had spent the last four hours sifting through. It had proven hard, eye-straining, confusing work and his brain was a chaotic jumble of fiscal workings. His initial hope of finding things fairly straight-forward had dissipated after the first half hour as the computa-tions and the mode of recording had become increasingly difficult to follow.

A cursory look through the box files revealed that one contained countless unsorted papers; letters, yellowed newspaper cuttings, receipts, several old black and white photographs and even a copy of the late Michael Parker's Last Will and Testament. The other was crammed with articles and magazines, pro-grammes and brochures, flyers and bulletins – all detailing the weird and wonderful lives and times of the deceased's so-called 'luvvies'.

Salford stood, debating whether he should call it a night and resume his task in the morning or try and get another few hours work in. Draining his whisky in one gulp, he resumed his seat, checked his watch, lit another cigarette and decided to work until midnight. As the minutes ticked by, he found himself ruminating on the fact that on the other cases he had worked on it was usu-ally the paucity of documentation which held him back—this time, however, there seemed to be too much.

It was the classic case of a needle in the haystack and there was no certainty that there was a needle there to be found.

Methodically and meticulously, Salford had checked each page of the ledgers as they had been compiled, going through them in chronological order from earliest to most recent. They presented to him a highly accurate picture of the volatile, ever-changing financial fluctuations of Parker's clients. Most were securely within the boundaries of what most people would term extremely well-off; their portfolios extending into six and even seven figure values.

The finances of one or two had obviously not fared quite as well and there were several instances where scribbled, indecipherable markings in red ink, which appeared to have been documented in some form of code or shorthand, possibly highlighted this.

Going purely on the volume of red ink written alongside a pair of individuals who were referred to simply as O & M, Salford decided to try and concentrate on these two, reasoning that it was as good a place as any to begin. Now that he had finally ascertained a starting place, his spirits lifted somewhat. If there was anything to this investigation then at least he had something, no matter how tentative, to go on. Now that he had singled out this pair, he began to note their conspicuous recurrence.

It had now gone midnight.

Like a bloodhound with a scent, Salford delved deeper, purposefully seeking out anything pertaining to the mysterious O & M. The fact that Parker had always referred to them in such a manner, consistently using the old-fashioned ampersand, whilst freely using the word *and* for all others was in itself slightly unusual. And, although he was unable to comprehend their full relevance, the sheer preponderance of comments ascribed to their financial status suggested to him that the deceased accountant had become increasingly concerned about something or other.

Was it all just about money?

Salford removed his spectacles and nibbled thoughtfully at one of the arms.

Surely to God there was nothing here which could drive a man of sound mind and body to suicide?

Putting his spectacles back on, Salford sat up and stretched his arms out. Glancing at his wristwatch, he was surprised to see that it had just gone one o'clock. He lit himself another cigarette and turned his attention to the amassed documentation and other bits and pieces in one of the box files. Assuming correctly that there was no real order to it, he tipped the contents on to his desk and began rifling through it.

Much of it was personal effects; an old driving license, a marriage certificate, a school achievement for something or other, National Service papers and —

Salford's eyes were drawn to a small newspaper cutting.

It was typed in French, of which he could read little, and over twenty years old, dated to August 11th, 1955.

One line stood out: *Mademoiselle Ophelia & Mademoiselle Margaret.*

Were these O & M?

If so, then Salford knew of them. Lady Ophelia and Dame Margaret, as they were now known, were the stage personae of a rather clapped-out drag act still treading the boards in some of the less prestigious seaside playhouses; a poor man's Hinge and Bracket by all accounts whose act was often laced with a smattering of 'seaside postcard' innuendo. He seemed to recall they had once featured in a television advertisement for some lesser well-known brand of sherry or something similar, giggling like overgrown schoolgirls as they quaffed and cavorted. They had to be in their late fifties or early sixties by now. He scribbled something down in his notebook and decided it was now time for bed.

Two long days of searching through Parker's files had yielded nothing of note except for the mystery of the red annotations which Salford was certain had been written in some kind of code. With only this to go on, he determined to talk to each of those clients about whom there were red notes. If he were honest with himself, he was also becoming more than a little curious about Lady Ophelia and Dame Margaret and he had decided to start with them.

Despite a fairly intensive search, he had been unable to find out the real names of the two cross-dressing entertainers, which perplexed him. However, their address, just outside London, had been more forthcoming, contained as it was in some correspondence between them and Parker, and, as he turned into the private drive, he mentally tried to work out how he would initiate his inquiry.

There was little doubt in his mind, and indeed in the minds of those who were aware of them, that they were a homosexual couple; eccentrics—recluses who, aside from their flamboyantly camp and inimitably over-the-top performances, now shunned all contact with others. He had to assume that they had been informed of their accountant's death. If not, it would be up to him to break the bad news.

The fact that the duo did not appear to have an agent was something that also intrigued Salford. Admittedly they were 'getting a bit past it' but he still thought they would have had some form of representation.

It was not unprecedented but it was unusual.

After he had parked, Salford locked his car up and made his way to the main entrance.

It was a substantial house, set in grounds that may have been neatly kept in the past but were now running to seed. Few places looked their best in winter but it was clear that nothing had been done to keep the gardens in good condition for a long time and the gravel surrounding the building was patchy and weed-filled—a sure sign of years of neglect. From its steeply-pitched gables to the ornate iron conservatory, now missing several panes of glass, it must have been a perfect example of a grand Victorian house.

Salford had to supress a shiver. Places like this always reminded him of ghost stories. Looking up at the small windows on the top floor, he could imagine a despairing face looking out; silently screaming for help. He stopped at the door. On his right was an old-fashioned bell pull and he was just about to reach for it when he heard a series of bolts being drawn back.

The door opened.

The sight that greeted the private investigator was as strange as it was surprising. For he had never expected one of the middle-aged thespians to answer the door, dressed and made up in the Edwardian fashion they were known for; complete with beauty spot, a peacock feather in what was surely his wig, long jade-green dress, gloves, stylised cameo brooch, pearl necklace and drooping earrings. Yet, such was the case.

'Yes, what is it?' The man's voice was nasal, high-pitched and snobbish; condescending to the point of insulting. From the smell of it, he had doused himself in lavender.

Salford hesitated, unsure how to proceed. He had prepared himself for several eventualities but this had not been one of them. 'Pardon me for asking, but are you...Lady Ophelia or Dame Margaret?'

'As you ask, I am Dame Margaret.'

Things were bordering on the surreal for Salford. Despite his reluctance, he found himself scrutinising the transvestite, his face creasing with disapproval the more he saw. It was like something he had last seen at a pantomime when he had been a child; ghastly, yet at the same time strangely fascinating. However, it was one thing seeing individuals like this on the stage but to be confronted by them on the doorstep to their homes was quite an-other thing. Unless a performance was imminent—which, given the early hour of the day, he doubted—such things were far from normal. He opened his mouth to speak but no words came out.

'Margaret, darling. Have we a visitor?' called out a mellifluous voice from within the hallway. A moment later another made-up man, resplendent in a rich scarlet dress, choker, gloves and tiara stepped into view. Reaching into his handbag, he removed a monocle which was then deftly fastened to his right eye. With a giggle, he stepped unnervingly closer. 'Well, let's have a look. My, such a fine specimen of manhood.'

'I agree, Ophelia. Perhaps we ought to have him stuffed,' quipped Margaret in sudden good humour. 'You know how good I am at taxidermy. I daresay he'd make an excellent contribution to my collection.'

Ophelia smiled. 'But think of the mess, dear. We no longer have any servants to do the tidying.'

Salford raised his arms. 'Look, I fully get your banter or whatever the hell it is you guys are—'

'Guys?' The two drag queens turned to each other in shared confusion before turning their gazes on Salford.

'Am I right in thinking that you are of the opinion that we are...men?' asked Margaret. Undoubtedly offended, he drew in his cheeks so that it looked as though he was sucking on a lemon.

'Please, you can drop the act. Save it for your shows.' Salford was growing uncomfortable and impatient. There was little hope in getting much from these two weirdoes if they were to persist with their bizarreness. 'I'm here to inform you that your accountant, Michael Parker, is dead.'

'What a... tragedy,' commented Margaret.

'Yes indeed.' With actions that were as blatantly insincere and disrespectful as they were exaggerated, Ophelia withdrew a silk handkerchief from his handbag and began to wipe false tears from his cheeks.

'Now see what you've done.' Margaret put a comforting arm

around his other half. 'There, there, dear.' He fixed the private investigator with a scathing stare. 'Look! You've gone and given her the sniffles. I'll ask you to leave and take your bad news elsewhere. You're not welcome here. Begone and bother us no more!'

Not for the first time in his life, Salford found the door slammed in his face.

After Salford's failure to get any information from Ophelia and Margaret, he meticulously checked through the other clients whom Parker had left cryptic notes about. All had been extremely helpful and genuinely saddened to hear of their accountant's death, in stark contrast to the reaction of the two he had met the day before.

An elderly actress, who Salford vaguely remembered seeing on screen, had told him that they would all be hard put to find an accountant who had such a good grasp of show business. She had also given him a clue about Parker's notes.

Apparently she received a regular payment from an ex-lover who, though he was still fond of her, did not want their history to become public. When she had mentioned the name of a prominent, married politician, Salford pricked up his ears. What if the notes were all to do with secrets that Parker had either been told in confidence or had worked out for himself?

If so, then Ophelia and Margaret might have a lot to hide and possibly a lot to lose. He really had to decipher Parker's code and decided that the person most likely to know how to solve this conundrum was Sally. She agreed to meet him in a quiet coffee shop near to his office that he liked to use to relax nervous clients.

'You mentioned on the phone that you were planning to pay a visit to some of Michael's 'luvvies'. Do you have any news for me?' Sally asked, eager to hear of any developments.

Salford took a sip from his steaming coffee cup before returning it to the table. 'Not news as such but the visits have thrown up a few questions that I hope you can help me with. Some of the entries in your husband's records have coded writing beside them. It may be important that we decipher them and I wondered if you know how to read them.'

'Those scribbles?' Sally asked in surprise. 'No idea I'm afraid. Aren't they just to do with calculations?'

'The first few seem to have been but as I went further into the records they changed. The later notes look far more like coded writing. Let me show you.'

Salford removed a few photographs he had taken of the pages in question. 'See this one. These are all letters but I can't make head nor tail of them.'

Sally took the photographs. 'I see what you mean. It doesn't look like shorthand. I was a secretary before I married and I would recognise that.' She stared at the photographs for a few moments before shaking her head. 'I'm sorry but this doesn't mean anything to me. Michael often talked about his clients and he loved to tell me some of their anecdotes but he never discussed their finances with me. Do you think this might be important?'

'It could be. I'm beginning to think that your husband knew more about his clients than some of them would have wanted. I imagine that discretion is important in his line of work?'

'Of course! He would have needed to know all about their financial affairs to do his job and people don't generally want those facts to be broadcast.'

Salford lit a cigarette. 'Yes, but I was thinking more on the lines of embarrassing secrets or incriminating behaviour. Would he have come across anything of that nature?'

'Well, I think there were a few times when he had to ask directly for an explanation of money coming in or going out that he could not account for. Now that you mention it there was something. Something that he got worked up about.'

Behind his spectacles, Salford's eyes narrowed. 'What was it?'

'It would have been about two years ago, when he took on some new clients. He spent at least a week working through the files from a previous accountant and he was very distracted, worried almost. Then it suddenly got better and he was back to normal. I haven't thought about it since.'

'Can you remember who the clients were?' Salford asked eagerly.

'Yes, I'm pretty sure it was the musical comedy act, Ophelia and Margaret.'

Salford tensed. 'How sure exactly?'

Sally thought for a moment and then nodded her head. 'It was definitely them. He said they were the most colourful characters he had ever met. Personally, I've always thought them a little weird, creepy almost. Still, I'd be most surprised if they've got anything to do with Michael's death.'

'Have you ever met them?'

'No, but I've heard a bit about them and I saw them on television once or twice. I have the feeling they once starred alongside Morecambe and Wise, or was it Benny Hill?'

'Acting on a hunch, I went out to see them yesterday. I've met some strange people in my line of work, but there's something about those two that sets my teeth on edge.' Salford reached into his jacket pocket and removed his notebook. 'There are a few questions I'd like to ask you. Firstly, how's your French?'

'Reasonable...I suppose. Why?'

'As you know, your husband kept many articles and notes on his clients.' Salford opened his notebook and took out the small newspaper cutting which had steered him towards the two drag queens. He handed it over. 'I'm okay with German but I never got the hang of French. Can you read this?'

Sally took the cutting and quickly read it to herself, her eyebrows rising in surprise. 'Okay. It reads as follows: During a performance by Mademoiselle Ophelia and Mademoiselle Margaret a man barged on to the stage, shouting wildly and seemed about to attack the stars. Security men ran to stop him but he produced a gun and shot himself in the head. The authorities are currently investigating but no one apart from the gunman was hurt. This comes two weeks after the tragic suicide of the Mademoiselles' manager, Monsieur Guillaume Baschel.' She looked up from the cutting and there was a spark in her eyes. 'Two suicides!'

'It's certainly an interesting coincidence.' Salford tried to sound cautious and level-headed but he too felt a building hope that this could be a real lead.

'You need to go back and get some answers from them,' Sally insisted.

'I will, but I want to do some more checking first. There may be more about the incident in Paris and there must be people who can dish the dirt on them. Showbusiness is supposed to be gossipy. Hell, I haven't even be able to find out their real names yet.' The private investigator drained his cup and asked for the bill. 'You check at home to see if there are any other papers that might relate to all this.'

'Yes. If I find anything I'll call you.' Sally rose to leave and then sat down again abruptly. 'I've just thought!' she exclaimed. 'You should ask Ernest Harrington about Michael's notes. He was Michael's employer for twenty years and taught him most of what he knew.'

'Good thinking! I'll get straight on to it,' Salford agreed. He felt a renewed vigour as at last there was something to grab hold of in this case. He would put his friend, Gerry Lomas, on to searching old newspapers for anything about Ophelia and Margaret. Lomas worked as a librarian and was always glad of a supplement to his income, particularly if he could do his research when the library was not busy. His own time would be better spent at Harringtons.

'Oh, yes. I recognise these.' Ernest Harrington ran his finger down the page of the ledger that Salford had handed him. He was a thin, balding man who was fast approaching retirement age.

'Can you decipher them?' Salford asked.

'Of course! It's my own invention. Sort of a cross between shorthand and anagrams. Poor Michael picked it up very quickly. I use it when I need to make a note of something delicate that I would not want to become common knowledge but don't want to forget.'

'So, what do they say?' Salford tried to retain his patience but he was dying to know.

'Let's see. What have we got here?' Like an Egyptologist poring over a sheet of ancient papyrus, Harrington began to translate the cryptic notes. 'South American funds. Illegal brokers, check for implications. Payments to F. Moreau draining account. Clients refuse to reveal details. Etcetera. Hmm... interesting stuff,' he commented and moved on to the next section of red notes.

'This is from a few weeks later. Again more of the same. Chilean investments doing better than expected. Here Michael writes that the funds have been disposed of and payments ceased. What's this? O and M explained that F. Moreau had been a penniless relative whose medical bills they had paid but he had unfortunately died.'

Salford was disappointed. So far there was little to help with his case. He was about to thank Harrington for his time when the elderly accountant made a sudden exclamation and peered more closely at the page he was examining.

'This is the last entry and the last section of annotation.' Harrington pointed to the text he was studying. 'Michael writes that there was a large payment from Paraguay in October, far larger than any other the two had received before. It was from the same source as the ones he was concerned about when he took on their accounts.'

'Sorry, I'm confused. I don't quite understand the problem

with investing in South American businesses,' Salford confessed.

'Oh, mostly it's fine and there are some very good opportunities for long-term investors but there have been warnings of quite a high level of criminal activity, drug cartels and the like. I always advise my clients to be very vigilant about any investments from that area in case there's a connection. I'm sure Michael did the same and I'm not at all surprised that he flagged up this payment and was going to ask them about it.' Harrington returned his attention to the page. 'It says: Have arranged meeting with O and M. Eleven-thirty, November, First.'

'But that was the day before he died!'

Harrington looked at Salford with dawning horror. 'Do you mean to say that you suspect O and M, whoever they are, had a hand in his death? I thought he'd committed suicide. Leapt in front of a bus or something.'

'Maybe, maybe not. It's too early to jump to conclusions. Tell me, if Parker found evidence of a client taking part in illegal activities, and not for the first time, do you think he would have informed the police?'

'If he had real evidence, I'm certain of it,' Harrington answered with conviction. 'He was absolutely straight.'

Unlike some Salford thought.

It was proving to been an eventful day. After Salford's interview with Harrington, he had called on Sally to check if her husband had indeed visited Ophelia and Margaret on the day before his death. As she had been at her sister's at the time in question she could not confirm it either way.

However, she did have news of her own. She had shown him the latest edition of the *Radio Times* because there was an article about the forthcoming Royal Variety Performance. And, much to his surprise, near the end of the list of acts were Lady Ophelia and Dame Margaret.

How exactly they had managed that was beyond him. He knew the Royal Variety Performance was a rather eclectic mix but even so…

Leaving to do some research of his own, he had called Lomas and had felt a certain grim satisfaction at the librarian's discoveries. The records showed that the two performers had come to England, from France, in the early-Sixties and had left a mysterious trail of death in their wake.

It appeared that at least seven people who had some connection with them had taken their own lives: three stage managers, a theatre critic, a make-up artist, a cleaning lady and a journalist. Strange as the deaths had been, there did not seem to have been any suspicion on the police's behalf that the two drag artists were involved and the incidences had happened far enough apart that they did not pursue this.

Salford felt as if the pieces of the puzzle were finally falling into place although he still had no idea *how* the deaths had been made to happen. Was it all just coincidence or could they have used some kind of hypnosis to plant a death wish in their victims' minds? In Parker's case, could one of them have actually pushed him under the bus and just not been noticed by the witnesses? Were they guilty or innocent?

Of one thing he was certain, they were dangerous to know for death surrounded them. He knew it did not add up but there was definitely something to be discovered. He had debated whether to go to the police but felt that he simply did not have enough to go on yet.

He did not even know if Parker had in fact gone to see his cross -dressing clients as he had planned. They could always deny it anyway. What he needed was some hard evidence.

Sitting in his office, he wondered whether or not he should approach them directly. Given the reception he had got last time maybe not. What he really wanted was to take a look inside their house—see if there were any skeletons hiding in the closet amid the sequined ball gowns and cocktail dresses.

Remembering the article in the *Radio Times*, Salford had a sudden inspiration. The show was to be recorded tomorrow and there would surely be rehearsals before then. He telephoned the London Palladium pretending to be an electrician and ascertained that the main rehearsals were to be held today, before the main performance tomorrow and that all the acts would be there for several hours. The office manager had told him that they did not generally finish until late evening.

Salford's mind was made up. This was his chance.

The early evening air was bitterly cold and one or two stars were beginning to show through the breaks in the cloud as Salford emerged from the shadows and scaled the wall which surrounded the foreboding property. Stealthily, he dropped to the other side, pleased to see that all was in darkness. Now that he was inside the grounds, everything was suddenly ominous.

In the course of his numerous investigations he had only once before had reason to resort to breaking and entering. He took out his heavy torch, comforted by its solidity in his hand.

In the far distance an owl hooted.

Clinging to what shadows there were, Salford crept towards the house. Warily, he made his way around the back of the building. Removing a small jemmy from his coat pocket, he searched for a convenient window, then set about levering it open. Once done, he switched on his torch and shone it inside.

Aside from the dancing shadows there was no movement.

Nerves afire, Salford clambered into the room. It was small and had the appearance of a scullery. Shining his torch around, he saw a vast Belfast sink and racks for dishes to dry on, a large wooden tub and a mangle.

Moving through an archway to the kitchen, the feeling of

stepping back in time continued. There was a scrubbed wooden table and an old range for cooking on. Not a sign of any modern white goods was visible. More importantly, nothing to confirm his suspicions about the house's owners.

Exiting the kitchen, Salford went through to a wide hallway with several doors opening off it and a fine staircase. The first main room he entered was undoubtedly for entertaining. There were ornate, if slightly faded sofas, elegant chairs and a grand piano which was covered with photographs of Lady Ophelia and Dame Margaret at various stages of their none-too-illustrious careers.

Again, the room was stuck in a time warp. Two large, gilt-edged mirrors reflected his torchlight and every flat surface had valuable-looking ornaments on them. There was even a yellowing newspaper bearing the date 1910 which had been placed on a side table and countless other little period features which added to the genteel, yet decidedly strange ambience. He searched the room thoroughly but to little effect.

The other large downstairs room felt more private. It appeared to be a study, with two identical desks and chairs.

A well-stocked drinks cabinet showed a particular fondness for imported beers, port and brandy—clearly not the sherry Ophelia and Margaret were renowned for tippling on stage. There was a filing cabinet which took Salford's attention for a while but contained only information about requests for the duo to appear at various venues over the years and revealed them to be zealous in their pursuit of the highest fee they could command.

He noted that there had been a gap of several years between their last performance and the very recent letter inviting them to perform at The Palladium. This sudden renaissance in their popularity struck him as strange.

Leaving the study, Salford checked the last door on the ground floor but only found a broom cupboard. That puzzled him. In most houses of this era there was a cellar. Returning to the kitchen, he looked more carefully round the room.

Against one wall was a dresser with a few plates and cups on it. There would have been room for many more and given the excessive nature of the decoration elsewhere it looked out of place. Examining it more closely, he could see that there were concealed hinges on the far side of the dresser.

Wriggling his fingers between the wooden back and the wall, he pulled gently and was not altogether surprised when it swung smoothly open, revealing a door behind it.

There was a light switch behind the concealed panel and a little further down a modern strip light, incongruous given its environment, was fixed to the sloping ceiling. A short flight of stairs ended at a plain wooden door.

Cautiously, Salford crept down. His heart was thumping in his chest, though whether due to fear or excitement, he could not tell. Reaching the door, his heart sank upon finding it locked.

Fortunately, he was fairly adept at lockpicking, and, removing a fine set of picks from a back trouser pocket, he set about diligently trying to gain access. At any moment he half-expected one or both of the cross-dressing owners to appear at the top of the stairs – that he would hear a noise and, upon turning, would see some knife-wielding individual imitating Norman Bates from Hitchcock's infamous *Psycho* shower scene framed in the doorway above.

With a click, the lock sprang.

Salford put his lockpicks away then gently pushed the door open.

The room beyond was fairly small, perhaps twelve feet by eight, and had been closed and hidden for very good reason—for on the wall directly opposite was a photograph of Adolf Hitler beneath a large flag bearing the swastika of Nazi Germany!

'What the..?' Shaking his head in disbelief, Salford stepped inside. Panning his torch away from the photograph of the Führer, he could see that the room served as both an office and a private shrine dedicated to the Third Reich.

There were several large filing cabinets, two chairs, a desk atop which was a typewriter, a pending tray, some books, a stack of papers and a gilt-framed photograph. The latter showed three men in white jackets reclining in large wicker chairs.

The private investigator's eyes widened as he read the lettering in the small white caption at the bottom: *Schutzstaffel K. Werner, J. Mengele und E. von Koenig. Buenos Aires. 1952.*

Mengele. Josef Mengele. The infamous 'Angel of Death' who had presided over the terrible experimentation on countless Auschwitz concentration camp detainees.

Salford's jaw dropped upon realising that the other two men were none other than Ophelia and Margaret! Even through their disguise and the fact that the photograph was twenty-six years old it was possible to recognise them.

Unlike other prominent Nazi war criminals they had not gone to ground, altering themselves through plastic surgery and hiding away in the remotest parts of the world, but had rather done the opposite as, for over a quarter of a century, they had evaded capture and fooled the world by masquerading themselves behind the personae of two quintessentially English drag queens; rising above suspicion through their very conspicuousness.

Reasonably fluent in German, Salford began skimming through the papers on the desk. Most were letters; private correspondence between Mengele and his two agents. Others made repeated reference to the *Thule Society* and Heinrich Himmler's quasi-historical Occult Division—*the Ahnenerbe*. There were also details of not insubstantial payment from South American benefactors—Nazi sympathisers for the main.

In the pending tray was what appeared to be a scientific document. Expertly typed, it consisted mainly of a long list of names, and caught the private investigator's attention as that at the bottom was *Michael Parker*. Alongside, was a time: 27 hours and 32 minutes. Two other names Salford recognised. *Guillaume Baschel. Francois Moreau.* All individuals who had mysteriously committed suicide.

'Well, hello.'

Salford spun round.

Stood in the doorway was Ophelia or rather SS officer Klaus Werner. Dressed and made up as his feminine alter-ego, he took a casual draw from the slender cigarette holder he had clamped between the fingers of his left hand. In his right hand he held a Luger. 'Margaret dear, guess what I've found?' he shouted.

Gulping nervously, Salford raised his hands.

With an insane giggle, the other transvestite scurried down the stairs and looked over his accomplice's shoulder. 'My, my. It's a good job we decided to come back so that I could get a change of costume. I want to look my best in front of the Queen after all.'

'I... I don't understand,' Salford mumbled. Fear gripped him and he knew that, having discovered what he had, the chances of him getting out of here alive were minimal.

'Of course you don't, dear,' said Ophelia. 'And what's more, you never will. You think that the war ended back in 1945 and that your country, along with the USA and the Russians stamped out Nazism.' He pulled a sorrowful face and shook his head. 'How presumptuous of you and how utterly wrong you are.'

'But enough, Ophelia. What are we going to do with him?' asked Margaret.

Ophelia took another draw on the slim cigarette holder then gave an evil smile.

Margaret clearly understood the unspoken implication. 'Oh surely not? I thought we only reserved that kind of treatment for our fondest guests.'

*

At gunpoint, Salford was ordered to go upstairs. Once in the study, Margaret searched him, tutting with disapproval when he found and confiscated the lockpicks and jemmy. Then he was tightly bound to a chair.

Ophelia stood by an old-fashioned gramophone. 'Now then. Time for a little musical interlude as they say. But first I'd like to tell you a story. Back in 1945 a most gifted, though sadly short-lived, Hungarian composer called Zsiga Zsoldos helped Margaret and I in creating a truly amazing musical score. We had always had a deep fascination with music, sound in particular, and its potential use as a weapon. Through certain mystical means, which I'm sure wouldn't interest someone of your uncouth disposition in the slightest, we created the perfect weapon.'

Margaret came forward with a record. 'Do you remember Ophelia dearest how the little children would cry and beg: 'Uncle Josef, can we hear the pretty song?' they would say. How sweet.' Almost reverently, she put the record on to the antiquated turntable.

'I envy you,' said Ophelia, gazing into Salford's eyes, 'as you're going to get to hear the piece in its entirety. Which, for obvious reasons, is something we never have. We didn't manage to work out just how much of the music one needs to hear for it to be effective but I'd rather not take any chances. For your information, it was said that Zsoldos was in league with the Devil; that he came from Romany stock—accursed gypsies who could harness the powers of darkness. Whatever the case may be, through our perfection and the choral backing of those who were tortured and exterminated, it has the ability to kill; to drive those who hear it to take their own lives. It took long months of experimentation to perfect and unfortunately it has to be heard directly from the record of which only this one exists. Just think how useful it could have been to the Fatherland had we been able to broadcast it. Now, normally we just leave it playing as background music whilst 'entertaining' those guests whom, like the late Mr Parker, begin to get a little too close for comfort.'

'A suspicious one that. Methinks we should have done away with him sooner,' added Margaret as he poured himself a brandy.

'Bastards! You'll never get away with this!' Salford shouted.

'Get away with what?' asked Ophelia.

'Murdering me won't get you anywhere. People know I'm here. If they don't hear from me in a few hours' time this place will be crawling with police and you two can look forward to life in prison.'

It was pure bluff on Salford's part but he knew he had to try something.

'Really?' Ophelia purred. He nodded to his accomplice and the gramophone was switched on. 'Toodle-pip.'

The two Nazi drag queens left the study and closed the door.

A crackling sound came from the gramophone—a sure indicator that the record was old and well-played. Then the music began. At first, it was just a lone violin, playing a simple tune. It was reminiscent of many folk songs from Eastern Europe or Russia and seemed utterly unremarkable.

Salford found he could not take it seriously. Surely this could not be real? No mere music could do what the two claimed it could. He half-expected them to come back in with a loaded syringe or a spiked drink—something that would actually do the job. But if that were the case, then why had no drug been found in Parker's body? His heart lurched a little.

The music was changing.

The violin was joined by other instruments and a quiet background sound that seemed vaguely choral.

It was not unpleasant but Salford began to feel slightly unsettled. It was as if something was nagging at the back of his mind. There were no words that he could make out beneath the orchestral work but he had the disturbing sensation of someone muttering in his ear. The main melody was slow and melancholic and if he had not been strapped to a chair by two madmen he would have paid little attention to it.

With the knowledge of just who he was dealing with and what he had discovered, however, the effect was becoming hard to ignore.

Sweat beaded on his forehead and trickled down the sides of his face as his fists clenched. He now had no doubt that there was something hellish at work. Try as he might to blot the diabolical music out, even singing a different tune as loudly as he could, the sound wormed its way into his ears, subliminally implanting its message of doom deep within his mind. He imagined black, leather-gloved hands kneading his brain like dough.

After a few minutes more the unholy record came to an end.

The door to the study opened.

'Finished?' asked Ophelia. Monocle in eye, he regarded the panting Salford with scientific curiosity. 'That's interesting, Margaret. Look at the difference when they know.'

Margaret sipped from his brandy. 'I wonder how long he'll last?'

'Unfortunately we won't be able to time it accurately as we have other things to do. Can't keep her Majesty waiting.' Lovingly, Ophelia stroked the gramophone. He looked at Salford. 'You wouldn't believe how long it's taken us to get this far. No doubt you're wondering how we managed to secure a spot on the Royal Variety performance. Let's just say the current organiser is a big fan of our work. *All* our work.'

'Is that what this is all about?' Salford blurted out. 'You're going to play this at The Palladium?'

'Not a complete idiot after all,' Margaret said sarcastically. 'Yes, the final demonstration of our talents will be a very public affair, the climax of our act! At least, the beginning will be. However, the world will have to wait roughly twenty-four hours to see the full effects.'

'But, if you play this on stage, surely you'll be affected by it too?' said Salford.

'My dear boy! Have you never heard of ear plugs?' Ophelia exclaimed. 'We've been practising hard to do our entire routine with them in and I assure you that no one will notice. And then, Dame Margaret and I will gracefully retire and go somewhere nice and hot for a little holiday.'

'South America, no doubt.' Salford ground his teeth in fury.

Ophelia clapped his hands and laughed, a jarringly masculine sound. 'What a splendid suggestion!' He pulled out his Luger. Menace sparkled in his piercing blue eyes.

Margaret looked at his watch. 'I think we should get back to our hotel, dear. We do have a dinner reservation after all.' He produced a knife from his beaded handbag and slit the ropes holding Salford to the chair.

'Now then. Back downstairs with you, you grotty little man.'

Salford was in two minds about making a move, to try and overpower the two murderous transvestites. Swiftly coming to the conclusion that such a course of action would only hasten his death, he reluctantly followed instructions. He was taken downstairs and pushed into the secret room.

'We're not completely without pity,' said Margaret. He threw his knife into a corner of the room. 'I think you may need that before the end. But please, try not to make too much of a mess. From our observations of the many test subjects I can advise you not to fight against the compulsion. The results seem to be…most excruciating.'

'Auf wiedersehen.' With a nod, Ophelia slammed the door shut. A key was then turned in the lock.

'Bastards! Nazi bastards!' Salford yelled as he hammered on the door. Realising the futility of his actions, he went over to the photograph of Hitler, removed it from the wall and smashed it on the floor.

Three hours later, Salford had only succeeded in breaking the knife while trying to force open the locked door and had nearly broken his shoulder trying to batter it down.

It was while recovering from the latest attempt that he experienced the first wave of pain. It had taken him by surprise and it was a brief but intense sensation similar to the migraines he had sometimes had. It was gone almost before he had registered it but there was a strange feeling in his head that lingered for a few minutes.

Taking stock of the situation, Salford sat at the desk to think. He guessed that the performance the following day would start sometime in the early evening. If that were the case, then he might even be dead before then. He found the piece of paper that had Parker's name on it and looked at the numbers next to it: 27 hours and 32 minutes. Presumably that was how long it had taken between Parker hearing the record and killing himself.

Looking through the other names and numbers, the times of death varied between twenty-three and thirty hours. If he lasted to the outer limit that would give him time to stop the murderers, provided he could get out of this room.

The locked door had so far resisted his attempts to batter it down. Salford considered the possibility of going through the wall or ceiling. From what he could remember of the house, there had been no tell-tale low windows to indicate the existence of another cellar so presumably outside the walls of the room would be packed earth, almost impossible to get through in the timeframe.

The ceiling however offered possibilities.

Climbing on to the desk, Salford found the ceiling was only about a foot above his head. Using the broken blade, he began chipping away at it.

The first thirty minutes' work revealed that the ceiling was plasterboard suspended from wooden joists with floorboards above. He wiped his forehead with his sleeve. The work was awkward and the constant looking up made him feel dizzy but he was sure he could crack this, given time.

Whether he had enough time remained to be seen but given the circumstances there was no alternative.

There were obvious parallels with tunnelling out of Colditz.

It was the longest night of Salford's life and the most stressful. Many times he felt like he could not go on. The aches in his arms and back were dreadful and he was experiencing more of the waves of pain which left him light-headed and depressed.

At one point, in the early hours of the morning, he had simply succumbed to exhaustion and curled up on the floor to sleep, the torn down Nazi flag serving him as a pillow.

When he woke, he got back to work. Gradually, he uncovered the joists and found a gap that would be large enough for him to fit through. Then the floorboards had to be weakened enough to break.

This was the hardest part of all and he pulled the heavy carriage out of the typewriter to employ as a hammer. He almost gave up then. The effects of the record were taking their toll and he found himself looking speculatively at the knife several times, his eyes and mind regarding the sharp blade with a strange fascination; a longing almost. A swift, deep cut across both wrists and…there came a sudden image of his father, Salford senior, who had stormed the beaches at Normandy trying to rid the world of scum like Werner and von Koenig.

He was damned if he would give up while there was still a chance of defeating them. A fragment of Churchill's rousing 'We shall never surrender…' speech entered his head.

Eventually only an inch of carpet remained and the blunted blade made heavy work of the job.

Cutting through the last obstacle, Salford made an escape

route. Before leaving his prison, he took the photograph of Mengele, Werner and von Koenig and several incriminating documents that would prove who Ophelia and Margaret really were and what they intended to do.

Checking his wristwatch, Salford saw it was a little after five o'clock in the afternoon. He still had time. A visit to the bathroom served to clean him up a little and a quick search of the two Nazis' bedrooms turned up a second Luger and a large amount of money, in various currencies.

Leaving the money, he took the gun, fully loaded, and left the house, aware that there was a time bomb ticking in his head and that the final countdown was fast approaching.

A solution to the problem of how to get into The Palladium had come to Salford as he neared the centre of London and he pulled up outside a florists.

Armed with the most extravagant bunch of flowers they could make for him, he abandoned his car in a side street near the theatre. The waves of pain in his head were becoming more intense now and began to be accompanied by feelings of soul-crippling despair. His mind was drowning; the sensations threatening to overcome him completely. Reality blurred.

Stepping off the kerb on to the road proper, he was startled by the screech of tyres and the angry blast of a taxi's horn. A window rolled down and an irate taxi driver shouted angrily at him before speeding away.

In the distance there was the sound of police sirens.

Avoiding the grand entrance of the theatre, Salford made his way to the stage door in a dingy back alley.

Unsurprisingly, there was a doorman but he was leaning casually against the brick wall and smoking a cigar with every evidence of enjoyment.

'Delivery for Lady Ophelia and Dame Margaret,' Salford said

briskly.

'All right,' the man sighed. 'Give them here.'

'Can't do that,' Salford replied firmly and with a hint of self-importance. 'The boss was very insistent that I ensure the arrangement is properly presented. No offence intended but you'd probably just shove them in a vase or leave them on a table.'

'True enough, I suppose,' the doorman admitted. He considered the fussy-seeming man before him with his carefully combed hair and air of impatience. He also considered having to abandon his cigar to take the flowers inside and made up his mind. 'Okay, you can nip in but don't be long.'

Salford thanked him and slipped inside the theatre. Heart pounding, he checked that the Luger was still obscured by the swathes of tissue paper wrapped around the stems and set out to find the stage.

He should be able to find the murderous pair and shoot them before they had the chance to complete their 'experiment'.

The rabbit warren of corridors was busy with the many performers and their assistants, chattering and laughing as they waited their turn or relaxed having completed their acts. Trying not to stare at people he had only ever seen on the television, he followed directions to the stage, once having to squash himself against the wall to allow a group of glamourous dancers in spectacular feathered costumes to get past. Finally, he saw the wings of the stage up ahead.

A stagehand, carrying a clipboard, came over. 'Stay back there and keep quiet. Who are you looking for?' he asked.

'I'm to give these to Lady Ophelia and Dame Margaret when they come off-stage,' Salford lied. 'When are they due on?'

'That's them out there right now,' the man answered. 'Their set's about ten minutes so you won't have long to wait. May I suggest you go to their dressing room.' He turned and went back to his post.

Salford could hear raucous singing. He looked in horror at the sliver of stage he could see from where he was. Sure enough, there was a sofa and a standard lamp of the kind they had in their drawing room. Moving a little closer, he caught a glimpse of the green silk dress worn by Dame Margaret as he enthusiastically swished around the stage, conducting the audience in an exuberant rendition of *The Marrow Song*.

'Oh, what a beauty! I've never seen one as big as that before!'

The audience was loving it.

Heart thumping, Salford knew he had only a few minutes. Ophelia and Margaret had said that the record would be part of their finale—the ultimate swansong.

'Oh, what a beauty! It must be two foot long or even more.'

Salford checked his inside pocket. The incriminating photograph of Mengele and his protégées was still there, along with the handwritten letter from him, wishing the two good luck in their glorious endeavour.

As long as the police found the envelope it would put them on to the murderers, even if he failed. And if he succeeded in his assassination attempt, at least people would come to know why he had done it. His priority was to prevent the record from being played, whatever it cost him.

He was doomed anyway, if Ophelia and Margaret were to be believed, and he now knew enough to be convinced of that. How many poor wretches had died in agony to create the diabolical musical score? Grasping his head, he could imagine the terrified eyes, could almost feel the emaciated hands reaching out to grab him, beseeching him for help. Innocents; men, women and children who had been reduced to living skeletons; numbers, not names.

The wave of utter despair hit his mind with dreadful force, setting up a stabbing agony in his head. He only had to take the gun out, put it in his mouth, pull the trigger and it would all be over.

A roar of laughter from the auditorium broke Salford out of his dark contemplation. He stared blankly at his hand which had been reaching for the Luger and then thrust it back into his pocket. He had so little time left! The next wave might be the last. He turned his attention back to the stage.

Margaret was telling a long, humorous story about an aspidistra much to the audiences' delight. Ophelia had remained seated at the piano and was watching with a kind of restrained eagerness that turned Salford's stomach.

Then he heard it.

The unobtrusive background music that was accompanying the story. God knew how long the record had been playing while he had been caught in a fugue.

Still clutching the flowers, Salford pushed past the stagehands and rushed on to the stage, behind the two performers. With their earplugs firmly in place, they did not at first notice him, whereas the audience burst into a fresh bout of laughter, obviously believing he was part of the act.

Grinning inanely, he put his finger to his lips as if signifying a prank to be played on the two 'ladies'. Then, he wrenched the record from the gramophone and shattered it over his raised knee.

Noticing the change in their audience, Ophelia and Margaret turned round and Salford saw the flash of hatred in their eyes. He pulled the Luger from its hiding place and fired twice at Ophelia where he sat at the piano. Having never fired a gun before in his life, he missed and the next moment he was felled by a punch from Margaret that knocked a tooth out and sent him sprawling on to the sofa in the centre of the stage.

The transvestite was screaming at him in German, calling him all the names under the sun, hands clamping around his throat while the audience looked on in stunned disbelief.

At the gunshot, two policemen materialised as if by magic. One wrestled the Luger from Salford's unresisting grip whilst the other struggled with Margaret who looked ready to tear the private investigator to shreds.

Salford could feel the shroud of pain and despair descending again. He fell back on to the sofa. There was nothing else he could do and no way of knowing if the audience had heard enough to seal their fates. The royal box was empty now, its inhabitants doubtless spirited to safety as soon as the first shot had rung out.

He barely felt the policemen bind his hands and caution him. The sound of those tortured and killed in Auschwitz was taking over all his senses but he saw Ophelia tear off his wig, stand to attention, give the *sieg heil* Nazi salute and, with an insane fervour, start hammering out the tune to the *Horst Wessel Lied* on the piano.

'*Die Fahne hoch! Die Reihen fest geschlossen!*' Gone was Margaret's melodic singing voice as he defiantly bellowed out the Nazi Party anthem. Still singing, he was dragged off.

The sight made Salford start to laugh but soon there were tears running down his face. The awful, black despair was back and the relentless stabbing in his head was worse than before.

The urge to kill himself was immensely powerful now and resisting it as difficult as holding his breath continuously. The Luger was beyond his reach and, handcuffed, with a policeman on either side of him, he had little chance to make a run for it.

If only he knew whether the record had been playing long enough to implant its deadly message.

The scene before him was fading, the grandeur of the theatre turning into greys and blacks, with shadowy, writhing figures surrounding him. The pain swelled up to claim his mind and he lurched forward.

'How long had the music been playing?' he shouted to the stunned stagehand in the wings. Strong hands grabbed him and he felt himself being dragged to the side.

'What?' The stagehand stared at him in fear and confusion.

'The record! How long had it been playing?' Salford shouted.

'I... I don't know. A few minutes perhaps. I wasn't really paying attention,' the man stammered.

The policeman to Salford's right pulled him sharply away. 'You're coming with us.'

'*But how long?*' Salford's yell tailed off and his face began to twist in pain. Ignoring the police, he slumped over with his head in his lap. Sickened, he could see dead, white faces everywhere. They became clearer as the music in his mind crashed its way through his very being. Denied of the opportunity to take his own life, he felt a searing explosion of pain as blood vessels in his brain finally burst. Blood streamed from his eyes and nose. '*How long..?*' he mumbled before collapsing, face-first, to the stage.

Also available from
Shadow Publishing

Phantoms of Venice
Selected by David A. Sutton
ISBN 0-9539032-1-4

The Satyr's Head: Tales of Terror
Selected by David A. Sutton
ISBN 978-0-9539032-3-8

The Female of the Species And Other Terror Tales
By Richard Davis
ISBN 978-0-9539032-4-5

Frightfully Cosy And Mild Stories For Nervous Types
By Johnny Mains
ISBN 978-0-9539032-5-2

Horror! Under the Tombstone: Stories from the Deathly Realm
Selected by David A. Sutton
ISBN 978-0-9539032-6-9

The Whispering Horror
By Eddy C. Bertin
ISBN: 978-0-9539032-7-6

The Lurkers in the Abyss and Other Tales of Terror
By David A. Riley
ISBN: 978-0-9539032-9-0

Worse Things Than Spiders and Other Stories
By Samantha Lee
ISBN: 978-0-9539032-8-3

Tales of the Grotesque: A Collection of Uneasy Tales
By L. A. Lewis
ISBN: 978-0-9572962-0-6

Horror on the High Seas
ISBN 978-0-9572962-1-3

Creeping Crawlers
Edited by Allen Ashley
ISBN 978-0-9572962-2-0

Haunts of Horror
ISBN 978-0-9572962-3-7